THE VENUE

A WEDDING NOVEL

T.J. PAYNE

Published by Tunnel Falls

ISBN: 978-1-954503-05-2

This book is dedicated to Michael and his loving family.

For reminding me why I write.

PROLOGUE

Invitation — DRAFT #1

Sup Amy,

How are ya, buddy? It's been awhile!

I'm getting married soon and I'd love for you to come. It'd be great to reconnect and catch up. I'm sorry things got so weird between us back in the day. I didn't mean to push you away.

Lilith, my fiancée, really wants to meet you, as well. She's heard so much about you.

Are you still with Ryan Parker?

Not that it matters. If you are, he's invited too.

Or whoever you're seeing.

Please RSVP!

— Caleb

Dear Amy,

Although we haven't spoken since high school, I want you to know that I still consider you my best friend. I often look back fondly on our time together. You were there for me when no one else was.

It's in that spirit that I want to tell you some exciting news.
I'm getting married!

And let me tell you, Lilith is awesome. I've gone through some tough times, but I've never been happier than I am right now.

We found a place in the Alps for the wedding. Don't worry, I'll pay for everything — I'm doing okay for myself these days. :) I'd love it if you could attend. It would mean so much for me to share this moment with you. Your parents are invited too; it would be fun to see them again.

You can (and should) bring your husband or boyfriend or partner. You don't seem to be on social media, so I don't know who you're seeing these days. Unless you ARE on social media and blocked me. Haha! It sounds like I'm stalking you. I'm not, I swear. Just keeping tabs on an old friend. My best friend.

Anyway, Lilith is great. I'm very happy.

Please come. (I bet that's what you said to Ryan Parker! I kid, I kid.)

I'd love to see you again, buddy! But if you can't make it, no biggie. It's cool.

Please RSVP.

Love, Caleb

Invitation — DRAFT #3

YOU'RE A FUCKING WHORE, AMY.

I'M GONNA RIP OUT YOUR HEART AND MASTURBATE WITH IT!

FUCK YOU.

By the way, I'm getting married.
Hope to see you there!

Sincerely, Caleb

Invitation — FINAL DRAFT

Dear Amy Holgate,

You are cordially invited to the wedding of Caleb Hunt and Lilith Foley.

The ceremony will be held at an exclusive European resort. All travel and accommodations will be provided by and paid for by the bride and groom. This is our way of thanking you for being such an important part of our lives and making us into the people we are today. A special day needs to be shared with special people.

You will not want to miss it.

Please RSVP by clicking on the provided link. You will be taken to a secure website that will handle all arrangements.

You are allowed a plus-one.

We look forward to celebrating with you.

Love, Caleb and Lilith

It was hotter than normal that day.

The Event Planner felt the sweat forming on her brow and back. She squinted in the bright afternoon sun. The owners didn't allow the employees to wear sunglasses. Too distancing. It put a barrier between the staff and their clients.

The owners also didn't allow sweat.

Elegance does not sweat.

Luxury does not sweat.

Sweating was a common problem for common people, of which there were none at The Venue.

The Event Planner checked her watch. She knew the limousine would arrive in two minutes. She knew because everything at The Venue worked on-schedule. Down to the second.

The clients had been told that they would arrive at *exactly* 2:30 p.m., Zurich local time, despite the trip requiring an airplane, helicopter, and limousine ride up steep, unmarked roads.

The Venue liked to schedule a walk-through for their clients a year before an event. That way, the clients could see The Venue in the proper season. A snow-dusted winter event just felt different than the soft evening glow of summer. Winter and Christmastime were usually booked for reunions and holiday parties, but summer was wedding season.

The Event Planner knew that "The Venue" used to go by another, more sophisticated name. But the owners found that their clientele discovered this particular event space through word-of-mouth. Those hushed recommendations often referred to the location only vaguely as "The Venue."

The name eventually stuck.

Why force your American clients to mangle an obscure Romansh name? Calling it "The Venue" worked just fine.

The vast building, a cross between a ski lodge and a castle, sat nestled along the rising slope of the Alps. It easily held a hundred guests in the hotel rooms that filled the second and third levels of the spired, vaulted structure. With all its underground passageways and shelters, most of the staff assumed it had been built as a getaway for the Nazi High Command. But no one ever talked about that.

It was best not to ask questions at The Venue.

As the Event Planner tried not to sweat or squint in the morning sun, she heard the purr of the limousine's engine as it wound its way up the mountain. It would only be a few seconds now.

A hostess pulled a champagne bottle from its ice bucket, popped its cork, and poured two chilled flutes.

It was then, when the limousine rounded the final corner and came into view, that the Event Planner's gaze fell toward a rose bush that accented the front door. She didn't know why she looked there at that moment, except maybe she realized, subconsciously, that something was amiss.

Sure enough, on the dirt by the rose bush sat what looked like a pale, folded leaf. The Event Planner knew better, though.

Her glare darted to the various members of her staff, each of whom stiffened and grimaced in their red vests and bleached white shirts. They saw what she saw.

Nestled in the dirt was a human ear.

"Unacceptable," she hissed.

She plucked a white handkerchief from a nearby bellhop's breast pocket and bent down by the bush.

The ear was cleanly severed but speckled in blood. An army of ants marched in a line over the top of it, seemingly making plans for how best to carry it away for their dinner.

The Event Planner scooped up the ear in the handkerchief.

Tucking the ear in the folds of the cloth, she shoved the handkerchief back into the bellhop's pocket, taking a moment to adjust its corners into a proper triangle.

The bellhop and the rest of the staff kept their eyes forward.

The limousine came to a stop.

The staff rushed over, opening doors and unloading luggage.

A man and a woman stepped out of the limousine.

They were younger than most of the Event Planner's clients. She had a keen eye for "new money," and in this age of tech start-ups and venture capital, it seemed that fresh billionaires were minted weekly.

The man, barely into his 30s, shifted uncomfortably beneath his mismatch of designer labels. The Event Planner could see him constantly glance over at his fiancée, modeling his movements and excitement level on her own.

"Well... isn't this lovely," the woman said with a bit of a posh New England accent that struck the Event Planner as fake.

The woman had dark hair tied back from her angular face. The Event Planner could tell that the woman was fit. Months, perhaps years, of physical training had sculpted and toned her arms and legs, making her physique look quite impressive, even while draped in a loose summer dress. But the rest of her features pulled downward, as though gravity tugged at the edges of her nose and mouth, creating a perpetual, drooping glare.

The woman managed to pull her cheeks up into a smile that she directed at her soon-to-be husband. "This could work."

"Do you like it? Really?" the man said, his face lighting up.

"Perhaps. It's an option. Depending on the rental agreement, I suppose."

New money all right.

The Event Planner stepped forward. "Mr. Caleb. Ms. Lilith. It is my great honor to welcome you to The Venue."

The woman, Lilith, eyed her. "And *you* are?"

"The Event Planner assigned to your wedding. My job is to answer any questions you might have. May I interest you in champagne?"

Caleb reached out and took a bubbly flute from the hostess.

Lilith, meanwhile, made no such motion to accept the offered refreshment. Her gaze busily danced around, taking in the mountainous surroundings and the large, stone building.

After looking at her for a bit and concluding that she wasn't going to take a champagne, Caleb set his drink back on the hostess's tray.

"I hope your trip was comfortable," the Event Planner continued. "If you would like to be shown to your room and given an opportunity to relax a bit, we can continue discussing your event later this—"

"We'd like to finalize the agreement as soon as possible," Lilith said.

The Event Planner smiled. "Of course. Everything should be in order. Please follow me."

***

The Event Planner and her two clients sat at a table in the center of the otherwise empty ballroom.

Long windows stretched up one wall to the hall's high, vaulted ceiling. The evening sun cast an orange glow on the opposite wall — a wall decorated entirely with medieval weapons. Axes, scythes, ꞇ swords. Some blades were rusted, some were honed and gleaming.

"Naturally, it will look different at night when your reception occurs," the Event Planner said, her sharp voice echoing around the bare room. "The chandeliers will be lit. We like to keep the lighting somewhat dim as we find that it promotes interaction among the guests."

"Can we use that balcony for the bouquet toss?" Lilith asked, pointing to a spiral staircase that led to a small metal balcony that overlooked the ballroom.

"Many couples opt for that. The balcony provides an excellent overview of the festivities."

The couple nodded. "And any damages that occur..." Caleb began to ask.

The Event Planner smiled warmly, "All included in the price of your rental agreement. Broken windows, broken tables, linen stains — all included. If, by the end of your celebration, your party is... how do I say... 'well-behaved,' then we will refund a portion of your deposit."

"Well, that doesn't sound like much fun," Lilith said.

"I agree," the Event Planner said. "And let me assure you, a damage-free event is a situation that I have yet to witness myself."

"And, the, um, the estimate you told me... is that accurate?" Caleb asked.

The Event Planner saw Caleb shift his weight in his seat. She knew the look of sticker-shock when she saw it. Of course, they had run a background check on his finances and she knew that he could well-afford it.

With a reassuring smile, the Event Planner pulled a contract from her folder and set it on the table. "At this point, the remaining your guest list. No children are allowed, obviously.

re is an additional surcharge for any guests whom we

ıgh-profile. Politicians, media-personalities, wealthy

ıs owners, and so forth."

ıy?" Caleb asked.

"People of a certain visibility require more resources on our part. They tend to have lawyers, heirs, life insurance investigators. There might be fans or reporters who take an interest in the case. Nothing we can't handle, but there is a certain amount of clean-up involved."

"Most of our guests are from our childhood," Lilith said. "They're nobodies."

"Fantastic. That's always easier. And cheaper."

"What about photos?" Caleb asked as he reached over and grasped Lilith's hand tenderly. "I'd like to have something to remember it by."

"Of course. You will, naturally, want photos to post on social media or have framed at your house. Your children, if you so desire to have them, will want to see your wedding, I'm sure. We understand. We will provide you with a photo album filled with happy memories. But, to be clear, those will all be photo-manipulated. There will, sadly, be no evidence of the actual event. You will have to keep your real wedding photos in your head. As we like to say here, *'Discretion is Our Profession.'* You will be bound by a strictly enforced non-disclosure agreement."

"And what about any guests who go home?" Caleb asked.

Lilith's eyes narrowed and her face wrinkled in what seemed like disgust at the thought.

Caleb looked down and shrugged. "I mean, it's, you know, it's not fun if they don't have a chance. And if they go home afterwards, I

T. J. PAYNE

just don't get why they wouldn't, you know, say something about what happened here."

"A very valid concern," the Event Planner said. "In the past, money and pressure were enough to buy silence. With social media, things have changed. Anyone can be an investigative journalist. But we have a solution that has proven one-hundred percent effective. We have access to a psychotropic drug developed privately and utilized by the United States Government. It strips away the short-term memory. It is administered by a small dose of pills. All of your surviving guests must agree to take the prescribed pills upon departure."

"Will we have to take the pills?" Lilith asked.

"Goodness, no. It's your special day. We want you to remember it forever."

Sensing that the time had come to close the deal, the Event Planner slid the contract across the table and placed a fountain pen on top of it.

"We have relationships with several Swiss banks," the Event Planner said. "We also accept certain cryptocurrencies at whatever the exchange rate is on the day of your signature." Then she calmly folded her hands and waited. "Take your time. I am here for any questions."

Caleb picked up the pen. She saw his throat move in an involuntary gulp. His hand stayed still, but his eyes darted up and down the document, apparently not actually reading it but letting his mind race.

"Second thoughts?" he said, turning to Lilith.

If there was any hesitation in Caleb's face, it melted the moment he made eye contact with Lilith. That face of hers, which had always seemed to be scowling, became positively radiant. Her eyes lit up and her cheeks rose into a joyous grin.

"It's perfect," she said, pausing a moment, seemingly to breathe in the very aura of the room.

"It is?" Caleb said, his voice pitching an octave higher out of his own excitement.

"It's everything I ever dreamed of."

"Really? You really mean it?"

"It's the wedding I want. Here. Surrounded by our friends and family."

"Then it's yours. We're doing it."

Without waiting another second, Caleb picked up the pen and scribbled his signature on the document.

Lilith let out a joyous screech. "We're doing it!" She wrapped her arms around Caleb.

A waiter standing behind them opened a bottle of champagne. *Pop!*

"Congratulations," the Event Planner said. "I'm very excited for both of you. I have yet to see a client regret this decision."

As the waiter filled their flutes, the Event Planner took a moment to review Caleb's signature. The process of signing was a formality, of course. The physical document would be destroyed. But signing an actual paper was a little tradition that seemed to resonate with the clients.

"We need to get Save The Dates out," Lilith said, her eyes lighting up brightly. "I don't want anyone to miss it."

"I've already started composing some," Caleb said.

The Event Planner smiled. "I will be sure to include whatever wording you would like. But, in general, we handle all communication with your guests ourselves. I advise you not to send emails or physical invites. Nothing that can be traced back to you. Less paper means fewer problems down the road. Remember, when you rent The Venue, the only thing *you* worry about..." she stretched her smile even wider. "...is enjoying yourself."

Caleb and Lilith settled into their seats, finally relaxed enough to take dainty sips of their champagne.

"Have you finalized your guest list?" the Event Planner asked.

Caleb's face shifted. The change was slight. His grin became tighter. His eyes began to glow with a new intensity. It was a look the Event Planner knew well.

"Yes," he said. "We have."

CHAPTER 1

"Get in your hole, you little asshole. Get in your fucking hole!" Amy yelled at the tiny hex wrench in her hand.

It didn't help that after a day of carrying boxes upstairs and then assembling cheap furniture — two bookshelves, a night stand, a cabinet, and a table —her exhausted hands struggled to grip the little wrench that came with her dining chair.

Amy was sure that the manufacturers made the wrench too small on purpose. She had heard somewhere that the self-assemble furniture companies *wanted* the process to be difficult. Or, at least, a little difficult. Sure, they could design the pieces to slot together and be ready in five minutes. But some market researcher somewhere learned that customers were more attached to their furniture if they had to work to assemble it.

Supposedly, it gave customers a feeling of accomplishment. That they had created something. They had built this whole table with their own two hands!

The harder the journey, the more you appreciate the destination. Or some shit like that.

But right now, Amy didn't care about journeys or struggles. The hex wrench was too small to gain any true leverage. And the angle that she had to reach into the chair seat meant that she was only allowed a quarter turn at a time.

She reached in again.

Most people thought that her work as a yoga and aerobic dance instructor would provide her with some sense of inner Zen when confronted with life's challenges.

Nope.

She tended to deal with difficult situations by either giving up or swearing profusely.

The wood let out a creak as Amy twisted the hex wrench one final time. Her chair was finally finished.

"About effing time."

She flipped it upright and slid it under her new dining table.

She grabbed a slice of pizza from the box on the floor and shoved it in her mouth. Her back ached. Her face and arms were sticky from sweat. She wanted a shower and a beer.

But as she munched on pizza and gazed at her studio apartment, she couldn't help but bask in her accomplishment.

Aside from some unpacked boxes and the still-to-be-inflated air mattress, her new home was coming together nicely. She might not have enough space to host friends — not that she *had* many friends at this stage of her life; she was always too exhausted in the evenings for friends — but she had a place to shower and sleep.

Maybe the feeling of accomplishment that came from assembling one's own furniture *was* a thing.

In one day, she had moved on to a new stage of her life.

A new apartment.

A new Amy Holgate.

She was done.

But as she admired her new home, her gaze fell on the key that lay on the counter. Her old key.

She *wasn't* done. Not yet.

With a sigh, she walked over and picked it up.

"Damnit," she said, staring at the key. "Shit, shit, shit."

She was swearing again.

Another of life's challenges would have to be dealt with.

***

She hoped that Mariko wasn't home yet. She could leave the key on the table and slink off, telling Mariko goodbye through text, or something.

But the moment Amy stepped inside her old apartment, the spicy scent of Chinese takeout wafted over to her.

Amy walked in, closing the door behind her.

As she strolled through the living room toward the kitchen, she glanced at the furniture. Her pride at her day's accomplishments evaporated. Her old place was nicer. Much nicer. As was the furniture, the kitchenware, the TV. Everything.

But Mariko had paid for it all. It was hers. Not Amy's.

As she walked into the dining room, Mariko looked up from the table and leaned back in her seat. She still wore her gray blouse and skirt from her day at the office, having evidently just gotten home.

The two of them locked eyes with each other.

"You all moved out?" Mariko asked.

"Yep."

"If you had waited for the weekend, I would have helped. Or at least cheered you on."

"I had today off."

"Nice place?"

"No rat turds. No hypodermic needles."

"Schmancy."

"Anyway, I just wanted to drop this off," Amy said as she stepped over and set her old key on the table. "And, um, this as well." Amy reached into her pocket and pulled out a ring. She kept her head tilted down as she set the ring beside the key.

"I bought beer," Mariko said, disregarding the ring as she motioned toward the fridge. "Help yourself. You look hot and stinky. There's also an open pinot if you're feeling civilized."

Amy went over and grabbed a beer.

"Told my parents about the breakup," Amy said, trying to casually lean against the counter as she took a sip.

"How'd that go?"

"Dad grunted and muttered some 'whatever makes you happy' thing. That's about as much of a response as I can ever get from him anyway. My mom on the other hand..."

"Ugly?"

"Devastated. Did she call you? She said she was gonna when she stopped crying."

"Yep. She called," Mariko said.

"And? What did she say?"

"That she'll always love me like a daughter. That she wants to make sure that I keep in touch with her and Roger. That I'm invited to Thanksgiving and Christmas at their house every year because..." Mariko's words stumbled as she became a little choked up, but she quickly recovered. "Because... she knows how much it hurt when my family disowned me. She says that'll never happen with her. It was very sweet."

"Mom's a softie."

"That's our Candice."

"She say anything else?"

"Just that she hopes that I'm still going with you all to what's-his-butt's wedding."

Amy looked up. "And? What did you say?"

"I said I would."

"You don't have to. Really."

"Your call. If it'll be weird..." Mariko said.

"It won't be weird."

"You sure?"

"Yeah. We're adults. We're friends. But if you don't wanna come because *you* think it'll be weird..."

"It's a free trip to Europe. I'm willing to put up with large quantities of weird for that."

"Then come."

They looked at each other quietly, both seemingly trying to gauge each other's true feelings on the matter.

Finally, Amy shrugged and took another swig of beer. "It'll be fun. Besides, if I had to spend a week traveling through Europe with my parents by *myself*—"

"— you would fucking kill yourself."

"I would fucking kill myself."

They grinned at each other. Amy broke eye contact by forcing another swig of her beer. Her mouth was dry and the alcohol actually wasn't helping. It didn't cool her down either.

"But seriously, you don't have to go," Amy said.

"Stop it. I put in for the vacation months ago. If I don't go, I'm just gonna be sitting around the apartment. And if I sit around the apartment, I'm gonna end up with a cat. You don't want me to get a cat, do you? Because if I get one, I'm gonna feel bad that I leave it alone all day, so then I'll need to get it a friend. And then the hoarding begins."

"And I'm allergic to cats."

"It's all in your head," Mariko said. "Besides, your mom's been looking forward to this trip for months. If I'm not there, she's just gonna pester you about how you're gonna die alone."

"She's gonna do that anyway."

"That's our Candice."

The two grinned at each other.

Amy knew that Mariko was right, as was often the case. Amy's mom was a different person around Amy's girlfriends. Maybe because it gave her mom someone to talk to — Lord knows Amy's *dad* wasn't an engaging conversationalist. But Amy also knew that her mom simply wanted Amy to be happy, and she was incapable of fathoming the possibility that her daughter might be happiest alone.

"So, who is this guy who's getting married?" Mariko finally asked.

"Caleb? His family lived across the street from us. We were best friends when we were kids."

"You never talk about him."

"We dated in middle school. You know how that screws things up."

"Don't I."

"But it'll be fun," Amy said. "Caleb's a good guy."

She took another swig of beer.

"A good guy," she repeated, although she didn't know why. Amy hadn't spoken to Caleb in years. She honestly didn't know what kind of guy he was now.

***

Caleb had never loved Lilith so much.

He always heard that weddings were stressful for couples. So much to do. So many decisions to make. A minor disagreement on linen colors or centerpieces could open an irreparable rift.

But Caleb and Lilith were a good team.

Caleb deferred to Lilith, and Lilith made snap decisions.

Caleb didn't *always* agree with her choices, though. He thought the color scheme of red and black was a bit too unpleasant, especially considering they were having a summer wedding. Lilith also refused to grant the guests menu options other than filet mignon, *very* rare. That struck Caleb as lacking in all subtlety.

Still, the decisions happened quickly and painlessly.

They only argued about table assignments. It was primarily a math problem. The tables only seated eight guests, meaning that some parties had to be broken up and others combined. Caleb suggested moving Lilith's dad to Table Three to make room for Caleb's coworkers to sit together.

Lilith shot back that her father *must* be front and center. Nothing near doors, nothing near windows. It was Table One or nothing.

What should have been a simple statement of preference turned into Lilith accusing Caleb of not listening to her. She yelled that he was trying to ruin her wedding. She called him weak. She called him a loser.

He went back to their room and cried.

When he finally returned, Lilith acted as though nothing had happened. She pleasantly kissed his cheek and announced that she had figured out the seating math. She would seat her cousin, who played linebacker, next to Caleb's cousin, who was a first lieutenant in the Army. Two big alpha males seated together. That should create some sparks, Lilith figured.

With that task behind them, they went on to their evening routine of weight training, weapons training, and steroid injections. Caleb had gotten pretty good with a rapier. Lilith's preferred weapon was a long, spiked hammer. It was relatively light and maneuverable, but it still managed to deliver a significant amount of force.

That night, they tried to make love.

They weren't successful.

Caleb had been struggling to maintain an erection since he began their steroid regimen. At first, he was ashamed, but Lilith understood. It was a sacrifice for something more important.

Caleb was a lucky guy. Instead of a Bridezilla, he had found the kindest, most understanding, most loving person he had ever known. He lay awake that night, smiling to himself. Any day now, their families and friends would make the trek across the Atlantic.

Their perfect day couldn't come soon enough.

CHAPTER 2

Amy's tiny apartment wasn't meant for this.

Her parents and Mariko crowded together in the small space, making it seem all that much smaller which, in turn, made Amy's new life seem all that much more pathetic.

She sat on her airbed with her father. They both watched Amy's mom nervously pace in a tight circle around their stack of suitcases.

"Is there a flight number?" Amy's mom, Candice, asked as she stared at her watch. "Or tickets? Did you print out tickets? I always print out the tickets. I know they say the digital ones work just as well, but it's good to have something physical in your hand. Something you can show someone."

"It's fine, Mom."

The RSVP website had said a car would pick them up and take them to the airport. Candice had insisted that they all travel together.

"Maybe we should have printed out the screen. Something to show them if we need to," Candice said.

"The website said we only need to bring our passports."

"Did you get a confirmation email?"

"No."

"A confirmation number?"

"Mom—"

"Always print the confirmation number. That way, you have proof it went through. What if it didn't go through? Then we'll miss the flight *and* the wedding. It's always smart to check these things. Mariko agrees with me. Don't you, Mariko?"

Mariko put up her hands. "Don't drag me into this." She had perched herself on the dining table, watching out the window for the car while turning every now and then to take in the spectacle of a Holgate Family Vacation.

"Mom. Chill. The website said—"

"*The website. The website. The website.* I just don't understand what this website is. Is it a travel site? An airline site? I just don't get it."

Amy sighed. "You got the invitation via email, right?"

"Yes."

"And there was a link to a website to RSVP. Did you click on it?"

"No. Of course not. That's how you get viruses."

Mariko let out a laugh as she heard this. "Wait, wait, wait, Candice. You didn't clicked on the link because you were scared of getting a virus?"

Candice nodded. "I'm not a dolt, Mariko. I don't just go clicking on websites willy-nilly."

"So, you had *Amy* click on the link and RSVP for you and Roger?"

"Yes."

"So, you weren't worried about *her* getting a virus?"

"That's her problem. She's young. She can figure it out."

Amy let out a sigh and flopped backwards onto the airbed, splaying her arms out in the process. This would be the last time she would *ever* go on a lengthy trip with her mother. They hadn't even stepped out the front door yet and Amy felt like clawing the paneling off the wall.

She wondered why Caleb bothered to send an invitation to her parents to begin with. All of Amy's friends who had gotten married talked about how they had to rank their loved ones in order of importance. There always had to be a cutoff — a tier of friend and/or family that just didn't merit an invitation. The cruel math of weddings.

Amy couldn't believe that her parents made it into Caleb's "must-invite" tier. He probably invited them with the hope that they'd decline and thus free up a precious spot for someone closer.

But when Amy's mom saw the opportunity for an all-expense-paid European vacation with her husband, daughter, and daughter's (then) girlfriend, there was no way for Amy to talk her out of it. She had never seen her mother so excited.

Although, an excited Candice Holgate was a beast unto itself.

"Are we *sure* a car is coming to pick us up?" Candice asked. "Did we need to reserve it? Is there a phone number we can call to verify?"

An exasperated Amy covered her eyes with her hands. "Dad? Little help?"

Roger sat beside her like a block of wood that had been carved into a stout, balding man. "Candice," he said in his deep voice. "Relax."

Candice scrunched her face and threw up her hands in a *Just you wait. If this all falls apart, don't blame me!* motion.

But she didn't say another word.

There was the liberal side of Amy that didn't approve of how readily her parents slipped into stereotypical gender roles — how a single grunt from her stern, silent father was enough to quiet her chatty, worrying mother. But damn, that old school dynamic was useful when it worked!

For a few minutes, Amy enjoyed the glorious silence. But it was just long enough for her to actually start worrying herself. The RSVP website *was* a bit bizarre. Unlike most wedding websites and registries, Caleb and Lilith's page had no pictures and no event details.

The site only contained the name of Amy, her parents, and a blank space to fill in Amy's plus-one.

She clicked "Attending" for all of them and then filled in her pickup location. A message popped up stating that a car would arrive at 10:30 a.m. on August 8th. Bring a passport and formal attire.

That was it.

The website then faded to a screen that only read, *"We Look Forward to Celebrating With You."*

No "back" button.

No "return to main menu."

No additional details.

No nothing.

As Amy sat on her airbed, her mother's concerns started to overtake her.

Maybe she had missed some crucial detail. Surely, there was more information about where exactly they were going and what the trip would entail.

She pulled out her phone and searched through her emails.

There was no confirmation in her inbox.

She tried to find the original invitation email. Maybe there were more details there.

Amy scrolled through message after message but couldn't find that email either. Had she accidentally deleted it? As she searched deeper into her email folder, Amy couldn't find any evidence that this wedding was *actually* happening, that she and her family had *actually* been invited, that there was *actually* a car coming to pick them up.

God, maybe her mother was right.

What a terrifying thought.

As Amy opened her mouth to voice her suspicions to the group — *Honk! Honk! Honk!* — a horn sounded outside.

"Uh, guys?" Mariko said from her perch on the dining table. They could see her jaw hanging open as she gazed outside. "That ain't a *car* they sent."

Amy and her parents joined Mariko at the window.

A stretched limousine idled in the road, waiting for them.

The driver climbed out and tipped his hat toward their window. "Caleb Hunt's wedding?" he called out.

***

The limo ride lasted more than an hour.

Amy and her family didn't mind, though. They played with all the switches and consoles, running through the various lighting options and turning on all the TVs.

They didn't touch the mini-bar, though, despite the sign that read "Complimentary." None of them trusted that sign. As Amy's mom said, "There's no such thing as a free lunch. Or booze. They'll charge you one way or another."

It was only near the end of the trip that Amy began to wonder why they had been driving for so long. Her place was only thirty minutes from the airport. Unless they were flying out of a different airport. The windows on the limousine were all blacked out, so she couldn't even gauge what freeways they drove down.

Just as she pulled out her phone to check a map, the limo came to a stop.

The door opened and daylight streamed in, accompanied by the roar of an engine.

A smiling man in a suit motioned for them to exit.

"Right this way," the man said, having to practically shout over the noise.

Amy was the first to climb out.

She had to let her eyes and ears adjust to the blinding light and roaring engine. It was a small airport; Amy didn't recognize the area at all. They were standing on a tarmac only a few yards from stairs leading up to a private jet plane.

A ground crew jogged their luggage from the trunk of the limo to the plane's baggage loader.

Amy's group, still in a daze, wandered up to a flight attendant standing at the bottom of the stairs, holding a tray of champagne flutes. "Welcome," she said in a thick accent that Amy couldn't place. It might have been Russian. Maybe German. Amy wasn't exactly a world-traveler. "Champagne?"

"Do we have to go through TSA?" Candice asked.

The flight attendant simply grinned at her with a face that seemed to say, *I cannot answer your question because I don't actually speak English.* Then she motioned for all of them to walk on up the steps to the plane.

"If I'd known that I wouldn't have to go through the x-ray, I wouldn't have worn my slip-off shoes," Candice muttered as she gripped the handrail and pulled herself up the stairs. Roger and Mariko followed behind, their heads swiveling around, taking in the fact that they were about to have their first charter flight.

Amy lingered on the tarmac a moment.

"What airport is this?" she asked the flight attendant.

The woman only smiled in response. "Champagne?" she said.

Amy took a flute and walked up the stairs.

The inside of the plane didn't disappoint.

Rows of recliners.

Open bars.

A full movie lounge.

Scattered throughout the plane were small groups of people Amy assumed were also wedding guests. Mostly young women, probably a few years removed from college. They were all stylish and professional, like Barbie dolls who grew up to become lawyers. But even they couldn't fathom this level of luxury. They played with the remotes on their seats, giggling as personal televisions descended from the plane's ceiling.

"Wow," Candice said.

"I'm feeling a little insecure that I only got him a hundred-dollar Target gift card," Amy said as they claimed a grouping of recliners for themselves.

"Okay, seriously," Mariko said. "This dude's dropping stupid amounts of money on us. How good of friends *were* you?"

"Oh, Amy and Caleb were inseparable," Candice said. She began to recline her seat. "His mom and I used to joke that *they* were going to get married someday."

"We were just friends," Amy said.

"You obviously never saw the way he looked at you. Even back in third grade, that boy was head-over-heels."

"That boy was a creeper," Roger said. "Just a weird, creepy kid."

"Roger, be nice," Candice said.

Amy turned to Mariko and shrugged. "We grew up across the street from each other. We were best friends in elementary school. We kissed once in middle school."

"But you never talk about him."

"We grew apart. Started hanging out with different groups."

"That's it?"

"I mean, we were still cool. We'd say 'hi' in the hallway and stuff."

Mariko looked around the plane. "So, where does all *this* come from?"

"Caleb's grandparents owned a bunch of property in the Bay Area," Amy said. "When they died, it all went to him."

"Why not Caleb's parents?"

"Because they're assholes," Roger said.

"Roger, be nice," Candice said. Then she turned to Mariko and said softly, "It's true. They could be a bit unpleasant. But you didn't hear it from me."

"So, he made a fortune flipping houses?" Mariko asked.

"Kinda," Amy said. "I heard he took that money and put it into finance. Venture capital and tech start-ups and stuff. I know he invested in a few companies that got bought out by Facebook and Google. Probably some others."

"He was always a smart boy," Candice said.

"And a weirdo," said Roger. "Just seemed like a miserable kid."

"Roger..." Candice said while continuing to recline her seat. "Caleb is obviously doing very well for himself. Some kids are late bloomers. I'm glad he found happiness." Candice couldn't help but giggle as her seat went almost completely horizontal, practically transforming into a bed.

Amy looked around. The words of her mom nibbled at her. Had Caleb actually found happiness? Is this what happiness looked like? Could that sullen kid who glared at Amy whenever she dared talk to another boy actually be happy?

Yes. Of course, he could. Her mom was right. Caleb had made a couple hundred million before he hit thirty. Amy, meanwhile, was an aerobic dance instructor who lived alone and was vacationing with her parents and ex-girlfriend. Who should be judging whom?

The flight attendant walked by with another tray of champagne flutes.

"Please prepare for takeoff. Flight time is eight hours and thirty-five minutes," the flight attendant said. She seemed to be able to speak some decent English when she wanted to, Amy thought.

"Where exactly are we flying into?" Amy asked her.

"To Caleb Hunt's wedding," the flight attendant said, her English suddenly sounding broken again.

"But *where*? What country?"

The flight attendant smiled and shook her head, not understanding the question.

Before Amy could ask again, she walked off.

***

Even in the luxurious recliners, and even with the eye-masks, ear plugs, and complimentary slippers, Amy struggled to sleep. She tried watching a movie but couldn't concentrate. Same with reading a book.

One by one, everyone nodded off around her. Her father first, making that heavy purring sound he made when he slept. Her mother, meanwhile, slept silently, only to erupt in sudden fits of nasal snorts before going silent again.

And then there was Mariko. Her head cocked to the side, pulling her mouth open as she slept. It was as though the top half of her face was serene and peaceful, while the bottom half of her face was a ghoulish scream. Amy chuckled at the sight.

Feeling the need to stretch her legs, Amy stood and walked to the bathroom.

As she approached the rear of the plane, she passed the three young, stylish women she had seen earlier. They huddled together, playing some card game, but using it mostly as an excuse to keep drinking free martinis late into the night.

As Amy walked by, she accidentally made eye contact with one of them. Shit. Now she felt she had to converse.

"Are you all going to Caleb and Lilith's wedding?" Amy asked.

"Yep," one of the women said. "I'm Angela. That's Becky and Jasmine."

"Amy," she said, giving a shy wave. "You're friends with Lilith?"

"Sisters. Sorority," Angela said. On cue, all three women flashed some hand signal that Amy assumed had something to do with Greek life.

Amy had tried the sorority thing in college but ultimately rejected the notion of paying dues to have friends. Amy participated in Rush Week, got a few invites to join, and then promptly never responded. She preferred being by herself anyway. Throughout her life, Amy was the type of person who only maintained one or two close friends. There was no need for more.

"What was Lilith like?" Amy asked.

"She was a total disaster when she joined," Angela said.

Amy raised an eyebrow.

"We had a tradition. Every year, we would allow one project-girl to join. We don't tell them that, of course. But we'd bring the 'Eliza Doolittle' under our wing and we'd fix her," Becky said.

"Fix her?"

"Tough love," said Angela. "Lilith was just trashy. So needy and desperate. She clung to us. But we put up with it. And now she's marrying a billionaire."

Amy's mouth involuntarily twitched upwards in a grimace. She quickly converted it to a smile. So, Lilith was BFFs with girls who spent four years shaming her.

"You're good friends for traveling this far to support her," Amy said, trying hard to sound genuine.

Jasmine, the only one of the women who hadn't said anything, let out a laugh. "Fuck that. *I'm* here for the free Euro trip!"

Becky and Angela laughed with her.

Amy forced herself to join in.

CHAPTER 3

Amy stepped off the plane.

They had touched down in a small airport surrounded by snow-capped, jagged mountains.

The mountains were so perfect, so beautiful, so stunning that she was sure one must be the Matterhorn — the steep, pointed mountain that Walt Disney recreated in his parks. Of course, as Amy looked around, there were five or six mountains that could qualify.

She breathed in an air that was so crisp it made her shiver.

"Enjoy the rest of your trip," the flight attendant (who had rediscovered her ability to speak English, yet again) called out to them from the plane.

As Amy stepped onto the tarmac, a ground crew ferried luggage from the plane to a large, executive helicopter that waited nearby. Its spinning rotors added to the mountain breeze.

By now, Amy had stopped asking questions. She had stopped acting surprised. *Of course there would be a helicopter portion of this trip.*

Though, on second glance, perhaps it wasn't an executive helicopter. There were no windows except in the cockpit. It looked more like a repurposed military chopper.

They walked across the tarmac, angling their heads down to keep the blowing air from sending dust into their eyes. Then they climbed up the low staircase into the belly of the machine. Only Amy's mom paused to ask a question of the crew member who stood by to assist people up the steps.

"Excuse me," Candice shouted over the roar of the engines. "May I sit in front? I'd like to see the mountains as we fly over them."

"I am sorry, ma'am, but that's not allowed," the crew member said pleasantly.

"Rats," Candice said as she pulled herself up into the helicopter without another word.

Amy lingered a moment on the tarmac.

"Fun times ahead!" the crew member said to her with a big grin.

She nodded and climbed up the steps. As she took one final glance behind her, she saw another plane circle overhead. More guests must be arriving. *How many?* Amy wondered. How much did this all cost?

She ducked her head and went inside.

"Here's a seat. Sit next to me, Amy," Candice said as she motioned Amy to sit beside her.

Amy plopped down into the empty recliner.

"Your father ate fish on the plane. I told him not to. It always gives him the most dreadful gas."

"Mariko's in for a fun trip then." Amy glanced over to the seats across the aisle where Mariko and Roger settled in.

The doors sealed shut. The rotors sped up. Amy felt the helicopter lurch off the ground and climb into the sky.

"Do you have a moment to chat, sweetie?" Candice asked.

The helicopter was much louder than the plane and its roar drowned out all other conversation. This was obviously the opportunity her mother had quietly been anticipating for a full day now. Hell, probably for weeks.

"I don't know why you insist on pushing away anyone who gets close to you," Candice said, not waiting for an invitation to continue.

"Let's not do this, Mom. We're on vacation."

"I'm sorry. You're right; you're right. It's your life. None of my business. I fully and completely respect your ability to make your own decisions. I'll stop butting in."

Candice sat quietly for five seconds. Amy was impressed. It might be a new record. And then—

"But seriously, Amy, if you can't make *Mariko* work, then there's something wrong with you. You're my daughter, I love you, I think you can do anything you set your mind to, but you'll never do better than Mariko. Never. Not in a million years."

"Thanks, Mom."

"There. I've said my piece. I'm done. Feel free to continue ruining your life out of some deep-seeded commitment issues. Heaven knows where you got those from. But it's none of my business."

"Agreed."

"But *seriously*, Amy—"

"Mom!"

"Just tell me what went wrong. You're so good together."

"We had a fight."

"A *fight*? You and Mariko? Please."

"A disagreement."

"About what?"

Amy sighed. "I came home from work one day. It was a Saturday. I was sweaty and exhausted. And then Mariko shoves sperm donor paperwork in my face. She'd been researching it for months, kinda doing it behind my back."

"Probably because she knows you well enough to guess that you'd flip out and get trapped inside your head and become a little baby about the whole suggestion. But continue, sweetie."

"And then, mid-debate, she pulls out a ring."

"Isn't that sweet?"

"I don't know. It just made me think back to Caleb. He was my best friend, we did everything together. We were a good match."

"You were not a good match."

"Anyway, we kissed in middle school and everything changed. We barely spoke again. We lost track of each other."

"Well, you were gay."

"It's not about the sex side of it, Mom."

"Good. Because I cannot sit here and imagine *you* and *Caleb Hunt* doing... you know..." she scrunched up her face and shook her head at the mere thought of it.

"It's just that Mariko and I have fun. She's my best friend. But marriage and sperm donors... it felt like... it felt like kissing Caleb. Everything had changed. And I didn't like it. And when I moved out, we were friends again. And we can go on this vacation with you and be totally cool."

"Sweetie," Candice said, taking a long pause as she seemed to choose her words carefully. "I think you're full of it."

"Thanks, Mom."

"For this sliver of time, you and Mariko still love each other. And when she finally moves on, which you know she will because she's out of your league—"

"You are just a joy today, Mother."

"— then you'll really be hurt and it'll all be your fault because you never learned that things change. Relationships change. People grow up. You have to grow with them or be left behind. You're trying to hold onto your twenties, just like those poor souls who hold onto their high school days or their petty grudges."

Candice turned away from her and reclined her seat, signaling the end of her lecture. "But it's your life. Do what you think is best. Love is hard. Love is a fight. Relationships feed the best and the worst in people. If Mariko isn't bringing out the stronger, better person in you, then disregard this old nag. What do I know? Couples either give each other strength or amplify each other's weakness. It's always a risk. But sometimes, you just have to live with the unknown."

Candice closed her eyes and looked as though she were about to relax into a restful nap. Amy watched her. Suddenly, Candice's face wrinkled up. She bolted upright in her seat, waving her hand in front of her nose. "Good lord, what is that smell?!"

The pungent aroma smacked into Amy. She looked across the aisle as Mariko burrowed her nose down into the collar of her shirt. In the seat beside her, Roger raised his hand. "Sorry, everyone. That fish from the plane is givin' me the salmon squirts. I'd open a window, but..." he motioned around at the encased helicopter cabin.

"Ugh. Dad!" Amy cried out.

"Christ Almighty, Roger," Candice exclaimed. "I'm trying to make a point about love over here!"

"I said I'm sorry. Geez."

Amy covered her nose. She glanced across the aisle and made eye contact with Mariko. The bottom half of Mariko's mouth was still buried inside her shirt, but Amy could see the tips of Mariko's cheeks pull up and her eyes twinkle in a smile. Mariko was laughing.

Amy laughed too.

***

The helicopter touched down on a small landing pad in the mountains.

Everyone wearily stepped out and saw a line of limousines waiting for them. One of the drivers held a sign that read "Holgate Family and Guest."

They walked toward it. The other groups of guests wandered to their own designated limos.

The driver holding the "Holgate" sign seemed to sense their exhaustion. He flashed a big grin and did an exaggerated thumbs-up. "Heeeeey! Big smiles! This is wedding. Fun time. Happy-happy!"

They climbed in.

The ride was long and uneventful. The backseat had several TVs and a wide selection of movies, but nobody cared to watch anything. Mariko and Candice talked about a TV show they were both into. Roger took a nap. Amy just sat, zoning out.

After another hour, the limo came to a stop.

Amy momentarily wondered what leg of the journey they were about to embark on now. A boat, perhaps? They hadn't had to ride a train yet. Despite sitting on her ass for fifteen hours, Amy was exhausted. All she wanted was a shower and a nap.

But when the door of the limo opened and the soft evening light drifted in, Amy didn't hear the roar of an engine or the churning of helicopter blades. Just birds calling in the distance. She heard the breeze stir itself around the rocky peaks. Her agitation from the long trip vanished and a serenity washed over her.

She climbed out of the limo and took in the building.

It stood higher than the tree line of the mountains, built precisely on the separation between the blooming, lively forest below and the stark, beautiful mountain summits above. The stones of the building's walls seemed to absorb the sunlight, creating a dark, intimidating monolith on the natural surroundings.

Almost as an attempt to soften its powerful image, the front entrance was flooded with vibrant rose bushes, all tightly trimmed into perfect globes of color.

It was scary. It was strong.

But, oh, was it ever beautiful.

A team of bellhops, all wearing bright red vests, gathered the luggage from the trunk of the limo and trotted the bags and suitcases up the steps. Amy knew that her parents must be awed by the view because any other time, her dad would arm-wrestle the bellhops for the right to carry his own bag. Few things irritated him more than having to tip for a job that he could jolly-well do himself.

But Roger kept his lips sealed as his gaze roamed over the expansive scenery. Amy even saw him reach out and put his arm around Candice in a warm embrace. Candice nestled into his shoulder. It was the first public display of affection that Amy's parents had shown in twenty years.

The sight made Amy smile.

It was then that the doorman, clad in a crimson vest, tipped his hat to them. "Welcome to The Venue," he said.

CHAPTER 4

The front doors of The Venue opened into a large lobby.

Wooden furniture, stained and glossed with deep layers of varnish, dotted the area. Mounted up and down the ten foot walls were stuffed animal heads. Bears. Wolves. Elk. Large, scary beasts. Their dead eyes seemed to angle downward, staring at Amy and her family as they stepped across the stone floor.

The lobby bustled with movement.

Guests wandered up and down the grand staircase, wide-eyed as they explored the building. Various staff members, all wearing their signature red vests, moved around, performing their duties with precision. Some carried flowers and decorations. Others migrated through the crowd, offering refreshments.

A man in a crisp tuxedo at the front desk smiled warmly as Amy approached.

"Good afternoon. Welcome to The Venue," he said in a slight accent that Amy thought sounded Eastern European. "I am the hotel manager. May I have your names please?"

"Holgate," Amy said, pointing to herself and her parents. "Amy, Roger and Candice. And she's Yamazaki, Mariko."

"Thank you. One moment please."

The manager clicked around at his computer.

"I shall need a photo I.D. for each of you, please."

They reached into their bags — and in Candice's case, the money belt that she kept tucked deep inside the front of her pants — and pulled out their passports. The manager inspected the photos and held the passports under a scanner.

"It will just be one moment," the manager said.

***

The Event Planner kicked off her heels.

The Control Room was a tight space filled with computers and screens. The monitors received feeds from the cameras planted throughout The Venue. The Event Planner sat directly behind the two control operators.

Passport images tiled onto one of the operator's screens:

A childhood friend of the groom...

The friend's parents...

The friend's plus-one.

The Event Planner sighed. The groom paid for *four* guests just so his middle school girlfriend could attend? Whatever. It was his money.

Alongside the passport photos, security camera images of the guests' faces appeared. Each one flashed a green check-mark. *Identity Matched.* Good. On rare occasion, a guest might RSVP for a particular plus-one and then change their mind and try to substitute another plus-one at the last minute. That always led to a scramble on The Venue's part.

So far, Caleb and Lilith's guests were well-behaved and followed their instructions. And, as the bride and groom had stated, they were all a bunch of nobodies. This was shaping up to be an easy event.

Hopefully, the cleanup would be just as simple.

"Guests' identities have been confirmed," one of the operators said, reading from his list:

"Guest Forty-Five — Amy Holgate"

"Guest Forty-Six — Mariko Yamazaki"

"Guest Forty-Seven — Candice Holgate"

"Guest Forty-Eight — Roger Holgate"

"Check-in complete."

***

The manager smiled at Amy and her family.

"Thank you for your patience. Your reservation has been confirmed," the manager said as he handed them back their passports. "Being a relaxation resort, we encourage our guests to disconnect from society. With that in mind, we do require that all mobile phones, devices, and cameras be checked in at this time."

"Wait, what?" Amy said.

The manager maintained his smile and motioned to a sign that hung over his desk that read, *"Please respect the serenity. No mobile phones or cameras allowed."*

"Your devices will be safe. They will be returned to you upon your departure."

"I don't understand," Amy said. "It's not like we get service here. I haven't gotten a bar since we got on the plane."

"This is a very exclusive resort. The owners try diligently to prevent photos of it, and the events we host here, from appearing on social media. We like to keep our events private. We have professional photographers who will take photos of you and your party at the wedding. Prints and digital copies will be provided to you free of charge."

Amy looked over at her parents and Mariko. They all seemed to be holding a debate with their eyes. Who was going to hand over their phone first, and who was going to say *hell no*?

"Believe me, I understand how hard it can be. All of my staff adhere to the same restrictions. I'm sorry but this is the official policy of The Venue and is nonnegotiable."

Surprisingly, it was Candice who broke first. She sighed and said, "Rules are rules." Then, she reached into her bag, pulled out her phone and tablet, and set them on the counter.

Everyone else followed along.

The manager delicately placed all of the electronics in a metal box. "We will keep these very safe," he said. "We take our guests' privacy seriously."

The manager closed the lid on the metal bin.

"And now, your room keys," the manager said, flashing his wide smile again.

From some hidden rack beneath his desk, he pulled out four black bracelets. Each bracelet had a claspable strap and digital watch-face, making it about the size of a standard smartwatch.

The manager held the bracelets out.

"These will act as your keys. They grant access to your room as well as The Venue's many amenities. You can remove them whenever you so desire, but we do request that you wear them any time you are out and about, enjoying The Venue. They are waterproof, scratchproof and impact resistant. You can wear them in the pool or in the shower. They will also serve as your admittance to the wedding festivities. We take wedding crashing very seriously."

They took hold of the bracelets and inspected them.

The thought nibbled at the back of Amy's mind that they had just been required to hand over all of their technology to honor The

Venue's quaint atmosphere and yet, instead of room keys, they were being asked to use a fancy electronic bracelet.

"Oh, and I should mention that these key bracelets also grant you access to all the open bars, The Venue's café, and The Venue's restaurant," the manager said. "As long as you have those on you, all food and drink are complimentary, courtesy of your hosts, Caleb and Lilith Hunt."

"Score!" Mariko said as she put the bracelet onto her wrist.

Candice and Roger quickly followed.

Finally, Amy strapped hers on as well.

"Excellent. Your check-in is now complete. You will be shown to your rooms. Enjoy your stay at The Venue."

He rang a small bell on his desk. Immediately, four bellhops grabbed the family's luggage and carried it up the grand staircase — a wide, twisting structure of stone steps that wrapped around behind the front desk.

The family followed behind.

The bellhops exited the staircase at the second level and proceeded down a well-lit hallway lined with numbered rooms. The wood trim and crown molding softened the dungeon-like stone walls. Chandeliers hung from the ceilings, making the hallway bright and welcoming.

One of the room doors opened. Amy made eye-contact with the middle-aged man and woman who stepped out into the hallway.

"Mr. and Mrs. Hunt! How are you?" Amy said to the couple.

"Amy, dear. Hello," Mrs. Hunt said, drunkenly swaying on her feet ever-so-slightly. As long as Amy could remember, Mrs. Hunt was always teetering and slurring her words.

"You're looking fit," Mr. Hunt said. His own heavy drinking seemed to have unmoored his eyes. They roamed over Amy's body. She cringed.

"Have you ever seen a wedding this nice?" Mrs. Hunt said. "I said, 'Caleb, you're going to blow your whole retirement on this one weekend,' and he said, 'Mom, do you know how much money I have?' And, honest-to-goodness, I truly have no idea how much he makes; he's doing so well. I'm so proud of him."

"You should be," Candice said.

"And how are you, Amy?" Mrs. Hunt said.

"Good."

"I'm so glad to hear it. I got worried when I heard you were a dancer or something."

"I am."

"Oh," Mrs. Hunt burped. "Well, you have plenty of time to find yourself, dear."

"If you're looking for a real career, talk to Caleb," Mr. Hunt said. "This is why we didn't hand out participation trophies. If Caleb had gotten his way, he'd have gone to art school, or some fruity thing like that. You gotta push your kids. Right, Rog?" He elbowed Amy's dad hard in the arm.

Roger didn't react. He just zoned out and stared ahead.

"Anyway, we need to settle in," Amy said, glancing at the bellhops who waited patiently.

"Of course, of course. Treat yourself to some luxury," Mrs. Hunt said. "People like you deserve it most. It was so nice to see you all."

And with that, Caleb's parents turned and stumbled off down the hallway.

"Charming people," Mariko said as soon as they were out of earshot.

"Assholes," Roger muttered.

"Be nice," Candice said.

The family turned and followed the bellhops.

"Your bracelets are your room keys," the head bellhop said, stopping at one of the doors. "Rooms 103 and 105."

Candice held her bracelet against the magnetic pad at the room door. *Ding!* — it unlocked and swung open. She couldn't help but giggle.

As the bellhops carried the luggage in, Roger made a show of searching his pockets. More than once, Amy had sought out a service worker in order to supplement her dad's meager tipping habit. He was a good, honest, kind man. But boy, was he cheap.

"I, uh, didn't have time to exchange any U.S. dollars," Roger said. "If I can find an ATM, I could—"

"It is quite alright, sir," the head bellhop said. "We are not allowed to accept tips. Your host and hostess have already paid all gratuities"

"Oh. That's nice of them," Roger said, relief flashing across his face.

And with that, her parents disappeared into their room, closing the door behind them.

Amy turned and pressed her own bracelet to the door of the adjacent room. It swung open. The bellhops carried the suitcases inside and deposited them on racks.

"Please let us know if there is anything that can make your stay more comfortable," the head bellhop said, tipping his hat as he walked back out.

He then led his team to the end of the hallway, stopping at a door marked "Staff Only." He held his own red bracelet to the plate beside the door which beeped and then swung open.

Amy watched as the crew disappeared into the hallway beyond. Then she turned and stepped into her room.

CHAPTER 5

The actual hotel room was a letdown. It was relatively small. There was no TV, no amenities. Just some bottled water and chocolate bars on the night stand. All were complimentary, of course.

Even the view, which Amy had been looking forward to, wasn't particularly impressive. Iron bars mounted on the outside of the window threw their shadows into the room, creating a cross-hatch pattern in the orange glow of the setting sun.

It made her feel as though she were in a prison, filling Amy with a sudden, overwhelming urge to leave. "I'm gonna see if I can get a roll-away bed or something," she said.

"What? Why? It's a queen. We'll just share."

She didn't look Mariko in the eye, but she knew the face Mariko must be making — head cocked to the side and mouth slightly open to release a single, silent, exasperated sigh. The same look Mariko had when Amy insisted on paying for dinner, despite them both knowing that she had crippling credit card debt. The look that said *You're being silly, Ames.*

"It's fine. I wanna walk around anyway."

Before Mariko could respond, Amy walked out the door.

She wandered back down the grand staircase.

The noise level of the lobby had increased dramatically since her group had arrived. The boisterous conversations of guests echoed around the stone walls.

Amy rounded a corner and stood on the edge of the stairs, peering down into the lobby. There was now a bottleneck at check-in. Dozens of people, exhausted from travel, stood in line.

Waiters migrated among the tired guests, offering spa water, champagne, and hors d'oeuvres. It did little to placate them. The entire line was being held up by a wiry, middle-aged man in a track suit whose veins bulged on his bald head and red face as he fought with the manager.

"What if someone tries to call or email me?" the man said.

The manager replied in a pleasant voice, "Unfortunately, there is no mobile service or internet access here, and so I am afraid that you cannot—"

"I'm not giving you my phone."

"I am sorry, sir, but the rules state—"

"I got movies and books loaded on this. What the hell else am I supposed to do here? Someone should have put this rule on the website when I booked this trip!"

The people in the line behind the man groaned and muttered to each other. This argument had apparently gone in circles for a while.

Amy watched the interaction.

There was something about the man's voice... something familiar.

Amy tried to place it. She *recognized* that man. The voice, the face, the wiry frame, and most of all, the intensity in the way he spoke. As a memory formed on the tip of her brain—

"Hi, Ames."

The voice, so close behind her, made her jump.

She swung around.

There stood Caleb.

He seemed taller than she remembered. Or maybe it was his frame. As a kid, he had always been on the heavier side. He wasn't an obese child, or anything, but he always had a round, full face and a stocky build. Amy's mom often commented that little Caleb looked like a cherub, a sort of Cupid who never shed his rolls of baby fat. Candice, of course, meant it as a compliment, but it was never received as such.

The person who stood before Amy now, however, was hardly that same person. Those fat rolls had been carved into muscles, the contours of which could be seen pushing against the light blue t-shirt that tightly hugged his body. His round face had found cheekbones and a jawline. His chest bulged out, pulling the shirt away from what Amy could only assume was a tight stomach.

She gazed at his sculpted body, impressed by every inch of him. Until her gaze reached his eyes.

They looked down at her but didn't seem to quite focus on her face. He seemed to be looking *through* and past her, staring more at some speck in his memory than at the woman in front of him.

He smiled. But the smile on that face wasn't the one Amy remembered seeing so often from childhood. Caleb's face used to glow when he smiled. His toothy grin would merge into dimples that were so big that he had to partially shut his eyes to accommodate them. His nose would twist up and a joyful snort would sometimes escape.

When they were kids, Amy saw that smile often. She saw it when they had squirt-gun fights. She saw it when he'd beat her at tic-tac-toe with sidewalk chalk. She saw it when they played *Street Fighter*. She saw it when they watched *The Burbs*. She saw it every time he answered the door and saw her there, ready to go play.

She saw it less and less as elementary school turned to middle school turned to high school. By now, she couldn't remember when she last saw that smile.

Amy definitely didn't see that smile today.

This smile was strained. Pulled tight. Depending on the context, Amy would struggle to differentiate this smile from a grimace.

"Hey, man! Good to see you," Amy said after collecting herself. "Congratulations," she tacked on, trying to fend off another silence before it could overtake them.

She opened her arms for a friendly hug.

Caleb recoiled and took a step back up the stairs, putting space between them. "I'd better not," he said, motioning to her outstretched arms. "I'm in a committed relationship with Lilith."

"Oh. Uh, yeah," Amy said, dropping her arms. "I didn't mean to—"

"I see you brought a friend as your plus-one," Caleb interrupted. His eyes seemed to finally zero in on her and were now probing her, as a robot might. "I was hoping you'd bring your husband. Or boyfriend."

"Uh, nope. Not seeing anyone."

Caleb's smile seemed to get bigger, but that just meant that his lips pulled tighter, exposing even more of his teeth.

"Same old Amy," he said. "I get it. It's fun to play the field. I would too if I wasn't in love." He pointed to the ring on his finger as if offering proof of his affections.

"That's, uh, that's great. I mean, this is really incredible. The trip here alone was fucking fantastic."

"That's good to hear, Amy. I want you and your parents to have the time of your lives."

Amy shuddered under his unblinking gaze. "So, um, how are you, man?"

"Me?" Caleb's eyes went wide, seemingly surprised that anyone would ask anything about him. "I'm better than I've ever been. Lilith has changed everything for me. I see things so much clearer now. I finally found peace. And now I'm about to have the happiest day of my life."

"That's awesome. I'm happy for you."

"I appreciate that," he said. He stared at her for another moment. As Amy was about to say something else to end the silence, he suddenly broke eye-contact and began to step around her. "Now, if you'll excuse me, I have things to see to."

"Oh, yeah, of course. Sorry. Didn't mean to keep you."

Caleb took a few steps down the stairs and then turned to look at Amy again. "But I just want to say that I hope you and your parents really get into the spirit of the occasion."

"I'm sure we will. My mom's been looking forward to this for months. She *really* likes you."

"Really?"

"Uh, yeah. She always asks if I've heard from you. Sorry I've been a flake. Adult friendship is hard, you know? But we're all really happy for you, Caleb."

Amy couldn't tell, but it seemed that, for the first time in this conversation, a different emotion cracked through Caleb's stiff face. It almost appeared to be a look of confusion.

"And you're looking good, man," Amy stammered on. "I've never seen you so fit."

"Lilith and I are on steroids," Caleb said.

Amy let out a laugh. *Finally,* it was the Caleb she knew and missed. The one with the quick, dry wit. Always a sarcastic comment.

But his face didn't seem to register that this was a joke at all. He just looked at her with that blank expression. It was then that Amy realized that he wasn't joking. Those arms, that chest, that neck of his... Heaping, lumpy muscle mass like that didn't just happen.

Caleb turned to walk away again.

Amy wanted to call after him, to invite him to her room for a drink, to do anything to see if she could break through this weird mound of fleshy emptiness in front of her and find the old friend from her cherished childhood memories. She said the first thing that came to mind.

"Is that Coach Sanborn down there?" she asked.

She didn't know how or when the pieces had finally snapped together in her brain, but she suddenly remembered where she knew the bald man with the bulging forehead veins and the tracksuit from. Coach Sanborn. Their high school cross-country coach.

Amy had joined the cross-country team sophomore year.

When she showed up for the first practice, she saw that Caleb had also signed up. It was like that a lot in high school — Amy would start a new activity, walk through the door on the first day, and Caleb would already be there waiting.

Unfortunately, Coach Sanborn thought that "coaching" meant "break teenagers apart and then build them back up." He ran them until they were nauseous. His theory was that the harder he pushed them, and the more horrible the circumstances, the better runners they would become.

Cross-country fucked up Amy's body. Her left knee still ached if she didn't stretch it daily.

In truth, Coach Sanborn wasn't even a trained coach. He was just an English teacher who did it as a part time gig and seemed to learn most of his coaching techniques by watching inspirational sports movies.

"Yep. That's him," Caleb said with a smile. "He made me into the man I am today."

With that, Caleb walked off down the stairs.

Amy watched him go.

***

Amy walked back into her room.

Mariko had flopped out on the bed and was idly flipping through a magazine.

"There was a line at the front," Amy said. "I didn't get an extra bed."

"Tough shit, loser," Mariko said as she shimmied her body to the center of the mattress and then spread out her arms and legs to take up as much space as possible.

Amy sat on the edge of the bed. She stared off.

"You okay?" Mariko asked, sitting up.

"This whole thing feels weird," Amy said.

"Weird like how?"

"Our high school cross-country coach is down there."

"So?"

"Caleb shit himself in practice once."

Mariko let out a laugh. "Wait, wait, wait. You mean, like, *literally* shit himself?"

"Like poop came out his butt, ran down his leg and soaked into his sock. Yeah. *Literally.*"

"Oh shit. Literally."

"It's not that big a deal. It happens a lot with runners."

"One more reason to take that half-marathon off my bucket list."

"A good coach would *know* that runner's diarrhea happens. A good coach, hell a good *person*, wouldn't make it a thing. But Coach Sanborn used it as motivation for everyone else. He made an example of Caleb. No one wanted to run slower than 'Shit Streak.'"

"Good runner's name."

"It was a bullshit thing for an adult to do to a kid."

"Yeah."

"Who invites their asshole high school coach to their wedding?"

"Shit Streak, apparently."

"It's not just Coach Sanborn."

"What do you mean?"

"There are other people I recognize down there. Caleb's cousin Rick is here. He tore Caleb's shoulder out when they were wrestling as kids. Caleb's childhood priest is here. He accused Caleb of stealing and told Caleb's parents. There are the girls on the plane. They sounded like they were complete bitches to Lilith in college."

Mariko let out a loud sigh that Amy knew meant she wasn't convinced.

"That's all petty kid stuff," Mariko said. "It happens to everyone. You move on."

"Caleb hated these people. There are only so many seats at a wedding reception. So many plane flights you can book. A wedding is cruel math. There are people who don't make the cut. Friends who just aren't close enough to be invited."

"Maybe there was no one else to invite."

Amy nodded. *That* actually made a bit of sense.

There was the part of her that was surprised that Caleb had actually invited *her*. They hadn't spoken much since high school, and if she was being honest, they hadn't been "friends" since middle school.

But when she thought about it, there wasn't anyone else from their childhood whom she would have expected him to invite. Caleb didn't make friends easily.

"And what horrible thing did you and your parents do to poor Caleb?" Mariko asked.

Amy thought. "Nothing," she finally said. "Except wanting his fucking wedding to be over."

C H A P T E R 6

The next day, Amy woke up refreshed.

She apologized to Mariko for being so weird about wanting a second bed. They had slept — each on her own side — without excessive tension, sexual or otherwise.

Then she apologized for being weird about the wedding in general. Mariko told her that she now needed to apologize for being so weird about all these apologies about being weird.

They laughed. Things felt like they were back to normal.

Amy chalked it up to jet lag messing with her mind and emotions.

They met up with Amy's parents for breakfast, free of charge at The Venue's café. Most of the menu options contained French words that Amy was afraid to pronounce, but she tried anyway. She ended up with some sort of pastry and egg dish that melted the moment it touched her tongue, releasing its rich flavors to swirl around her mouth. Hands down, it was the best unpronounceable French pastry and egg thing that she had ever eaten.

After breakfast, they wandered around the outside areas of The Venue, taking in amazing views of the jagged valley below.

That short walk made them feel they had earned a little relaxation. The spa at The Venue offered three different styles of massage. They tried them all; Amy fell asleep through most. At the end, she decided that she still preferred the good old shiatsu. She didn't need anything fancier than that.

She didn't see Caleb at all that day. She hoped he was off enjoying himself with his bride-to-be.

Every now and then, Amy would wander past the front lobby and see more guests arrive for the wedding. She thought she recognized some people — an uncle or cousin of Caleb's whom she had met decades ago. They were all friendly. And they were all drunk.

Amy got pretty drunk too. Expensive booze went down smoothly. She wondered if her bottom shelf liquor back home would taste like rubbing alcohol now.

Occasionally, at the pool or at the café, she would strike up a conversation with another guest. Some people knew Caleb from work. Some from college. Nobody had any particularly interesting stories or memories of him. Mostly the conversations were of the *Can you believe how nice this place is? He rented out this whole building for us? He must be doing really well!* variety.

All in all, it was a perfect day. Amy didn't even miss her phone. While drunk, she commented to Mariko that life without a phone was so satisfying, she vowed to lock hers away every weekend from then on. Mariko bet that Amy wouldn't make it through one month back home. Amy's parents sided with Mariko.

They parted ways to take afternoon naps.

When they woke up, it was time to get ready for the wedding.

***

Amy checked herself out in the mirror.

Her dress was a whopping eighteen bucks from the Target clearance rack. It had a nice floral pattern that paired well with her beige cardigan and blue heels. Nothing too fancy. She wasn't trying to impress anyone, especially at a wedding with her parents and ex. But the dress did have pockets, which was always a deal clincher.

As she was putting her hair into a simple bun, the bathroom door opened. Mariko stepped out. Her black hair was straightened down to her bare shoulders. She wore a sea-green gown that effortlessly flowed across her figure.

"You look nice," Amy said after she realized that she had been staring for a moment.

"You too."

There was a knock at the door. Amy broke her gaze away from Mariko and went to answer. Standing there were her parents. Candice wore a purple, short-sleeved dress that Amy recognized as being the same one she wore to Amy's grandma's funeral. It was probably the only dress Candice owned. Roger, meanwhile, despite having probably gotten dressed five minutes ago, had already taken off his suit coat, loosened his tie, unbuttoned his top button, and rolled up his sleeves.

"Let's get this over with," he said.

Roger offered his arm to Amy. They all stepped out of the room and walked off down the hall.

Other doors opened as they passed. Wedding guests in suits and gowns filed out. Nobody spoke to each other. There were just nods of recognition, an acknowledgment that they were all here for the same reason and going to the same place.

A sign had been set up at the end of the hallway:

"6pm. Hunt/Foley Wedding Service in the Chapel. Please proceed this way."

They followed the arrow down the grand stairway.

***

The chapel was a rounded room off of the main lobby.

It felt small and modest, particularly by The Venue's standards. The only light source came from flickering votive candles in crystal bowls that lined the aisle and altar. One wall had stained glass windows, but with night settling in outside, the room felt particularly cave-like.

Rose petals draped the aisle and benches, but in the faint light Amy struggled to determine if the petals were crimson or just black.

She led her parents toward an open pew, knowing that her father would want a seat as far to the rear of the chapel as possible. Amy wouldn't mind either. Anything to decrease the probability of having to interact with Caleb's parents.

They took their seats on the hard bench.

A strange hush fell over all the guests as they entered this petal-covered and candlelit tomb. They came in small groups and quietly found places to sit.

Bit by bit, the pews filled until no one else arrived.

For several minutes, the congregation sat in the darkened room, the only sounds being the rustling of their clothes as they shifted their weight on the pews. A whispered word or two occasionally drifted among the crowd, but the murmur would fade away before it became an actual conversation.

Just when Amy felt that her butt was going numb from sitting on the flat wood, the chapel doors slammed closed with a deafening *bang*. The couple in front of Amy jumped. A nervous laughter drifted out among the gathering. And then, like a leaden blanket, the silence descended over the crowd again, smothering out sound and conversation.

They sat in that stillness for another minute.

The door swung open again with a loud clang.

Caleb emerged from the darkened hall beyond. His mom clutched his arm as he escorted her up the aisle. Caleb's stone-faced father staggered on after them, swaying a bit on his feet. He evidently had begun celebrating early.

Behind them came a man in a suit, clutching a Bible. Amy recognized him as Father Dave. She had never met the man before, but she knew his face from the baptism photos that had adorned Caleb's childhood home.

The procession silently marched up the aisle, their footsteps muffled by the rose petals beneath their shoes. An unease moved through the crowd as no one knew whether to stand or remain seated. Ultimately, everyone opted to just watch.

Caleb made his way to the front, deposited his parents in a pew, and then stood by the altar with Father Dave.

A stringed quartet then played out from a darkened corner of the room; Amy didn't even realize they had been there the whole time. As the guests heard the familiar notes of *The Wedding March*, they rose to their feet, this time without hesitation.

All eyes were on the door as Lilith emerged from the darkness.

Her white, form-fitted gown was elegant but simple. A white veil hung over her face. Amy suddenly realized that she had never actually *seen* Lilith's face on any of the invitations. It filled Amy with a weird sensation, being unable to imagine what Lilith looked like beneath that veil. It felt as though a ghost were walking down the aisle, one steady step at a time.

Instead of watching the faceless bride migrate to the altar, Amy chose to look over at Caleb. His face beamed. *That* was the smile that Amy had missed. His lips gently curled up, softening his cheeks and his eyes as he watched his love float toward him. His mouth hung open slightly and Amy was sure that he was holding his breath.

In spite of herself, a knot welled in Amy's chest and a tear rolled toward the edge of her eye. In that moment, she felt nothing but joy toward her dear, old friend.

The violins pulled her out of that moment, though. Partway through the song, they transitioned from *The Wedding March* to *The Ride of the Valkyries*. At least, Amy thought that was what the song was named. She had heard it mostly in movies over scenes of helicopters swooping in to machine-gun down a village.

But after a few measures of the sinister, angry song, it transitioned back to the soaring strains of *The Wedding March*.

Amy looked around; nobody else seemed to have noticed. Or at least, she couldn't tell if anyone noticed — most people's faces were hidden behind the shadows that the flickering candles threw around the room.

When Lilith reached the front of the chapel, the music stopped. The group stood in silence for a moment.

"Let us pray," Father Dave said.

Although Amy was not a particularly religious person, she bowed her head anyway.

The wedding of Caleb and Lilith had begun.

CHAPTER 7

The service itself was fairly unremarkable.

Amy figured that Father Dave probably wrote a single wedding service twenty years ago and had been recycling it ever since. He recited from First Corinthians and then he told some story about empty shoes and open hands, or something. Amy zoned out. She felt the service leaned a bit too far toward the patriarchy — a lot of stuff about a wife being dutiful. Amy wasn't going to raise a fuss about it, though, as she was always a bit too lazy to be a true feminist.

And so, her mind drifted to thoughts of how thirsty she was, and how at the same time she kinda needed to pee. Eventually, she started wondering if she had ADHD and maybe that explained why she never finished the things she started in life.

Her attention only returned to the service when Father Dave announced that the bride and groom had written their own vows.

Amy sat up straight. She was going to hear Lilith's voice for the first time.

"I, Lilith, choose you, Caleb, to be my husband from today until eternity." Lilith said. Her voice wavered slightly, as though she were unaccustomed to speaking louder than a whisper in front of people. It made Amy smile a bit — Lilith must be a shy girl, slightly overwhelmed to have all eyes on her for once. Adorable. And probably a good match for Caleb, who Amy knew could get steam-rolled by a stronger personality.

"From the moment I met you, I knew that you had everything I needed to be happy," Lilith continued.

As she said that, Roger rubbed his fingers together in the "money" motion in front of Amy's face. Candice quickly swatted her husband's hand down.

Amy swallowed her giggle.

"With you in my life, I can achieve all my ambitions. All my dreams. All my fantasies." Lilith's voice seemed to be gaining strength as she continued. The tremble had vanished. "You have allowed me to be the person I was always meant to be. The real Lilith is now freed because of you. And everyone will soon see how strong she truly is and always was. Together, we are something greater and more powerful than anyone here has ever known. Those who laughed at us, will learn to cry. Those who hurt us, will be in pain."

Amy glanced at Mariko whose own face had wrinkled up in a *WTF???* expression.

"I will be with you, by your side, through ecstasy and agony," Lilith said, her voice now so passionate and forceful that she seemed to be shouting her words. "Fighting with you. Conquering with you. Overcoming all obstacles with you. Until death do us part."

The chapel sat in an uncomfortable silence for a second or two before Father Dave said, "Uh, thank you, Lilith. And now Caleb's vows."

Caleb cleared his throat. "I, Caleb, choose you, Lilith, to be my wife. From now until eternity."

Amy could hear his voice break as he spoke.

"Throughout my childhood, I always felt alone. I'd make friends, and they'd abandon me. I'd try to find lovers, and they'd reject me. I'd try to make connections with colleagues and coworkers, and they would shun me."

The benches in the room creaked as people shifted their weight. Amy herself had to look down for a moment. But after a breath, she forced her eyes back up. *I never abandoned him*, she thought. *I never shunned him or rejected him. I was his best friend and I dragged my whole family to support him at his weird-ass wedding.*

With that in mind, she sat up even straighter and looked directly in Caleb's direction. But his gaze didn't seem to register that there was an audience. He was locked in on Lilith, still hidden behind her veil.

"I thought I could reinvent myself in college," he continued. "But it was more of the same. Rejection. Isolation. Depression."

The room stayed silent.

"I was told that money was the answer. When I looked around at the guys who had girls, I saw that they drove fancy cars. They wore nice clothes. They radiated success and people were drawn to them for it. And so, I went into finance. And investing. I poured myself into my work in the vain hope that I would finally be seen.

"But it was more of the same. I had never been lonelier. Conversation didn't come easy, especially with girls. True connections weren't meant for people like me. Finally, I'd had enough. I was determined to be seen. Seen by everyone who ignored me. Who walked all over me. Seen by the people who didn't even know I existed.

"And so, I bought a forty-four Magnum. I carried it down into the building's lobby. I was going to shoot myself. I planned to do it by the elevators, at 7:55 a.m. so that everyone who came to work that morning, carrying their coffee and talking to their friends, would know. The elevators would be roped off as a crime scene. All my 'friends' would have to take the stairs. One final inconvenience for everyone whom I had inconvenienced my whole life."

Amy found her mouth hanging open. She slowly closed it, fearing that the slight click of her teeth coming together might be deafening in this silent chapel.

Mariko whispered in her ear, "Is this for real?"

"I... I don't know," she managed to stammer out.

"I stood there," Caleb continued. "I reached into my briefcase. I pulled out my gun. As I was about to bring it to my head, it... something happened... a *miracle* happened. An angel reached down from Heaven and grasped my hand. I couldn't raise it. I couldn't complete my task. She pushed the gun back down into my briefcase. I stood there, stunned. I looked into the angel's face. Her eyes burning with the brightness of a sun. Of *the* sun. The sun whose warmth I had not basked in since I was a child.

"I had seen the angel's face before. Every day, in fact. The face of an intern. An intern who always arrived early, who always stayed late, who rarely spoke and yet always seemed to be watching and seeing everything. I had passed this intern many times. We had said hello to each other as strangers do in the elevator. But I had never *seen* her, truly seen her and her love and her beauty and her fire until that very day. She shattered the darkness that had swallowed me and filled my life with a light so bright that I see nothing but her, now and forever."

Caleb reached out and grasped Lilith's hand.

Amy could see Lilith's lips stretch into a thin smile beneath her veil. The faint, stoic grin of the bride felt disproportionate to the outpouring of emotion from Caleb.

"The angel opened her mouth and spoke to me," Caleb continued. "She communicated not just in words but in emotions. Her eyes told a thousand stories of love and longing. She made me realize that I had more to live for. More to accomplish. More of a mark to leave upon the world. There was a plan for me. For us.

"Lilith, that angel was you. We left the building right then. We went back to my home. And then we made love. True love. I had been with women before. Mostly women, I'm ashamed to admit, I had to pay for. But I had never been *one* with someone else. Until that day."

Caleb's voice cracked. His throat seemed to twist up from the emotion. Amy could see the tears rolling from his eyes and on down his cheeks. He made no motion to wipe them away.

"Lilith, I promise to be one with you forever," Caleb said as he regained some composure. "Everything in my life has led me to this moment. This is my redemption. I promise to love you forever. I promise to cherish you forever. I promise to defend you, to fight for you, to bleed with you. Until death do us part."

Despite his voice building to that triumphant conclusion, none of the assembled guests cried. None of them clapped. The closest thing to a reaction was a drunken hiccup that Amy thought came from the vicinity of Caleb's parents.

At the altar, Father Dave — seemingly lost for words — stared at the young couple before him. He shifted his weight and blinked, looking unsure of what role he actually had in this bizarre ceremony. Caleb and Lilith looked at him.

"By the, uh, power vested in me, I, uh, now pronounce you husband and wife," Father Dave said. "You may, uh, kiss the—"

Before he could even finish the sentence, Caleb lifted Lilith's veil, grabbed her face and pulled her mouth toward his. Even from her seat near the back of the chapel, Amy could see their tongues spring out of their mouths and slosh around on each other like two wrestling sea lions.

At least it's passionate, Amy thought. *That's for damn sure.*

The other guests seemed to realized that the silence had gone on a bit too long. Someone, somewhere, started clapping. Everyone else joined in. But in a few seconds, the applause faded away again.

"The, uh, the bride and groom would like to invite everyone to the ballroom for the reception," Father Dave flatly announced.

It didn't seem that anyone actually heard him.

They were all glued to the sight of Caleb and Lilith groping each other amidst their wedding kiss.

CHAPTER 8

Being in the back row of the chapel meant that Amy and her family were the first out the door, after the exuberant bride and groom, of course.

Amy stepped out of that dark room and into the well-lit foyer, her eyes blurring a bit from the sudden change in light.

She stopped for a moment.

All the staff — dozens of them clad in their crimson vests — lined either side of the chapel door, forming a pathway across the foyer to the ballroom on the far side. Large smiles stretched across their faces as, like a rowing crew, they waved their arms in a synchronized motion to guide the guests along the path.

As Amy led her family, she occasionally made eye-contact with the staff. They looked right back at her, that smile constantly plastered on their faces. Unnerved by the intensity of the eye-contact, Amy found her gaze drifting toward her feet as her heels clacked on the polished stone floor.

The manager from the front desk stood at the ballroom door.

"May I see your guest bracelet, please?" he said to Amy and her group. One by one, they held out their wrists and presented their bracelets. The manager waved some sort of sensor wand over the devices.

The wand dinged and flashed a green light.

"Welcome Holgate Family and Ms. Yamazaki," the manager said. "You are all seated at Table Ten."

With a flamboyant tug, one of the bellhops swung open the wooden door.

Amy stepped into the ballroom.

She had to orient herself at first. The chapel had been relatively tight and confined, as had their rooms and all the connecting hallways. The ballroom, meanwhile, was massive. Its open, exposed-beam ceiling was so tall that a layer of haze seemed to drift around it. Crystal chandeliers hung above the seating area, casting their light down on the vibrant red linens and black and white tiled floor.

A string quartet sat on a stage at the far end of the ballroom, merrily playing sprightly classical music. A DJ stood to the side. He bellowed into a microphone, "Welcome to the par-tay, folks! The bar is open! Don't forget to swing by the photobooth."

Amy led the way to Table Ten, situated in the dead-center of the room. They found their place cards, although Amy had some difficulty actually reading her name through all the ornate, looping, hand-drawn calligraphy.

As she sat, her eyes were drawn to the side of the room they entered through. A metal, spiral staircase ascended to a small balcony that overlooked everything. Beneath the balcony was a bar, seemingly built into the wall and connected to a kitchen beyond. But she barely registered it because she couldn't help but stare at the wall itself which was decorated, floor-to-ceiling, in all manner of medieval weaponry.

The light from the room reflected off the blades of the arsenal. Despite their ancient design of wooden handles wrapped in leather, many of the weapons looked new. And deadly.

T . J .   P A Y N E

The sheer variety impressed Amy. She didn't know the names of all the weapons. There was a crossbow, of course. A battle axe that looked too heavy for her to lift. There was that spikey ball thingy. *Is that a mace?* Amy wondered. Or was the mace the spikey chain thingy? And what was the difference between a lance and a spear? Or a rapier and a saber?

"Well, that ain't gonna pass through TSA," Roger said, one seat over.

Amy looked. Her father had opened the little box that waited at each guest's seat. The wedding favor. He pulled out a metal throwing star. He tested its edge but quickly withdrew his finger at the sharpness. It was real. As he held it up, Amy could see the engraving:

"Make Memories — C & L"

"Did we all get one?" Candice asked, although by the time she finished the question, she had already opened her own box and revealed that, yes, she too received a throwing star.

"Come on now," Mariko said, a note of feigned disgust on her voice. "You can't mix ninja throwing stars with a medieval European theme. Pick a lane, people."

Amy laughed. But it was a forced laugh. She was now busy examining the centerpiece — a framed portrait of Caleb, probably when he was fourteen or so. Early high school. His slicked hair and collared shirt framed a face that scowled back at the camera. The flowers of the centerpiece wrapped around the frame, making it look almost like a memorial. A handwritten inscription was scrawled across the photo. *"Thank you for making me who I am."*

CHAPTER 9

To Amy's surprise, she actually enjoyed the reception. Maybe it was because whenever her back was turned, a waiter swooped in and topped off her glass. She had long ago passed the tipsy stage of the night and had entered the stage where she knew she would have regrets the next morning — just not enough regrets to do something silly, like promise to quit drinking.

The string quartet had transitioned from classical music to classical renditions of pop songs, forming a fun background noise. Amy would forget the quartet was even there until she would catch the familiar hook of *Celebration* or *Love Shack*.

Classic wedding songs, indeed.

As for the company and conversation, the other guests were fine. With a few exceptions.

Seated at their table was a middle-aged alpha dog of a man who insisted on being called "Big O." Amy gathered that his last name was "Ortiz." His wife was much nicer, much prettier, and much younger.

At one point, Big O jokingly threatened to leap across the table and punch Amy's dad in the face for mistakenly confusing the Pittsburg Steelers with the Philadelphia Eagles (Amy still didn't know which team Big O rooted for; she just knew not to confuse them).

Big O was Caleb's boss at one of the first companies Caleb worked for out of college. Amy met a few people from those early jobs. They were mostly frat boys turned stock traders. The kind of people who were accustomed to this level of luxury (or at least pretended to be). They seemed downright entitled to it.

She struggled to imagine Caleb working alongside these men, all of whom brought trophy wives and girlfriends to the wedding. They flaunted their money as easily as they flaunted their willingness to use the c-word. *I'm just kidding! Lighten up,* Big O would say when Amy or Mariko shot him a glare.

Lilith's side of the reception, meanwhile, appeared to all be middle class, or even lower-middle class. They seemed quiet. Somber. As if the weight of money troubles had slowly squeezed out their joy in life. Whenever Amy briefly chatted with one of them in the line for the photobooth or while walking to the bathroom, she found them to be pleasant but humorless.

It struck Amy that she didn't see anyone escort Lilith down the aisle. No father or father-figure. She wondered if Lilith still had parents. Or maybe she wasn't on good terms with them.

At some point, a waiter set a plate in front of Amy. Steak so rare that the pink juices had already pooled out to the edges where the plate curved upward. She picked up the knife, noticing how heavy it was. The knife might have looked expensive, but as she slid its serrated blade across the meat, it caught.

She held up the knife to inspect it.

Dull and rusty.

Also seated at the table was Mrs. Crawford, Amy and Caleb's third grade teacher. The woman must have been in her late 60s, yet she looked very much like Amy remembered — a gray beehive of hair and thick glasses draped with a homemade, beaded lanyard.

Mrs. Crawford had recognized Amy instantly (she seemed to have a photographic memory of every student she ever taught) and made a comment that she was surprised it wasn't Amy with Caleb up at the altar.

During dinner, when Mariko prodded her to talk more about Little Amy, Mrs. Crawford launched into the story of how Amy and Caleb danced a tango in front of the entire school for the third grade talent show.

"The *tango*? You?" Mariko exclaimed.

"I've always been into dancing."

"Did you even know what you were doing?"

"Sure. I whipped my head around, looked all sexy, and passed a rose from my mouth to Caleb's while our entire class laughed at us."

"Seriously?"

"It ain't a tango if it doesn't leave emotional scars."

"Whose idea was this?" Mariko asked.

"It was mine and it was adorable," Mrs. Crawford said. "And I swear, the other teachers and I, we never thought we'd see Caleb grow out of his shell like that. He was a silent child. Obviously very smart but he would never raise his hand. He'd freeze up if you asked him a question. The other teachers thought he was a lost cause. One of those kids who would slip through the cracks if you let him. That's where smart kids go to vanish. But I said, 'Amy Holgate is special and this boy is in love with her. He would do anything for her, including opening up.'"

"*That's* why you made us do that?"

"Oh, yes. He didn't want to, but I made him. We had a pool going in the teachers' lounge on whether I could get Caleb on stage. I won a hundred-dollar Macy's gift card."

"And?" Mariko asked. "How did it go for Caleb?"

"Horrible," Amy said.

"Sure, some kids laughed," Mrs. Crawford said. "There will always be a few knuckleheads."

"*All* kids laughed."

"But look where he's at now," Mrs. Crawford said while leaning back in her seat and motioning around the cavernous lodge. "Need I say more?"

"He burned the VHS copies of that tango. He never talked about it again."

"Well, that's the way you handle introverts. You need to shock their systems. That's how they realize that when the other kids laugh at them, it's not the end of the world."

There wasn't much more Amy could say to that.

"Are you done, ma'am?" a waiter asked, motioning toward Amy's plate.

"Yes, please." Amy glanced toward the large chunk of raw beef that remained. The waiter removed the steak knife from Amy's plate, polished it with a napkin, and then set it back on Amy's place-setting. Only then did he take the bloody steak away.

Amy looked around. Most of the plates around the ballroom had been cleared. But the knives remained.

"Caleb Hunt, the big ol' cunt!" Big O suddenly exclaimed as he rose from the table.

Amy grimaced at the word but managed to force a smile.

Caleb and Lilith, doing their rounds of welcoming and thanking all their guests, had finally made their way to Table Ten. Everyone, Amy included, stood to greet the bride and groom.

Big O intercepted them first, giving Caleb a bone-crushing handshake while slapping him on the back so hard that it might have dislodged a molar.

"It's our little nickname. Hunt the Cunt here loves it," Big O said to Lilith with a hearty laugh. "It's okay, I can use that word, 'cause I got a wife."

Amy could see Caleb's jaw clench slightly beneath his smile.

Lilith went over and gave Big O a warm hug.

"I'm so glad you could make it, Big O," Lilith said sweetly. "Caleb talks fondly about his time at Hartworth & Company. It was the job he had right before I met him. You set the stage for what he would become."

"I hope he hasn't told you too much. That's proprietary information. If he's giving out trade secrets, then—" Big O mimed swinging a punch right at Caleb's face. "Wham! My reflexes just gonna kick in. Can't be held responsible for what I might do."

Even before Big O finished speaking, Lilith had turned her back to him and faced Mrs. Crawford. Big O whacked his wife on the shoulder, pretending the joke was meant for her. She laughed.

"You must be Caleb's third grade teacher," Lilith said, grasping Mrs. Crawford's hand.

"Why, yes."

"Thank you for breaking him out of his shell."

"Glad to do it. As I was 'splaining to these folks, the way to handle introverted children is you have to shock their system—"

Once again, Lilith cut the conversation short.

Now her gaze fixed squarely on Amy. Lilith clutched a hand to her heart, the breath snatched from her lips as she stared in wonder at Amy's face.

"And you. You must be Amy. *The* Amy. The one and only Amy. Amy, Amy, Amy."

"Yep," Amy said after a pause. She shifted her weight and looked around her. "I'm Amy."

Lilith walked up to her, arms outstretched.

Amy opened her arms too, waiting for the hug.

But Lilith didn't embrace her. Instead, she reached over and grabbed Amy's bicep in a firm grip. Her hand travelled up and down Amy's arm, massaging it, feeling her muscles. Amy just stood there, not sure how to respond.

"My, you *are* fit," Lilith said, her hand on Amy's arm and her eyes on Amy's face. "And so pretty. So very, very pretty." Lilith released her arm and put her hands up to cup Amy's face. "You're an aerobic dance instructor, correct?"

"Uh, yep."

"You must have so much endurance. I bet you're fast. Agile. Slippery, even."

"Um, sure?"

Lilith removed her hands from Amy's face.

"I don't have much use for dance," Lilith said, a curtness in her voice now. "It's fun in a childish way. No useful skills, though. There are other ways to get aerobic exercise. I train with an ex-Mossad agent. He taught me Israeli hand-to-hand combat techniques. Much better for strength and cardio."

"Sounds intense."

"Oh, it is."

Caleb, having extracted himself from Big O, stepped toward Mariko.

"You're Amy's friend, right?" he asked her.

"Mariko." She held out her hand, but Caleb made no motion to shake it. Instead, his eyes traveled up and down Mariko's slim frame, taking her in. His brow wrinkled and his head nodded, like a handicapper sizing up an athlete.

"You seem pretty fit," Caleb said finally. "You also do dance?"

"She's got a real career," Amy said. "She does HR. Director of hiring."

Caleb's eyes went wide. "A head hunter! Fantastic."

"Uh, thanks," Mariko said.

"A director of hiring knows how to size people up immediately. A few words, or a handshake, or their body language. That's all you need to know everything about a person. That's what Big O always taught me, ain't that right, Big O?"

"Totes, bro," Big O said, raising his glass, although he probably didn't even hear the question.

A smile lingered on Caleb's face as he kept his eyes locked on Mariko. "You can see people's strengths and weaknesses. You can tease apart the leaders from the losers. Strong from the weak. Survivors from the chaff."

Lilith now seemed to be interested in Mariko too. She angled her way in, her eyes wide. "Ooh, I like this. Tell me, HR Girl, who in this room is strong?"

Mariko looked around. "Uh, well, I—"

"I don't mean physique or muscle strength. My cousin Brad over there played linebacker at UCO. He might look strong, but he's weak in other ways. I don't think he has what it takes to survive."

Amy looked toward the guy she pointed at, Brad. A big, hulking man whose muscles pressed against the fabric of his dress shirt.

"When we were kids, he came to stay with us for the summer. We did everything together. Including shoplift. Just candy from a big store. They wouldn't miss it. Wouldn't hurt their bottom line. But something about the 'Thou Shall Not Steal' really wormed its way into Big Brad's soft brain. Despite all his promises, the little prick tattled on me." She shook her head in disappointment. "Weak."

She motioned toward another of the biggest guys in the room. Amy recognized him as Caleb's cousin, Rick.

"And Rick, well, he's Army," Lilith said. Amy believed it. Rick had that military build and posture. "He's fit and well-trained. Should be calm under pressure. One of the few people here who could lift that battle axe on the wall. But I don't know how he'll react in a real emergency. How dark of a place is he willing to go to? Sweetie, what do you think?"

Caleb shrugged. "Dunno."

"The thing about Rick is that he's twenty-eight, never been promoted and never will be promoted," Lilith continued. "Because despite all of his skills, he's a bit..." she whacked her hand against her head a few times and crossed her eyes to make the point.

Then she turned her attention back to Mariko.

"So, tell me, Mariko the Headhunter, did you spot those weaknesses?"

"I... I haven't interacted with them."

"That's fair," Lilith said with a grin. "Before the night is over, I'm sure you will."

"What about me?" Caleb said. "You and I have talked. You've sized me up. I'm sure Amy's told you all about me. What's *my* weakness?"

Mariko glanced from one of them to the other. They seemed to genuinely expect an answer.

"Do tell," Lilith said.

"Yeah. What's my weakness?" Caleb pressed.

"You're, um, you're too damn charming?" Mariko finally said.

Caleb let out a chuckle. It rolled around his mouth and built in intensity until it was a full laugh. Lilith joined in too. Together, they stood there and laughed. Alone. Amy and Mariko could only look at each other.

"Delightful," Lilith said as the laugh died down and she wiped the tears from her eyes. "Did you learn to make jokes at Caleb's expense from Amy?"

Amy felt her mouth hanging open at the comment.

"What? No," Mariko said. "I just—"

"Your last name is Yamazaki, right?" Caleb asked. "Japanese?"

"Yeah."

"Don't the Japanese have repressed anger issues? Flip a switch and they go crazy."

"I was born in Charleston."

"Banzai!" Lilith shouted. She suddenly raised her hand as though she were going to slap Mariko's face. When Mariko flinched, Lilith let out a little giggle. "Just having fun, HR Girl."

At that moment, a woman wearing a headset and a pantsuit appeared behind Caleb and Lilith.

"It's 8 p.m." the woman said to Caleb.

"Excellent. Thank you."

With that, the woman slinked away, pausing only to pass some instructions to some of the wait staff.

Lilith looked back at Amy and clutched her heart again, seemingly saddened that their conversation had to come to an end.

"Dear, dear, Amy," was all she said.

Then she turned to the rest of Table Ten.

"It was so lovely to meet you. All of you. You've been such an important part of turning Caleb into the man he is. Always remember that I love each and every one of you."

And then, with a little bow, Lilith strolled off.

But Caleb lingered for a bit, standing beside Amy. His eyes stared down at her. She couldn't place that look of his. It didn't seem to be fondness or even resentment. His face seemed relaxed and his eyes did that thing again where he seemed to be focusing through and behind her, as though he were watching a movie projected onto her of all the memories of their childhood together.

"It was a beautiful evening," Amy finally said. "I had a great time."

"You're a liar," Caleb said. "But I won't hold it against you."

He winked at her and then walked off to chase down Lilith.

Amy lowered herself back into her seat.

Candice leaned over toward Amy. "We only heard snippets of the conversation. What were you all talking about?"

"Whole lotta weirdness."

"Well, thank god he didn't talk to us, then," Roger said. "It's nice being invisible."

Candice smacked him on the arm.

The string quartet suddenly stopped playing. The conversations at the other tables went quiet.

"Please turn your attention to the main stage," the DJ announced from his little booth in the corner of the room. "The bride and groom have some announcements."

Caleb escorted Lilith up the stage to a microphone. Big grins formed on their faces as they looked out at all their gathered guests.

CHAPTER 10

"First of all, from the bottom of our hearts, we want to thank each and every one of you for making this journey," Lilith said into the microphone. "This night means a lot to us."

Someone in the crowd began tapping their wine glass with a fork. *Clink-clink-clink.*

Others joined in.

In response, Caleb placed his arm around Lilith, dipped her down, and laid a passionate kiss on her lips. The crowd cheered and applauded, the unending stream of free booze having apparently loosened everyone up.

Lilith righted herself and caught her breath as she mouthed, "*Wow.*"

She cleared her throat to collect herself and then continued with her speech. "There are a few special guests we want to give a shout-out to. First, is my perfect little sister Trina. Everything comes so easy to her. Everybody loves her."

Amy craned her neck to see where Lilith pointed. At a table near the stage sat a young woman who looked very much like Lilith. Their features were similar, and they were very clearly sisters, but Trina had been blessed with the slimmer frame and perfectly angled face.

Amy had noticed the woman earlier and even pointed her out to Mariko. Trina was easily the most attractive woman at the wedding.

"She looks so beautiful today, doesn't she everyone? I'm glad that I finally found a man who isn't just going through me so that he can bang my little sister."

Trina's lips tightened and her smile became strained.

"Or are you?" Lilith said, gently elbowing Caleb.

He laughed along and jokingly made the *Call me* motion toward Trina.

A few drunken uncles chuckled, but the predominant sound in the room was of people shifting in their seats.

"Let's hear it for Little Miss Perfect!" Lilith announced.

The guests responded with a tepid applause.

"I also want to thank my father for coming," Lilith continued. "And he brought his lovely secretary... I mean *wife*, Hazel."

Amy tried to view the man she pointed to, but too many heads blocked the way.

"I'm sure most of you here don't know this, but today is actually their eight-year anniversary. I remember the date they moved in together vividly. Here's a funny story about Dad," Lilith said, already laughing at the mere memory of it. "I don't think I ever told anyone this. I saved it just for today — my special day.

"So, Dad had moved out and was living with Uncle Ben at the time, right Uncle Ben? Anyway, Dad wanted to come back to the house to get his things, but he didn't want Mom to see him because he didn't want a fight. And so, he timed it so that he came to the house while I was taking Mom to her treatment. You see, Mom had ovarian cancer at the time. I think Trina was the one who told him Mom's treatment schedule, right Trina?"

Trina kept her head angled down, not looking at her sister.

"Anyway, Dad didn't know I changed the locks in the house. When he couldn't open the door, he broke in through the bathroom window. And he stepped down *right* into Mom's chamber pot, which I hadn't cleaned because I was running late to get her to her chemo."

Lilith's smile had taken over her face by now as she took heaving breaths to try to quell the laughter that threatened to bubble out. "And so, I come home, pushing Mom's wheelchair, and we both wrinkle up our noses. I didn't even know Mom had much sense of smell left at that point. Full of surprises, that woman. Anyway, I look around and our stuff — I mean *Dad's* stuff — is all gone. The computer, the TV, even the router. But you know what he left us in its place? Stinky footprints! Everywhere! On the carpet, on the floor, in the kitchen."

She doubled up in laughter. Her heaving cackles filled the otherwise silent room. Bit by bit, she managed to calm herself. With a tear in her eye, she stood up straight and stared at her dad, a little smile dancing on her face.

"You're my father. I know you feel bad for how it all went down. I appreciate the letters you sent, and the apologies. I'm just busting your chops because it's my wedding day. I forgive you, Dad. And I'll always love you."

The words felt strangely earnest. A spontaneous applause broke out.

A tear rolled down Lilith's cheek. She had to turn away to wipe it. She held out the microphone for Caleb.

"Well, uh, I don't have as much to say as Lilith," Caleb began, shifting his posture back and forth in a way that reminded Amy of the nervous slouch he used to have whenever he had to do a presentation in front of class. "I want to thank my mom and dad. They always pushed me. I want to thank all my old coworkers and college buddies and my high school friend who made the trip. All my extended family as well. Thank you for being here. It means the world to me."

Another respectful round of applause.

"And now is the time when toasts usually happen," Caleb said. "Lilith and I don't have bridesmaids or groomsmen. No one has been asked to prepare a toast. We figured we would provide a kind of open mic opportunity if anyone wants to come up and say something nice about us."

The room went quiet.

Everyone's heads swiveled around, looking for someone else to raise their hand and volunteer.

Amy felt her father jokingly grab hold of her wrist and start to pull her arm up. She jerked her hand away and swatted him in the chest.

"Anyone?" Caleb called out.

No takers.

"Last chance. No pressure."

Silence.

"That's a-okay. There'll be opportunities for toasts later," he said. "Let's start the festivities!"

Lilith stepped forward and grabbed the mic.

"We need three volunteers for a little contest," she announced. "The winner will receive an amazing grand prize. But the losers..." her face creased into an exaggerated frown as her voice got low and menacing. "The losers will be severely punished." She smiled again. "Three people! Who wants to volunteer?"

Dance pop music blared out through the speakers as the bride and groom climbed off the stage and made their way through the crowd, cajoling their guests to participate.

"Who wants in?" Lilith called out.

Lilith danced toward her immediate family's table. She reached out and tried to grab the hand of the woman Amy guessed to be Hazel, Lilith's father's new wife.

Lilith gave a tug on Hazel's arm, but Lilith's father, avoiding eye contact with his daughter, simply put a beefy arm across Hazel's front, like a seatbelt restraining her to the chair. His other hand waved Lilith off, telling her to go elsewhere.

Meanwhile, Caleb had already found a volunteer. He guided one of his coworker's dates out of her seat. Amy sort of remembered the woman introducing herself as Yolanda. She was young and pretty, but in the brief interaction Amy had with her in line for the photobooth, she seemed dumb as a tuna. Mariko theorized that the woman might be a paid "escort" for one of the obnoxious day-traders with whom Caleb used to work.

In any case, Yolanda, in her too-tight and too-short blue dress, shimmied up to the stage.

Lilith then dragged the second volunteer up. "Uncle John, everyone!" she announced into the mic. Uncle John was a squat, middle-aged man whose face glowed bright red from alcohol. Twenty years from now, if he grew a white beard, he would make a wonderfully lecherous Santa Claus, Amy thought.

As Amy scanned through the crowd to see who else might get picked, she made the mistake of locking eyes with Caleb. She tried to turn away, to pretend to be adjusting her napkin or stifling a cough, anything to not draw him toward her. But she sensed his movement.

With his hips swaying to the beat of the music, he danced over. "Come on up, Ames," he said as he got near.

"Hard pass."

T . J .   P A Y N E

"Come on." He stood beside her now, his shoulders and elbows swinging to a cha-cha that didn't quite match the genre or beat of the music.

She smiled and waved him off with one hand while motioning toward her stomach with the other. "Too much to drink. I have gurgle-tummy."

He reached out anyway and grasped her arm.

"No," she said with a forcefulness that shocked even her.

And for a moment, Caleb stopped dancing. He stopped smiling. His face turned cold. Amy wanted to look away from him, but his eyes transfixed her. Those eyes burned with an anger she had never seen before. A hate.

"Yeah, Grandma!"

The shout from Lilith seemed to snap Caleb back to the moment. Everyone turned and watched as Lilith pulled an elderly woman up to the stage.

"Your loss," Caleb said to Amy with a shrug.

And then he danced back to the front.

"Please give a hand for our volunteers — Yolanda, Uncle John, and Grandma Foley," Lilith announced into the mic.

Everyone clapped.

"Remember, winner gets an amazing prize. The losers get punished. And the contest is... A DANCE OFF! Show us your moves!"

The DJ cranked up another dance-pop song. The three contestants on the stage looked at each other for a moment.

"Dance, dance, dance," Caleb and Lilith chanted.

The crowd joined in. "Dance, dance, dance..."

And so, the contestants started to dance.

Uncle John pulled out the only move he seemed to know — riding a pony while slapping an imaginary ass in front of him.

Yolanda seemed to go into her own world as she slid her body up and down a pole that wasn't there while sensually rubbing her hands over her breasts and hips.

The crowd recoiled a bit. No one wanted to outright boo, but definitely no one wanted to cheer on this display either.

The whole time, though, Grandma Foley stood back and watched her competition. Then, judging the moment to be right, she jumped to the front and center of the stage and started performing the moves she evidently just learned by watching Yolanda and Uncle John.

She rubbed her breasts and hips.

Then she rode the pony.

Then she slapped some ass.

Amy, along with everyone else, began to applaud. As the cheers rose in intensity, so did Grandma's moves. Before long, she was shimmying and twerking on the stage.

The crowd ate it up. Everyone laughed.

Caleb walked behind the contestants, pointing to each.

"Vote for your favorite. Yolanda!"

The crowd went quiet.

"Uncle John."

Still quiet. Someone, perhaps even his own son or brother, let out a low, good-natured boo.

"Grandma Foley!"

Thunderous applause. Everyone rose from their seats.

"And our winner is... Grandma Foley!"

With that, to the side of the stage, a white door swung open. Four red-vested staff members carrying a throne on poles marched out and up to the stage. They set the throne behind Grandma as they stood at attention.

Grandma blew kisses to the crowd as she took her place on the throne.

"For her Grand Prize, Grandma Foley gets..." Caleb announced, letting the anticipation build. "TO LIVE!"

The cheers faded into a confused murmur. Everyone looked to their neighbor, trying to understand what Caleb had just said.

The staff members lifted the throne.

Grandma Foley, sitting atop it, looked around, as confused as anyone. In the quiet, the staff members carried the throne and Grandma Foley through the white doors which swung closed and locked behind them with a noticeable and loud *click*.

Everyone lowered themselves back into their seats.

"And now, we have some very important announcements to make," Caleb said with a smile.

CHAPTER 11

Amy heard a soft beep.

A single vibration shook her wrist.

She looked down at her arm. The hotel bracelet's LED light had been intermittently flashing green since Amy had put it on. It now glowed a solid red.

She tried to loosen the strap, but the clasping mechanism wouldn't budge. It had locked shut.

"Mariko..." she said quietly, holding up her bracelet for Mariko to see. But Mariko didn't even look. She was too busy trying to pry open her own bracelet's strap. Its light also glowed a steady red.

Throughout the ballroom, other guests had noticed the same thing. At every table, people made futile attempts to remove their bracelet.

A murmur rose among the crowd.

"Please, please. Calm down everyone," Caleb announced. "If you accidentally break your bracelet, it will only make things worse for you, I guarantee."

Everyone looked up at him.

"A good wedding is never about the bride and groom," Caleb said. "It's about the people in their lives who made them who they are. It's about bringing those family and friends together in celebration of what they, as a community and as a village, accomplished. It's a time for reflection. A time to acknowledge the past so that the new couple can join together to create a brighter future.

"In essence, this wedding is not about us. It's about you. You are all very special people who had very special roles in our lives. Lilith and I want to pay each and every one of you back for all that you've given us.

"Now, I know some of you out there are thinking, 'Maybe I wasn't so nice to Caleb and Lilith. Maybe I could have been a more supportive person, a better person, a more loving person. Maybe I should take this special opportunity and tell them how I really feel about them. Maybe I should apologize for the awful, hateful person that I was.

"If anyone wants to come to the stage and say, 'I'm sorry,' in front of all our gathered friends and family, please come on up. We'll give you time to think about it and prepare your thoughts. Two minutes, in fact. You have two minutes to come up here and apologize. If you do, it will be water under the bridge. We're forgiving people, Lilith and I. We're loving people. Two minutes."

He looked out at the crowd. Everyone sat silently.

But then, the sound of sobbing drifted over the ballroom.

Lilith had taken a seat on the edge of the stage and now her hands covered her face as she wept.

"Sweetie? What's wrong?" Caleb asked, walking over to stand behind her. He rested his hand on her shoulder.

"I... I can't go through with it."

"Why not?"

"I don't have what it takes."

"What do you mean?"

She lifted her head and motioned out at her gathered guests. "They all see me as weak. As cold and passionless." Her voice seemed to enunciate in a strange, forced manner, as though she were performing in a play.

"Sweetie..."

"Just leave me alone. No one will ever love me."

With that, Caleb removed his hand from her shoulder, bowed his head, and walked off across the stage. He stood there on the far end, hands in his pockets and shoulders slouched.

Lilith slowly rose to her feet, looking away from him. They wandered around the stage in a synchronized manner, avoiding eye contact, pretending to be alone in their own little worlds.

The violin from the string quartet played out a few sad notes.

Then the other instruments joined in.

On their opposite ends of the stage, Caleb and Lilith swayed. Their arms motioned around, feeling the emptiness that surrounded them. Little by little, perfectly timed to the music, their flailing limbs and bodies approached each other until, seemingly by chance, their hands touched.

They quickly jerked their hands away, as if burned by the sparks that flew between them. They danced around each other, stealing furtive glances at one another.

The guests simply stared. No one had anything to say. Except Mariko. "This is the weirdest fucking thing I've ever seen," she whispered to Amy.

Amy couldn't argue with that assessment. They both kept their eyes glued to the bizarre spectacle on the stage.

The music swelled.

T . J .   P A Y N E

Caleb and Lilith, having fully explored the space between them with all their souls, suddenly came together in a firm embrace. The music seamlessly transitioned to a new tune. A familiar meter.

"Is that a... a tango?" Candice asked.

Amy nodded.

Caleb and Lilith were now arm-in-arm, dancing a well-choreographed and rehearsed tango. She lifted her leg all the way to his shoulder as he dipped her low. Then, with their eyes locked on each other, their mouths inches apart, they broke apart to spin and twirl. An unbridled passion burned between them as they danced their way up the metal spiral staircase.

"They're much better than you two were at that talent show," Mrs. Crawford said.

Again, Amy could only nod.

The waitstaff, who were busy topping off glasses and clearing dishes, ceased their work and raised their chins. Then, with beautiful choral voices, they sang out to the music. They didn't sing words, just notes, adding an air of intensity and build.

Caleb and Lilith reached the balcony at the top of the stairs. With the staff singing and the instruments straining, Caleb dipped her over the railing of the balcony, bent down and...

They kissed!

The singing waiters popped champagne bottles.

The guests all sat, stone-faced, as the string quartet played its final notes.

For a moment, the room sat in a dead silence, broken only by a few confused guests clapping a few sad claps.

Caleb and Lilith didn't seem to mind the muted reception, though. They held hands and smiled down from the balcony at the crowd.

"Your two minutes are up!" Caleb said, tapping at his watch. "The opportunity to apologize has officially ended. You're all locked in now."

"We're playing a little game from now until midnight," Lilith said. "Feel free to help yourself to any weapons on the wall. Anything at all, actually. Use your imagination. This place is your playground. You're free to go anywhere inside The Venue. But if you go outside, you will face a penalty."

It was at that moment that a sound caught Amy's ear.

A quiet, humming motor.

Beneath the balcony, at the cocktail bar that had been built into the wall, a glass partition rose up out of the counter and sealed the bartender off from the rest of the ballroom. The bartender barely seemed to notice. He went about his business wiping down his glassware.

Another glass partition rose up through the stage area, isolating and protecting the DJ in the corner of the stage. The string quartet picked up their instruments and carried them out the door to the side of the stage. Elsewhere, the waitstaff quietly migrated toward the various exits.

A weight developed in Amy's stomach that seemed to grow and expand, cutting off her oxygen. She struggled to fill her lungs. Tendrils of bile snaked up into her throat and filled her mouth and nose.

She had never experienced this before, but she knew the name of the sensation that had begun to burn through her. Dread. Her gaze swung from the balcony to the faces of all the other guests.

The brief pause in Lilith's speech, perhaps lasting only a second, allowed enough time for a million thoughts to swirl through Amy's mind.

All those feelings that had been building for several days now seemed to tug at her legs, prodding her muscles to jump up, to run to the door, to get out of there. Now. Part of her realized that those doubts, those nibbling terrors had been massaging her muscles this whole time, but her brain had successfully subdued those impulses.

And yet, no one else seemed to be jumping up and running away. They all sat there, their faces holding looks of bewilderment rather than fear. They seemed to view it all as another bizarre twist in a bizarre night from an eccentrically bizarre couple.

As everyone sat and waited for the punchline to play out, Amy did too.

"This night is about you," Lilith continued. "All of you. How you all demeaned Caleb and me. How you toyed with us, laughed at us. How you stomped on our faces, our hearts, and our souls. The worst part is that each of you accepted an invitation to the wedding of someone you've been horrible to.

"You don't even have the introspection to acknowledge your own cruelty. Because that's what you are. Cruel. Deeply, deeply cruel.

"But tonight, we are offering you a wedding favor. We are providing you the opportunity to see yourself the way that Caleb and I have always seen you. You have permission to uncage the darkness of your hearts. Let all of your repressed vileness go free. You will see who you really are."

An intense fire seemed to dance behind her eyes as she smiled down upon the group from the balcony.

"The rule of the night is simple," Lilith said. Despite not having a microphone, her voice came across loud and purposeful, like a ringmaster preparing to start the show. "By midnight, you must kill someone in this room." She paused, seemingly waiting for a gasp to rise from the crowd. None came.

"That's it," she said. "Kill someone by midnight. Do that and the staff will take you to a backroom. They will put you to sleep and remove this nightmare from your memories. You'll wake up in town. The local police will tell you that the other people in your party died in a car crash on a slick, mountain road. You won't remember anything, but you'll take their word for it because they have all the paperwork and evidence. You'll grieve, you'll mourn, and you'll return home.

"You'll be alive, but you'll be changed. You may not remember the specifics of the act that saved your life, but somewhere, in the back of your mind — a place only accessed while you dream — you'll remember the emotion. You'll smell the deep decay that has always existed in your soul."

She glared down at the guests, letting those last words linger.

Caleb seemed to sense that Lilith's speech had, more than anything else, confused the crowd. He stepped toward the railing of the balcony, by his wife's side.

"That's it. Kill someone and you will live. But anyone who doesn't have blood on their hands by midnight will face a penalty," he said. "Anyone who tries to leave The Venue or tries to remove their bracelet will also face the penalty. And that penalty? It's the same penalty as losing a dance competition."

Amy heard a rapid beeping.

She scanned the room, trying to zero in on where the sound came from.

Yolanda and Uncle John — the dance contest losers — had both returned to their seats at some point, unnoticed and forgotten among the guests. They now stood in panic. Whereas the light on everyone else's bracelet glowed a solid red, the light on Yolanda's and Uncle John's bracelets flashed quickly. The bracelets beeped a furious warning.

T . J .   P A Y N E

Uncle John tried to undo his strap, but no matter how hard he tugged, it wouldn't budge.

Yolanda, meanwhile, stood petrified, merely holding her bracelet arm as far away from her body as she could. She took steps backwards, seemingly trying to put distance between herself and her own hand.

Sensing what was about to happen, the people around them stumbled out of their own seats to clear space between themselves and the dance-off losers. Even Yolanda's date and Uncle John's wife refused to approach them.

In that final fraction of a second, Amy met Yolanda's gaze. Her wide, terrified eyes had stopped searching and locked onto Amy, pleading for help from the only person to make eye-contact with her. The edges of Yolanda's mouth had frozen, twisted upward into a grimace.

Amy wanted to mouth *I'm sorry* to her. Sorry that she joked to Mariko that Yolanda looked like a hooker. Sorry that, in her mind, she deemed Yolanda dumb. Slutty. Trashy.

Sorry that she didn't dare try to help.

But before Amy's mouth could form the words...

BOOM!

Yolanda's bracelet exploded.

The world seemed to move in slow motion as Amy watched the skin ripple away from Yolanda's left wrist, exposing the muscles beneath. A millisecond later, the blast sliced through that too, sending shards of bone and flesh sailing outward in a gloppy cloud of red.

It splattered over Yolanda's face and dress. More remnants struck the white chair coverings, accenting them and matching the red of the centerpieces.

As the blast knocked Yolanda backwards, Amy could see her face turn to look upon her fresh stump. The blast had sent slivers of the black bracelet into her cheek which had turned red from burns and blood.

She watched the blood flow from Yolanda's arm in gulps and bursts, like water from an old well-pump.

Yolanda's eyes rolled back into her head as her body completed the fall.

She thumped down onto the floor, unmoving. Unconscious. Perhaps dead.

It was then that a sound penetrated Amy's ears which, after the explosion, had momentarily stopped registering noise. At first she thought someone was performing a seal impression. Loud bursts of wailing and honking.

But as Amy's vision widened from its myopic focus on where Yolanda had just stood, she realized that the sound came from Uncle John. He lay on the floor, his body twisting around in the pool of blood that formed from the stump where his own arm used to be. He was trying to scream but didn't seem to have the capability. All he could produce were gargled yelps of pain and shock.

Chaos overtook the room.

Some of the guests dove beneath their tables. Others, like Amy, sat and stared, as though in a trance. Their brains seemed to want to make sense of what they had just witnessed.

This can't be real.

What a weird joke.

My arm didn't blow off. I'll be safe if I keep sitting.

Other guests weren't as numb.

Amy saw Big O leap up from the table and run toward Yolanda's body. He took his necktie off as he did and began to fasten it into a tourniquet.

Likewise, Caleb's cousin Rick, the one who was in the Army, rushed toward Uncle John.

But still, Amy sat.

She didn't know how her parents or Mariko had reacted. Somehow, she couldn't see them. Her peripheral vision had blacked out anything beyond where her eyes directly looked.

"Let's get this party started," someone shouted. A woman. Lilith.

"You heard the bride, ladies and gentlemen," the DJ said, speaking through a microphone in his new glass booth. "Let's get this dance floor rockin'!"

He turned up music. Some Kanye song that Amy could have named if that part of her brain were still functioning. But she had shut down.

It felt as though Amy's eyes and ears had become unmoored and she now observed the world not through her own body, but by floating around it at some distance.

"Give it up for the new Mr. and Mrs. Caleb Hunt, everybody," the DJ said. "And now, they're off to their bridal suite."

People screamed and shouted.

Some even ran.

Amy felt as though these panicking people were part of some other world, someone else's reality. She made eye contact with a woman a few tables over. An older, elegant woman. The woman looked back at Amy. They smiled at each other. That woman's mind also seemed to have shut down, unable to process the situation.

"Caleb? What's happening? Caleb, please. What have you done?"

Amy turned toward the voice.

Caleb's mom ran up the spiral staircase, toward the balcony.

But Caleb and Lilith ignored her.

They blew their final kisses to the crowd. A door behind them opened and they stepped off the balcony and out of the ballroom. The door slammed shut right as Mrs. Hunt arrived at the top.

She tried the knob. She pounded on the door. She wailed.

"Caleb! Caleb, please!"

Nothing. They were gone.

"Amy? Amy? Amy, can you hear me?" The voice was close. It belonged to her mom.

Amy turned to face her. Candice reached over Roger so that she could grasp Amy by the shoulders.

"You need to focus," she said. "We all need to focus."

The urgency in her mother's voice hit Amy on some primal level. It reached deep within her and grabbed hold of her consciousness, floating somewhere above her body, and then jerked her back to reality. The fog cleared from Amy's mind and her view of the room widened.

She was back.

And she knew they were all in danger.

CHAPTER 12

Amy might not have liked him, but she was glad when Big O took charge.

Caleb's old asshole of a boss had been the first to rush toward the injured. His tourniquet had saved Yolanda's life; she lay on the floor, pale but conscious and still breathing. Big O got the rest of Table Seven to tend to her, covering her with coats.

Army Rick had managed to stabilize Uncle John too, although he seemed worse off than Yolanda. He had passed out and Rick was unable to revive him. All his flailing, screaming, and alcohol-thinned blood probably didn't help stop his bleeding.

Conversation reached a crescendo as people argued in their own small parties over what had happened, what it meant, and what they should do. Occasionally, someone let out a loud wail, overcome by the moment.

Big O took the stage. He picked up the microphone.

"Calm down!" he shouted into the mic. "Everybody, calm down. Quiet! Quiet, please."

A hush spread across the room.

People lowered themselves back into their seats.

"Let's work the problem," he said. "First, we gotta get these bracelets off."

At the mere mention of the bracelets, some people started tugging on their wrist straps.

"Don't force it," Big O shouted. "Stop, just stop. Take it easy, people. We need an engineer. Are there any engineers here? Electrical engineers, computer engineers, I dunno. Someone who understands how a device like this might work."

Amy glanced toward her father. He slowly raised his hand.

"Roger, my man!" Big O said, pointing at him. "What do you need to work on this?"

Roger stood. "If, uh, if I had a screwdriver... I could pry open the casing. But I don't know what sets them off. If they're remote detonated—"

"Good point, good point," Big O said, thinking. "There must be a detonator board somewhere. A main control room. We need to get into the staff area."

Lilith's cousin Brad, the linebacker from UCO, burst out of his seat and grabbed a steak knife from the table. "I'm on it," he said as he marched to the staff door.

Cousin Rick jogged to join him. "Me too."

Brad and Rick inspected the door, running their hands over its edges.

"There's no lock," Rick said. "It must be magnetically sealed. We need like a keycard or something."

A murmur rose from the crowd.

"Stay calm, stay calm. Let's all work together, people," Big O said.

***

The Event Planner walked down the hallway to the bridal suite.

She resented the journey. It took several precious minutes of her time that she could be using to coordinate the festivities. But she reminded herself that *The Customer Is Always Right.* Her presence had been specifically requested by the clients.

She reached the door at the end of the hall and banged on it with the large, metal knocker.

The door swung open. There stood the scowling bride.

"Took you long enough," Lilith said.

"My humble apologies. How may I assist you?"

Lilith stepped to the side and let the Event Planner into the bridal suite. It was a beautiful series of rooms. The furniture was mostly fourteenth century French design. The staff had tastefully sprinkled crimson rose petals over most surfaces. The flickering light from dozens of large candles was absorbed by the dark wood and stone. Stepping into this suite was like being transported back in time.

Except for the TV, of course.

A large flat-screen sat inside an oak cabinet. The light and hiss of its gray static drowned out the romantic, medieval ambiance. Caleb stood in front of the TV, mashing the buttons on the remote, trying to look like he was trouble-shooting.

"This isn't picking up anything!" Lilith said. "We're missing my wedding."

"I am so sorry. May I?" The Event Planner held out her hand. Caleb passed her the remote.

"I better not have missed any good kills," Lilith said, crossing her arms while she took a seat on the edge of the bed. "The balcony's right there," she said, pointing to the side door. "Why don't you just put a viewing window here? Then we could watch it live."

"I will convey that request to the owners."

"Hurry up. We're paying for this."

"It's okay, sweetie," Caleb said, sitting beside her. "I'm sure we didn't miss much."

He tried to put his arm around Lilith, but she knocked it away.

The Event Planner hit a few buttons on the remote. Obviously, in the bride's haste to start watching, she had toggled the input settings. Of course, the Event Planner wouldn't *blame* the bride or groom, but it was definitely their fault. It consistently amazed her that despite how wealthy — and, therefore, presumably intelligent — every client was, they somehow were also the dumbest, most helpless people in the world.

After resetting the HDMI input and putting the TV back to Channel Three, the screen tiled with feeds from the innumerable cameras hidden throughout The Venue.

"You can select individual cameras here. This button will get you back to the main selection screen," she said, handing back the remote.

"How many bodies? How many bodies?" Lilith clapped her hands in excitement.

Caleb switched to a wide angle of the ballroom. Everyone sat at their tables, listening as Big O gave out directions.

Lilith leaned forward. Her head cocked to the side and her face scrunched up in confusion. "Is this from earlier?"

"I assure you, we are watching a live feed."

"Why aren't they killing each other?" Lilith asked.

"Every group behaves differently."

"We paid to have them murder each other."

"In my professional opinion, it's best to give these things time. As the night wears on, people's impulses tend to adjust. Some of our clients find it a fascinating study in human behavior."

"I don't want to study human fucking behavior! I want blood!"

"Maybe it's heating up, sweetie," Caleb said as he turned up the volume.

But the only voice that came through was Big O calmly controlling the situation. "Are there any radio experts here?" he asked. "We need someone to get to the roof and try to send out an S.O.S."

Two people in the audience raised their hands.

"This is bullshit," Lilith said. "This isn't what we paid for."

"Just wait, sweetie."

"Just wait?! This is *my* wedding. And everyone's just *talk-talk-talk*."

Caleb turned to the Event Planner. "What can we do? Can we blow up some wrists? Create some chaos?"

"I'm afraid that's against the pre-established rules of the evening. I understand how frustrating that can be. But we set the rules and insist on you agreeing to them because we find that changing the rules lessens the client's experience. Integrity is very important to The Venue's reputation."

"But they're strategizing. And planning. And working as a team."

"Nothing we haven't dealt with before." She pushed a button on her headset. "I'm with the clients," she said into her walkie-talkie. "They feel the energy at the reception is lacking. They would like less conversation and more engagement."

"On it, boss," came the reply from the DJ.

***

"Everyone needs to have a prepared tourniquet," Big O announced to the crowd. "Do we have any nurses or doctors—"

"It's that time of night, ladies and gentlemen," the DJ hollered into his microphone.

Amy, along with most of the guests, had forgotten that he was still in the ballroom, standing to the side of the stage in his glass booth, laptop and turntables in front of him.

"You know the song, you know the dance. I wanna see you all on your feet!"

He cranked up the volume as *YMCA* blasted from the speakers, completely drowning out Big O and all other conversation. The DJ raised his hands and danced along in his booth.

Amy watched Big O storm across the stage. He tried to open the door on the booth but it wouldn't budge. He pounded on the glass.

"That ain't how the dance goes, bro," the DJ smiled back at him. "I wanna see all you all's hands up now!"

He put his hands above his head in a giant Y.

One of the other guests picked up his chair, carried it across the stage, and slammed it into the glass booth.

The chair bounced off without leaving a scratch.

As all eyes were on the booth, Amy saw movement to the side. Coach Sanborn — the high school cross country coach — crept toward the wall of weapons. He reached up and grabbed a crossbow and quiver of bolts. He studied it for a moment, trying to figure out how to make it work. Then, he placed it on the ground and held it with his foot as he pulled back the bowstring until it cocked. He placed a bolt in the barrel groove.

Amy bit her lip. She scanned the rest of the wall. All the other weapons were hand weapons. Blades and blunt objects. Weapons that required close quarters.

Except the crossbow.

Coach Sanborn now had the only weapon with range.

With his locked and loaded weapon, Coach Sanborn pressed his back to the wall. His eyes darted from side-to-side. One slow step at a time, he backed his way toward the ballroom's exit.

"He's trying to escape!" Hazel, Lilith's step-mother, shouted.

All eyes turned to Coach Sanborn.

Lilith's father burst up from the table and jogged toward the coach.

"Put it down! Drop it!"

"It's for self-defense," Coach Sanborn pleaded.

Amy could tell from the waver in the man's voice that he wasn't a threat. He was terrified, like everyone else. He didn't even aim the crossbow at Lilith's dad as the man marched up and grabbed him by the arm.

***

Lilith and Caleb leaned forward, inching their faces closer to the TV.

"Is there a better angle?" Lilith asked, an excited sweat beginning to glisten on her face. Her breathing came in quick, sharp gulps, and her eyes were wide and unblinking. She looked like a child who had finally been granted permission to tear into her mountain of birthday presents and just didn't know where to start.

Caleb held up the remote and clicked around to the different camera feeds. At last he found a good one. A wide-shot from the opposite wall that clearly showed Lilith's dad grabbing at the crossbow.

But Coach Sanborn wouldn't let go. A struggle began.

"Money on Coach Sanborn," Caleb said.

"Shoot him in the balls, Coach."

Big O ran in between the two men. "Stop it! Stop it! We're not doing this. We have to work together."

Lilith turned to glare at Caleb. "What the hell is up with this tool? You said he was an asshole."

"Big O? He is."

"Then why isn't he killing people, *Caleb*? He's keeping everyone calm. He's ruining my wedding!"

As the three men wrestled for the crossbow a bolt shot out of the weapon. It flew across the room.

Gasps and screams rose from the crowd.

"Did it hit someone?" Lilith asked.

"I think so."

"Who? Who?"

"One of your sorority sisters. Jasmine."

"Hells yeah, bitch!" Lilith grabbed a champagne bottle from an ice bucket beside the bed. "Let's pour one out for Delta-Gamma-DIE." She tipped the bottle over and poured its bubbly contents all over the rug.

The Event Planner kept her expression neutral. She made note to have that rug cleaned.

***

Amy's mouth hung open.

A hush fell over the ballroom.

For a moment, Jasmine remained in a proper, sitting position. Her wide eyes seemed to go a bit crossed as she stared at the shaft protruding from the center of her head. A steady bead of blood ran down past her nose, over the crest of her lips, before dripping onto the floor.

Gravity seemed to kick in and she toppled over.

All eyes then turned from her to the man who held the crossbow.

"I... I'm sorry. I didn't mean to..." Coach Sanborn stammered out.

"And we have a murder!" the DJ announced. "Hold up that wrist-band."

Coach Sanborn obeyed the request and raised his trembling arm. His bracelet light glowed red like everyone else's. But then...

Click!

He flinched and shut his eyes. After a moment, he opened them to look. The bracelet hadn't exploded. In fact, the light had turned off.

Everyone quietly stared at the coach as he inspected his bracelet. At that same moment, the staff door beside the stage swung open.

"Right through those doors, coach," the DJ's voice bellowed out over the silent ballroom. "Congratulations on winning the first kill of the night award. We promise to get you home safely. Let's hear it for Coach Sanborn, everyone!"

The coach didn't move. He stood there, glancing from the mysterious door to the shocked faces of the rest of the guests.

"Hey, we get it," the DJ said. "You got trust issues. But that's what weddings are all about, man. Learning to believe in someone other than yourself. Learning to take a leap. Just know that this Venue has a perfect five-star review rating from our customers because we guarantee our word."

The DJ swayed in his booth as he spoke, as though he had a soundtrack constantly playing through his head.

"We say 'no tipping,' we mean 'no tipping.' We say, 'free booze,' we mean 'free booze.' No catches. No hidden fees. So, when we say we're just gonna wipe your memory and let you go home, our word is our bond. What kinda establishment would we be if we went back on that? Now come on, people, join me in a countdown before that door closes."

He waved his arms for everyone to count with him.

"Ten... Nine... Eight... Seven... Six..."

No one joined in.

"It... it was an accident," Coach Sanborn said. Then he turned and jogged across the ballroom toward the door.

***

Caleb and Lilith watched the coach run out of the ballroom.

The staff door swung shut behind him.

The crowd sat in silence.

"This is bullshit. Why do these people suck so much?" Lilith's face settled into a glare. "I want blood. I want to stare into their eyes as they realize how savage they truly are. When all their preconceived notions of themselves fall away like charred leaves, I want to be there. To watch their souls abandon them. To leave them with nothing but a black emptiness."

"I mean, sure, me too," Caleb said.

"My wedding is a disaster."

"Sweetie, don't say that. This is what we signed up for. I really wanted Coach Sanborn to die. I had dreams of him cowering and hiding, and now, he gets to go home. But that's fine. It's what we planned."

She crossed her arms and stuck out her lower lip. He remembered the first time she made that face during the early months of their relationship. He thought it was adorable. It didn't appear to be a conscious decision on Lilith's part to imitate a pouting baby; it was just the way she responded to frustrating circumstances.

It reminded Caleb of the face that Amy used to make when he couldn't come out to play; his mom was always making him do extracurriculars to boost his college application chances. Never mind that he was only in fourth grade at the time. He always had violin lessons or conversational French classes or a specially arranged permission to observe the high school's Model U.N. debates. He'd tell Amy he couldn't have a squirt gun war and she'd cross her arms, make an exaggerated pouty face, and kick out her legs.

He didn't even realize how endearing he found those goofy Amy faces until he saw Lilith do them.

Not that he thought of Amy when he was with Lilith.

That would be a betrayal.

Of course, soon he learned that when Lilith crossed her arms and creased her face into that deep scowl, it was because a true seethe had taken control of her muscles. And if he didn't diffuse whatever angered her at that time, she would explode.

"I believe I have a solution," the Event Planner spoke up. She had been hovering by the door. "I know that sometimes it's challenging to get the guests to participate in the festivities. From my experience, it's best if the event's host and hostess set the example and show everyone how to engage."

With that, she threw open the door.

A bellhop, who apparently had been summoned to wait outside for just this moment, wheeled in a cart. Displayed atop the cart were two matching archery sets. The bows were compound bows, sleek limbs held taut by pulleys, cables and cams. One was pink. The other blue.

"A wedding gift, from The Venue to you," the Event Planner said as she took the bows from the cart and offered them out to Caleb and Lilith.

"The grips are formed to your hands. Our armorist guessed at the most efficient draw weight for each of you. I apologize that the modernistic design doesn't match the medieval theme of the night. But special people deserve special weaponry."

She held out quivers of arrows.

"Go have fun. Because that's what weddings are all about."

C H A P T E R   1 3

Amy kept her body still, but her eyes darted back and forth, trying to take in as much of the situation as possible.

People were quietly positioning the steak knives near where they could quickly grab them.

The throwing stars that everyone received as a wedding favor were subtly hidden in pockets and laps.

Eyes glanced frequently from the wall of weapons to the various exits.

The sounds of whispering could be heard, and although Amy couldn't make out the exact words that people were saying, she figured that every group must be strategizing for their own survival.

Amy kept quiet, but she made a plan in her head. She wouldn't rock the boat. She wouldn't be the first to break ranks. But if things got ugly, she and Mariko would grab her parents and run. They'd race to their room, barricade themselves in, and plan from there.

Because her parents and Mariko were the only people Amy trusted right now.

She pretended to wipe her nose with her napkin. As she brought the napkin back to the table, she calmly set it on top of a knife. With a subtle, almost dainty motion, she slid the napkin and knife into her lap.

She looked around to make sure that no one noticed.

That was when she saw *them*.

She saw the balcony door swing open.

She saw the bride and groom step out.

She saw them raise up bows, nock arrows, and take aim.

Her dad was the closest to her; Amy threw her arm around him and pulled him below the table. "Get down!" she shouted, although her voice was so weak that it barely carried.

Mariko, who had been sitting completely still the whole time, now showed that her statuesque posture was actually her way of winding her internal spring tighter and tighter, readying herself to leap to action at a moment's notice. She dove under the table.

Candice, meanwhile, continued sitting, trying to make sense of the scene.

Amy heard the fluttering sound of arrows flying through the air and thudding into their target. Big O's calm, authoritative voice cut off and was replaced by a gurgle — the sound of a man trying to scream but finding that his lungs were filling with his own blood.

Yells rose from the crowd.

Chairs toppled as people dove under their tables.

Amy reached up from the ground, grabbed her mom's wrist, and pulled her down to safety.

It was tight — seven adults crammed together beneath a circle of wood. They pressed up against each other and pulled their legs in, not wanting an inch of their bodies to be exposed.

Amy found herself squished against Big O's wife. The woman seemed to know her husband had been shot, but she sat there, clutching her knees against her chest. She didn't seem to know if it was her duty to go out into the line of fire and help him or stay hidden. Amy put a hand on the woman's knee, gently communicating that she should stay.

The arrows flew rapidly. Their fletching caused a soft sound of rippling air as they sped down from the balcony before embedding in a table... or a shoulder blade.

From her position, Amy saw guests fall to the floor, screaming as they gawked at an arrow that had appeared in a leg or chest. Some of the injured continued crawling for cover. Others squirmed on the ground where they fell.

The faces of the wounded, initially bright red from screaming, quickly turned pale. Their blood oozed out over the black-and-white checkerboard floor, only to be trampled and smeared by the frenzied feet of people seeking shelter.

Amy could hear Caleb and Lilith laughing.

"Check it out. I call this 'The Legolas,'" she heard Caleb say moments before three arrows sailed out from the balcony in rapid succession.

"This is 'The Robin Hood,'" Lilith responded. Her bowstring twanged and Amy soon heard three arrows simultaneously thud into various tables.

The arrows rained down in a steady stream.

Caleb and Lilith barely seemed to be aiming now. And they certainly didn't seem to be running out of arrows anytime soon.

The injured writhed on the floor.

Amy watched one man try to drag a woman under his table. The woman screamed in delirium, incapable of assisting in her own rescue, as she grasped the arrow sticking out of her left hip. Another arrow sliced into the man's forearm as he reached out.

The man let out a yell and withdrew his hand.

"Was that you, Curtis?" Lilith called out. "Whoopsie-daisy."

Amy needed an escape plan. She kicked off her shoes. She made eye contact with Mariko who did the same. Candice had worn flats, which was good. If they had to make a run for it, it would be easier without heels.

She looked toward the ballroom's entrance.

Their table was centrally located. It would be a long run to the door. She might be able to zig-zag. Caleb and Lilith seemed to be well-trained with a bow-and-arrow, but they couldn't be *that* well-trained. To hit a moving target? She liked her chances.

Mariko was also nimble enough to probably make it out.

But what about her parents? Candice and Roger couldn't sprint. They couldn't zig-zag, at least not with any speed.

Amy swore under her breath. She looked around for something they could possibly use as a shield.

The arrows stopped.

The panicked screams subsided, replaced only by the moans of the injured.

"Hey, Daddy!" Lilith called down. "Where are you, Daddy? Don't you wanna kiss me on my wedding day?"

Amy heard a heavy breathing behind her. She craned her neck to look. She hadn't realized it but Lilith's dad, Mr. Foley, had left his seat to wrestle the cross-bow from Coach Sanborn, and in the chaos that followed, had evidently dived under the nearest table — Amy's table.

"Come out, come out, wherever you are!"

Mr. Foley was a big man. He took up more space under the table than anyone else. The back of his heaving neck glistened with sweat. He had removed his coat at some point, and now, large wet patches had consumed his entire backside as well as under his pits.

"I'll make you all a deal," Lilith yelled out. "Whoever tells me what table he's under gets to live."

The DJ's voice came out through the speakers. "You hear that, boys and girls? We got us an offer! Whoever tells the bride where her father's hiding gets a free pass. Don't ask me what happens if the father gives *himself* up. I mean, that would just be—" he pressed a button and a "*cuckoo-cuckoo*" effect sounded out.

"But here we go," he continued. "This will be the easiest save of the night. Your freedom in exchange for the father of the bride. Offer expires in five... four... three..."

Amy felt herself going completely still. Everyone under her table did as well. Not that it made a difference, but somehow, it felt as though making a sound or moving a muscle would endanger them all.

"... two..."

"Over there! He's over there!" someone shouted.

Amy looked. It was Angela, one of the sorority sisters, pointing toward Amy's table.

"Sold!" said the DJ. "Let the record show, she pointed to Table Ten. Madam, you may exit the ballroom."

Angela scampered to her feet and ran off.

"Thanks, love!" Lilith called out.

Suddenly, an arrow slammed into Amy's table. Its point sliced through the wood and came within an inch of Mariko's ear.

More arrows flew in. Most of them embedded into the top, creating loud thuds that echoed underneath. But some arrows found the weak spots in the wood and broke through a few inches, their tips coming perilously close to someone's head.

Everyone crouched down, trying to move as far away from the tabletop as they could. But there was barely any space.

"Get out! Get!" Mrs. Crawford yelled. Amy watched her elderly third grade teacher brace herself on her back and kick out her legs to push Mr. Foley from under the table.

More arrows thudded into the tabletop.

"No, please, please," he cried out.

Amy only stared. Somewhere in her mind, she heard a voice pleading with Mrs. Crawford to stop. But that voice never managed to make it through to Amy's mouth. She tried to reach out and hold Mrs. Crawford back, but similarly, her muscles seized up and never seemed to get the message.

Thoughts bubbled through her head. Another voice rose up inside her that insisted that Mrs. Crawford was right. Any attention that Mr. Foley brought to Table Ten decreased everyone else's chance of survival. And, after all, this man had raised, had *created*, the monster that now rained arrows down on them all. Certainly, he deserved whatever happened to him.

But he was also a human.

A scared human.

And all he wanted was the shelter of their table.

In that moment, Amy felt herself retreating to a childhood place. She looked to her parents to let them make the decision on whether or not to allow this man to stay. But her parents looked right back at her. That same look that Candice and Roger had when they needed an app installed on their phones. Amy was deferring to them, but they deferred right back to her.

In that moment of indecision, Mrs. Big O joined with Mrs. Crawford and together they gave a firm shove.

Mr. Foley rolled out from under the table.

He tried to claw his way back in.

Fffffft! A single arrow flew out and a moment later, Mr. Foley let out a scream of pain.

The arrow had struck him in the thigh.

"Sorry, Daddy! Did you get a widdle boo-boo?"

Mrs. Big O and Mrs. Crawford had already filled the space he used to occupy, forming a barrier to prevent him from crawling back to safety. He might have been able to push through them, but an arrow plunged into the floor next to him causing him to give up on the table.

Instead, he rose to his feet and hobbled off on his gimpy leg.

He grabbed a chair and held it up as a shield. An arrow struck it. Then another. Amy watched as he backed up, frantically looking for any avenue of escape. The windows were closer than the doors and so he took the chair and threw it through the glass.

He pulled himself onto the window sill.

But the moment his wrist breached the perimeter, his bracelet beeped.

The arrows stopped. "Whoopsie," Lilith called out.

The beeping intensified.

Mr. Foley scrambled down off the sill. His gaze darted from his wrist to the balcony. "No, no, no. I'm back inside. Lilith—"

In a flash of light, the bracelet blew his arm into a pink mist. The blast knocked him onto his side. He flopped around the floor, moaning out in pain. Several people in the crowd gasped and cried out, the explosion seemingly jarring loose a terror that they had been suppressing.

"*Hazel! Oh, Hazel,*" Lilith sang out. "Daddy needs you, Hazel. Don't abandon him now. You were always there for him. When his wife was sick, you were so comforting and supportive. You kept him company. You helped him move. Where would Daddy be without you, sweetie?"

From her spot, Amy could see Hazel. She had curled into a ball under her own table, hugging her knees to her chest like a child in a lightning storm. She didn't seem to be breathing, let alone moving. Her eyes weren't looking at her husband who squirmed and moaned on the floor across the ballroom. She just stared ahead, seemingly at Amy.

But then an arrow thudded into the table above her and Amy saw Hazel jump. More arrows rained down. Hazel's only response was to hug herself tighter as everyone else at her table screamed.

Hazel's body suddenly lurched forward. Someone behind her had either kicked or shoved her. The poor woman was so in shock that she hadn't braced herself at all. She didn't have the strength to fight back.

And so, Hazel easily tumbled out from beneath the table and plopped face down on the floor.

Even then, she lay still, apparently hoping that Lilith's vision might be based on movement, or something. That strategy lasted for all of two seconds before an arrow plunged into her shoulder blade.

Hazel cried out.

Another arrow struck her in the arm.

"Lilith, I'm sorry," she screamed, her face pressed against the floor. "I'm so, so sorry. Please. I made a mistake. I never meant to break up your family."

"Can't hear you, sweetie. Please grovel louder."

"I'm sorry!"

Another arrow struck her arm, almost in the same spot as before. She let out a whelp and sobbed into the floor.

"Hazel, run!" Amy finally shouted.

That seemed to awaken Hazel. She climbed to her feet. The arrows paused, as though Lilith wanted to wait and see how this all would play out. A little wobbly, Hazel stumbled around, looking left and right but seeming unsure of what to do or where to go.

"Don't run in a straight line!" Amy yelled. "Zig-zag!"

Hazel took the direction well. Or, at least as well as her disoriented mind was capable of taking it. She staggered around in an objectiveless zig-zag, like a drunkard trying to walk a straight line.

An arrow struck the table beside her.

"Get out of their line-of-sight," Amy called out. "Under the balcony where they can't shoot you."

Hazel did as told and ran to the bar beneath the balcony.

She threw herself against the shield that had risen to enclose the bar and pounded on the glass.

The bartended looked up. "What can I getcha?" he asked.

"Help me! Please!"

"I'm sorry. I only have drinks and melee weapons available. Can I interest you in a scythe? Or perhaps a mace?"

"Hazel? Oh, Hazel?" Lilith called out. Amy heard her shoes clanking against the metal staircase.

Lilith was coming down.

From her spot, Amy could see Lilith's tight, silky wedding dress descend the stairs. Calm and purposeful steps. She reached the bottom, the ballroom floor, and scanned the crowd. Lilith's face lit up with a broad smile that seemed to open her eyes wide with a crazed excitement.

Her bow and quiver of arrows were now slung over her shoulder, their straps cutting a black line diagonally across her white dress.

By her side, she carried some sort of medieval hammer. The handle was two feet of thin, shining metal that tapered to a head with a blunt striking-face on one side and a barbed spike on the other. She effortlessly wielded it with one hand, keeping it ready by twirling it in small circles.

Rick — Caleb's Army cousin — rose up from under one of the tables, grabbed a chair, and charged at Lilith.

Amy had a clear view of Lilith's face. Lilith's eyes narrowed, but her smile widened as the military-honed soldier ran toward her. He swung the chair, but she expertly side-stepped it. As Rick's momentum carried him past her, Lilith swung the hammer.

It cracked into the side of Rick's head, bursting the vessels in his eyes.

He wobbled on his feet for a moment and then crashed to the floor.

Before Lilith could revel in her kill, she had to side-step an axe swing from one of her uncles. She crouched like a snake ready to leap up and strike, but an arrow suddenly appeared in the uncle's neck. Caleb was firing from the balcony, covering his wife.

More guests saw their opportunity to attack. Mostly the men. Several of them grabbed whatever weapons they could and charged forward.

Chaos overtook the ballroom.

"They're distracted. Run!" Amy said. She grabbed her parents by the hands and bolted out from under the table.

They sprinted toward the ballroom doors. Plates clattered behind her as other guests left their hiding places to either run for safety or try to fight Lilith.

There were screams.

Falling chairs.

Feet trying to find grip on the bloodied floor.

Amy didn't look back toward any of the commotion.

"We got people on the dance floor," the DJ announced. "Let's get this place swinging!"

He turned on some swing-revival song from the 90s. It only partially drowned out the commotion of screams and fighting. Amy barely registered that there was any music playing at all.

The only thing on her mind was the door. She was getting closer.

A swift rush of air brushed past her cheek.

An arrow. Shot from the balcony.

It thudded into the doorjamb as she threw her weight against the door.

Her weight sent her tumbling through the exit and out onto the foyer floor. A hand, probably her dad's, grabbed the back of her dress and hoisted her to her feet.

Barely missing a stride, she ran.

CHAPTER 14

Amy led her family from the foyer to the front lobby.

The lights were all turned to full strength. The bulbs, no longer looking like dim, flickering candles, now illuminated the building better than even full daylight could.

The harshness of the light threw deep shadows against the animal heads that adorned the lobby's walls. The eyes of the dead elk and bear seemed empty and cavernous — large pools of blackness that watched Amy and her family run.

Behind them, the screams and crashing of plates rang out from the ballroom. Amy heard more stampeding feet, as though a wave of fleeing humanity were about to crest and crash over them.

As they passed the front desk, Amy felt a chill. A stiff, mountain breeze. The front door had been propped open. The dark world outside awaited them with open arms.

Candice veered off, seeming to assume that the open door was their destination.

"Mom! No!" Amy said.

Roger grabbed his wife's wrist and pulled her toward the grand staircase.

"Get to the room!" Amy said. It was the only place Amy could think to go. They could be safe there once they fortified the doors. Her

T . J .   P A Y N E

dad might figure out how to get the bracelets off. Maybe they could implement Big O's plan of getting to the roof and sending a distress signal.

If nothing else, they could have some protection. Some time.

Being away from the big group already felt safer. As the running loosened her muscles, Amy realized how tense her shoulders and back had been sitting at that table, surrounded by sixty or so people, any of whom might slit her throat to save their own life.

It was better this way. Being alone with family.

Amy led them up the steps of the grand staircase.

They stepped off at the hotel level and ran down the empty hallway. Amy swiped her bracelet at her room door.

No green light. No red light. No error beep. No nothing.

She jiggled the handle. Locked.

Mariko tried her bracelet on the pad.

Nothing.

"Step back," Roger said.

He raised his foot and kicked hard at the door, right beneath the lock. The noise of the kick made them all jump, but the door absorbed the blow. He tried again. And then again.

Amy looked up and down the hallway. Did the sound of those kicks give away their position? The hallway had no place to hide if it did. They were completely exposed and vulnerable.

"We have to keep moving," Amy said.

Her mind raced to think of where else they could possibly hide.

She ran back toward the grand staircase.

The staircase curved around on itself. Amy couldn't see down to the ground floor, but she could hear it. There were screams and shouts. Footsteps thundering up the steps. Some people moaned in pain, apparently dragging themselves forward despite their injuries.

They were getting closer. If she wanted to avoid them, there was only one direction to go. Up.

And so, she did. She ran up the staircase.

Her family followed at her heels. They came to the third-floor landing. They took a left, toward the gym.

As Amy passed a window, she heard an explosion outside. Amy looked.

A man in a suit lay on the ground by the front entrance. He pulled himself down The Venue's front path. His left arm hung in tatters behind him. It didn't bleed out, though. Amy saw that the man had secured his necktie into a tourniquet over his arm, seemingly anticipating this moment.

He pulled himself back to his feet and stumbled forward a few yards before collapsing.

Amy wanted to keep watching. She wanted to see if the man could get to his feet once again and continue his escape. How hard could it be? Running down a mountain with one arm? Surely, it was possible. But her family had rounded the corner on their sprint to the gym.

"Amy! Come on!" Mariko said as she disappeared around the bend.

Amy followed.

The door of the gym stood wide open.

It wasn't so much a gym as a weight room. No treadmills, no exercise bikes, no ellipticals. Just iron weights. Racks and racks of weights and bars.

Mirrors encircled the room, leaving no place to hide.

Mariko tugged on the door, trying to close it behind them. It wouldn't budge.

"Give me a hand," she said.

They all gathered at the door, grabbing hold of it.

"On three," Mariko said. "One, two... three!"

Together, they pulled and pushed at the door. They strained. Their feet slipped on the slick, polished floor. The veins bulged on Roger's neck and Candice's forehead. Mariko's face turned red from the strain.

The door still didn't move. It was as if it had been glued to the wall. Open for anyone and everyone.

"It's locked in place," Roger said, catching his breath.

Amy could hear banging out in the hallway. People were trying to get into their hotel rooms. They were trying to hide.

She reached out, grasped her parents' hands and gave a gentle tug. They backed away from the door, deeper into the open gym.

Mariko picked up the bar from the bench press and held it ready, as a staff. Roger picked up some of the smaller bench press weights, the five-pound iron discs. He stretched his arm, ready to hurl the heavy chunks of metal at whoever came through that door.

They stood and waited.

CHAPTER 15

There was no one left for Caleb to shoot.

Even those who crawled around on the floor, moaning and bleeding, were apparently off-limits.

His freshman college roommate, Alfredo, had tried to attack Lilith with a machete and had taken a blow to his spine from her warhammer in the process. As he lay on the ground, paralyzed, Caleb decided to do some target practice to put him out of his misery. Maybe he could pull off a headshot from fifty feet.

He missed.

As his arrow plunged into Alfredo's chest, Lilith shot Caleb a glare. She stood in the center of the ballroom, shouting up at him that he was being weak by showing mercy.

Caleb swore he wasn't, but Lilith just spit in his direction and marched off, stabbing some squirming girl Caleb didn't know in the leg. Lilith wanted the deaths to be as slow as possible.

It made sense, Caleb supposed. They had paid for the night. May as well get their money's worth.

But he didn't feel that Alfredo, of all people, needed to be excessively punished. Not like the others. He used to like Alfredo. Being randomly assigned freshmen roommates meant that Alfredo had been Caleb's first attempt at reinventing himself. They drank together, they went to parties together, they watched TV and porn together. Alfredo definitely had a charisma that drew in other dormmates. Caleb found himself going to parties and making friends, all because he was Alfredo's roommate.

There was no one moment when things changed. Eventually, Caleb realized that the people he assumed were his friends *and* Alfredo's friends started to hang out only with Alfredo. When Caleb packed up for winter break, no one swung by his room to say goodbye.

By spring, Caleb was spending his Friday nights eating pizza and playing games by himself. Except for the nights when he'd come back from class and find a sock on his door knob — the universal sign that Alfredo was busy hooking up with someone and was not to be disturbed.

Caleb and Alfredo kind of kept in touch after that. Throughout college, they'd wave to each other if they passed on the Quad. They were friends on Facebook and later Instagram. Alfredo had gotten married and become a special needs teacher in Ann Arbor.

His wife seemed nice. Caleb had met her for the first time the other day.

Alfredo and his wife had attacked Lilith together. It was a nice display of teamwork. Lilith bashed in her knee with the flat end of her warhammer and then struck her through the temple with the spike.

Caleb was glad Alfredo's wife died quickly. He bore her no ill will. That was the sucky thing about letting people bring a plus-one.

Caleb wasn't even sure if he had ill will toward Alfredo anymore either. In their brief interactions that weekend, Alfredo had seemed friendly and earnest; maybe being lower-middle class and working with special needs kids had softened the brash lacrosse player.

Or maybe that was the kind of sociopathic act that guys like Alfredo pulled to get away with all their bullshit. He was probably the type of teacher who made fun of his mentally challenged students the same way Caleb was sure he made fun of him behind his back. Caleb could faintly recall that Alfredo did a mean "disabled" voice as a joke, complete with thumping his hand against his chest.

The guy probably cheated on his wife too. A sweet, trusting, mousey girl like that? How could he not? Sure, she was attractive, but guys like Alfredo were never satisfied with *one* attractive thing to bang. *Oh, hey, hon. Sorry I'm home late. Had some faculty development to take care of with Charlene. What's that? You think Charlene is pretty? Hadn't noticed. Anyway, I'm spent. Goodnight.*

What an asshole.

As Caleb reached the bottom of the spiral staircase and set foot on the floor of the ballroom, he made a point of walking past Alfredo's prone body. He stepped on his old roomie's neck, feeling the tendons slide and pop under the weight of his heel.

Alfredo didn't move or react. Must be dead.

Pity, Caleb thought. Lilith was right. Guys like Alfredo deserved to suffer more. He shouldn't have given him a quick end with an arrow. It was a mistake that Caleb didn't plan on making again.

After rolling his foot around Alfredo's neck a bit more, Caleb wandered around the ballroom, trying to avoid the pools of blood.

He felt tired. Drained.

He convinced himself that the empty feeling, like some sort of black hole spreading out through his chest, was wedding-related stress. He needed to perk himself up. This was supposed to be a fun day. There was a lot of wedding left to celebrate.

He pivoted and walked back across the ballroom toward the bar. The DJ had transitioned to some funk song that Caleb had heard before but didn't know the title of. It brought a bounce to Caleb's step. A little bit of swagger and sway.

T . J . P A Y N E

Ordinarily, Caleb was too self-conscious to dance in public. He was even too self-conscious to provide the DJ with a list of his favorite songs; he didn't want to be judged on his taste in music. The DJ had settled on a generic list of wedding songs instead.

But today Caleb found himself cutting loose, swinging his hips and twisting his arms to the beat.

His shoes tracked through the blood oozing out of someone's stomach wound. It was slick. Caleb twirled around in that blood and used it to aid his feet in what he assumed was some sort of electric slide.

He glanced over to Lilith to make sure that she wasn't judging him. No. She was busy dragging Hazel around the room by the hair. Lilith paused only to bash one of Hazel's legs and then started throwing the screaming, bawling woman around again.

That would keep Lilith busy for a while.

Caleb danced his way up to the bar.

The bartended smiled from behind his glass wall. "What can I getcha?"

"Do you serve coffee?"

"Of course."

"Can I get a latte with a triple-shot espresso?"

"Comin' right up."

Caleb thought for a moment. "And how about cocaine?"

"I got powdered, freebase, crack, and speedball. Pick your poison."

"Uh, just powder. Two lines, please."

"Right away, sir."

Caleb stood and idly watched the bartender get the espresso running while he cut two perfect lines of coke on a small mirrored tray. The bartender went back to the espresso, frothed up some milk, and then poured it into the mug. The espresso and foam settled into a heart formation.

The bartender put the whole order into a small booth in the glass wall — the type of two-doored compartment that Caleb assumed one would find at the banks in poorer neighborhoods.

Caleb opened the door and took his coffee and cocaine. He didn't know which one he wanted to do first, but he definitely felt he needed a pick-me-up.

"Will that be all?"

"Honey?" Caleb called out. "You need anything?"

He looked across the ballroom. Hazel seemed to be clinging to her last moments of life, and Lilith seemed to sense it. Lilith picked her off the ground and slammed her onto one of the tables. She pulled Hazel's hair until her head hung over the edge of the table, then she picked up one of the abandoned steak knives and began to saw through the woman's neck.

Lilith's expression never changed. She didn't smile or even grin. Her mouth just kind of hung limply open, catching her breath from the strain of her task. Caleb knew she hated to be distracted when she was concentrating on a physical activity.

And so, he watched her for a moment, not interrupting her.

Some strands of her hair had worn loose and hung around her face, held down by a fine layer of sweat that also glistened on the tip of her nose. Her wedding dress had stayed surprisingly clean. Only the bottom hem, as well as the cuffs near her wrists, were tinged with blood. It accented the white. He didn't know how, but Lilith had kept the splatter to a minimum.

Because Lilith was perfect.

Always perfect.

And beautiful.

And strong.

Caleb felt his heart beat faster.

"Sweetie? Can I get you anything?" he asked again, sensing that she was at a good stopping place.

"Another quiver of arrows," she said.

He turned back to the bartender. "A quiver of arrows. Make that *two* quivers of arrows."

"Two quivers of arrows, comin' right up!"

Caleb reached into his pocket and pulled out a roll of cash. He knew that the gratuity would be handled at the end, but he didn't care. He always believed in tipping well. These guys deserved it.

He laid a thousand dollars into the doored compartment.

Then he sipped his espresso, leaned against the bar, and took in the beautiful sights of the room. Some slow dance from the 80s was now playing. In high school, the slow dances were the only dances Caleb felt comfortable doing. You just sway.

Too bad he never had anyone to sway with.

But tonight was his night. And so, he stood alongside the bar and swayed to the smooth rhythm of the music.

And the smooth rhythm of blood gushing from Hazel's throat.

CHAPTER 16

The Event Planner was glad to be back in the Control Room.

She kept a pair of flats in there and always relished the opportunity to slip out of her heels and plop down into a chair.

In front of her, the two control operators transitioned the screens between the various camera feeds. There were a few hundred cameras positioned throughout The Venue and since they only had eight screens to monitor everyone, it was an intricate dance of scrolling through feeds to land on the most entertaining bits.

They had started with sixty-four guests.

Three guests had won immunity and were being held in the green room.

Nine guests were confirmed dead.

Another ten or so had sustained injuries that were probably life-ending.

But those were still low numbers. The night would be long.

She found that the parties that were primarily composed of Americans were hit-and-miss in terms of bloodshed. But at least they weren't causing much damage to the facilities. She had been keeping an unofficial list of all the windows and furniture that would need to be replaced, as well as all the holes that would need to be patched. This was nothing.

She glanced at the screen. The bride certainly seemed to be enjoying herself, although she wasn't exactly smiling or laughing. If anything, she seemed almost robotic as she hacked through some woman's neck with a steak knife.

That'll take a while, the Event Planner thought.

The bride paused to catch her breath. She was a little less than halfway through the neck now and all the cartilage had started to clog up the serrated blade. There were plenty of other objects in the room that could cleave that head off with a single swipe, but the bride seemed to be the type of woman who liked to finish the tasks she started, even if that task involved sawing through a human neck with a five-inch steak knife.

The Event Planner didn't quite know how the bride planned to cut through the bones of the neck, but that was her problem. At some point, she would probably have to pull the whole head off.

That might be fun to watch, the Event Planner thought.

The groom, on the other hand, tried to find something to do to keep busy. He was sipping a latte, which the Event Planner actually thought sounded really good about now. She could go a shot of caffeine.

But otherwise, the groom's energy seemed to be sagging. The Event Planner made note that she might need to push some of the other events earlier to accommodate.

"The guests in the gymnasium may be attempting to remove their control devices," one of the operators said.

The four guests who were hiding in the gymnasium — three Holgates and one Yamazaki — had been the first to run out of the ballroom. Since then, two other groups had also gone to the gymnasium for refuge, but when they saw it was occupied, they left without so much as a word. No shouting, no pleading, no fighting.

They hadn't needed to smash anyone's head with a barbell to defend their territory. They got to keep the entire gymnasium to themselves without spilling an ounce of blood.

It was going to be that kind of night. The finishing crew was going to have their work cut out for them sweeping the building and disposing of the stragglers who didn't die from their control bracelet detonations.

Right now, the gymnasium group huddled together near the bench press machine. They were examining the control bracelet on one of the younger women. The Event Planner recalled her name started with an M.

"Turn on the sound. Let's listen in," the Event Planner said to her operators. "Be prepared to issue a warning."

***

Amy peered over her dad's shoulder.

He was busy studying Mariko's bracelet, holding her wrist in one hand while moving his glasses forward and back with the other in an attempt to create some sort of magnifying effect.

Candice, meanwhile, watched the door.

Part of Amy wanted to chuckle at the sight of her sweet mother with her teeth bared and a bench press bar in her hands. Candice hadn't wanted to be the one to scare away anyone who walked through the door. If Candice had her way, she would have welcomed everyone in so that they could all hide together. Hell, she would have brewed them coffee and baked cookies if she had the supplies.

It was Amy who forced her to be a mean, threatening bitch.

The only people Amy trusted were all within arm's reach.

Everyone else might *seem* nice, but Caleb and Lilith obviously chose their guests for a particular purpose. "Murderous tendencies and cruelty" might not have been written on the RSVP, but it must be a unifying characteristic among the guests. If Caleb — sweet, awkward Caleb — could be such a snake, then certainly, his parents, cousins, coworkers, and college friends could too.

And no matter how much these friends and family pleaded their decency now, once the clock inched toward midnight, all bets were off.

Mariko and Roger agreed with Amy.

Despite her objections, Candice was ultimately a team player and went along with the majority vote. When it was clear that her family had no interest in forming alliances with strangers, she took quickly to her role of mama bear, protecting the den from all intruders.

This allowed the rest of them to focus on getting the bracelets off. Because if they couldn't...

Well...

According to the announced rules (if those were to be believed) there was only one other way out:

Kill somebody.

Anybody.

Amy had started mentally compiling a list of the four people they could sacrifice. At the top were Caleb's parents. They were partly responsible for this anyway. Next would be Lilith's sister Trina, as anyone who shared a bloodline with that psycho must have problems of her own. And then, maybe Mrs. Big O. She had pushed Lilith's dad out from under the table to his certain doom. She didn't deserve any sympathies, despite her own husband having just been killed.

The list went on, but Amy tried not to think about it too hard. She knew it was a bit of a fantasy. In all likelihood, they'd have to select their victims based on opportunity.

Did she have it in her to kill some random person if it meant saving herself?

Maybe.

But did her mom?

It had occurred to Amy that their best opportunity would have been to hang around the ballroom and finish off someone who was already dying. Surely, that would fulfill the requirements. Perhaps it wasn't too late. There might be four people in the ballroom who were a few heart pumps of blood away from death.

Four tickets to freedom.

It would be easy. Amy's conscience could be clear.

She hung onto that idea, waiting for the proper moment to convince her family that their only option was to slink back into the ballroom and quietly finish someone off. Someone who might even deserve to die anyway.

But for now, her dad and Mariko had settled on trying to get the bracelets off without having to take a life (or lose an arm).

"The casing is held together by screws, but they're all on the underside," Roger said. "Even if we had access to them, it's not like I have a screwdriver."

"Could we, I dunno, do something to absorb the blast," Amy said. "I mean, how much of an explosion can be in that little thing?"

For a moment, no one answered her. Probably because the question itself brought to mind the only evidence they had of the device's explosive capabilities — the memories of people's arms disintegrating in a flash of light.

"We need them off," Mariko finally said. She bit her lip and took a deep breath. "Cover your faces."

With that, she grabbed her bracelet and tried pulling it over her wrist. It quickly became clear that it wasn't going to come off easily.

"Careful, Mariko," Candice said.

Roger gulped and backed away.

"We need some sort of lubricant," Amy said, looking around the gym. "If only we could get into the room and get some conditioner or something."

Mariko made a throat cleansing sound and spat a wad of saliva onto her wrist. "My mouth's kinda dry. Little help?" she said to Amy.

Amy couldn't help but grin. Mariko was the clean one in the relationship. The germaphobe. The one who religiously wiped down the house twice a week. Whenever they fooled around, Mariko always insisted on taking a shower afterwards, which at first Amy found a bit insulting.

But that was just Mariko.

Although, to be fair, when coming home after teaching three dance classes, Amy would often be covered in a decent layer of sweat and funk. And she had a habit of depositing her socks, bra and underwear wherever she happened to take them off, whether it was on the kitchen table, the couch, or Mariko's pillow — which, of course, was Amy's way of teasing her once she discovered how much it bothered Mariko.

And now, at Mariko's urging, Amy's tongue scraped around her mouth in search of new saliva to fling at her old roomie's arm.

"Ok," Mariko said, spreading the saliva around her wrist with her free hand. "Amy, you pull."

Mariko sat down on the floor. She braced her legs against one of the racks of weights and extended her bracelet wrist toward Amy. "Hard as you can."

Amy had no desire to grab hold of that thing. But Mariko had offered up her own device for the group to experiment on and Amy didn't want her parents to think that Mariko was willing to sacrifice more for the family than Amy. And so, she took a deep breath and grabbed the bracelet.

She took a wide stance, bracing her own feet on the floor. "Okay. One.... Two... three!"

She pulled on the bracelet as hard as she could.

"Careful, girls," Candice said, moving behind another rack of weights just in case.

Amy kept pulling.

The bracelet crushed up against the base of Mariko's thumb. Mariko scrunched up her face in pain but didn't tell her to stop. And so, Amy arched her back, dug her feet in and pulled harder. She could feel Mariko's thumb tendons sliding out of the way.

But they weren't moving enough.

Amy shook her head. She let go of Mariko's bracelet.

They all looked at each other for a moment as Mariko rubbed her sore thumb and wrist.

"We might have to cut someone's hand off," Amy said. She reached into the pocket on her dress and pulled out the steak knife.

They stood there quietly for a moment, looking at her.

"Let's try it," Roger finally said. "Do it on me." He knelt down at one of the benches.

Amy gripped the knife.

"Amy, this is silly," Candice said. "Roger, get up off the ground."

"Do it, Amy," he said.

"What's your plan, Roger?"

"I put on a tourniquet," Roger said, taking off his necktie and wrapping it around his arm. "Amy cuts off my hand, and I slide off the bracelet."

"Then what?"

"Then I run out the front door."

"And?"

"Get help."

"Where?"

"I don't know."

"Oh, Roger. It took us hours to get here. In a limo. You'll be bleeding out, in shock, stumbling down a dark mountain, looking for a town you don't know, with residents who speak a language you don't speak. The night'll be over by the time you get back."

"Then I'll take y'all with me."

"Oh yeah, sure. Four amputees bleeding their way down the mountain together. That'll make it much easier."

Roger suddenly stood, "Well, what do you want me to do then?! Watch you all *die*?!"

He glared at Candice, but she glared right back at him.

Amy had never seen this from her parents before. Their gazes locked in on each other, like two grown elk locking their antlers in combat, trying to force the other one down.

"I want you to not be a damned fool," Candice finally said through her clenched teeth. "We need to stay together. We're stronger this way."

Seemingly in defiance, Roger wrapped his necktie around his forearm, just above the bracelet. He put one end of the tie in his mouth and the other in his free hand, ready to pull it tight.

He knelt back down and laid his arm across the bench, exposing his wrist.

"Do it, Amy," he said.

Amy gripped the knife and knelt across from her dad.

"Ames..." Mariko started, but she had no more words besides that.

"That little steak knife'll never cut through your arm," Candice said. "You'll have to break the bone and *then* you'll still have to saw through all your skin and muscles and nerves. It'll hurt like the devil."

Amy looked to her father. He nibbled on his lip as he stared down at his wrist. She could see the sweat beading on his forehead. His face had become pale as his hurried breathing took in quick gulps of air.

She felt bile rise up to her mouth (it tasted of prime rib and pinot noir). She tried to push all thoughts from her mind, but she couldn't help but imagine the slow back-and-forth sawing motion she'd require to cut through her father's wrist. The image filled her head, playing on a continuous loop. She didn't think she could do it without throwing up.

Although she knew every piece of equipment and weaponry at their disposal — mostly weights and a steak knife — her eyes darted around the gym for anything else she could use. An axe. Or a machete. Something with a good blade with which she could chop through her dad's arm in one blow.

A quick strike, she felt she could handle. A surgical amputation with dinnerware, she couldn't.

"Maybe you could just crush his hand with one of these weights," Mariko offered, seemingly in response to Amy's thoughts. It didn't sound like a firm suggestion as much as an idea spilling out of her open mouth.

Everyone looked at her.

She seemed to feel the need to clarify, although everyone was on the same page. "If you just crush all the bones in his hand, then you can slide the bracelet right off," Mariko said. "Probably won't even need the tourniquet then." Mariko had a way of continuing to talk and offer advice when she was nervous.

"That, um, that's a good idea," Roger said.

Even Candice had gone quiet at this point.

"Use that twenty-five pounder," Roger said to Amy, pointing to the rack of dumbbells.

Amy robotically rose and went to the rack. She lifted it, immediately having to strain because she misjudged how heavy twenty-five pounds actually was.

Roger, meanwhile, took his hand off the bench and set it on the hard floor. He bowed his head, avoiding eye contact with Amy.

She carried the weight over, her arm suddenly feeling weak, almost nonexistent. It was as if the weight simply dangled from her shoulder by a piece of rope.

As she crouched down over her father's hand, she closed her eyes. She tried to pretend she was a little girl whose father was ordering her to clean up her room or turn off the TV. The last thing she wanted to do was disappoint him in an emergency.

"Do it, Amy," he said, his arm outstretched. Even with his head bowed down, Amy could see that his eyelids were clenched shut. The muscles on his face had already pulled themselves tight into a grimace, positioning themselves in preparation for the pain that was sure to come.

Amy raised the weight and lined it up over his hand.

"On three," she said. It came out a whisper, although she didn't intend it that way. She took a deep breath to steel herself.

"One..." she said, raising the weight.

"Two..." She was going to do it. She was going to crush all the bones in her father's hand.

"Three!"

She slammed it down. Her eyes involuntarily shut closed as she did. The weight seemed to move at a fraction of normal speed. She could practically feel every inch of air rushing past her hand as it sped downward.

Somewhere in that instant, the sound of her father shouting, "No, no, no! Wait!" reached her ears. But she couldn't stop.

The weight whacked into the hard floor, sending shockwaves rippling up through Amy's hand, arm, shoulder, and finally teeth. The sharp sound of metal on floor ricocheted around the gym.

Her eyes snapped open.

Her dad's hand wasn't beneath the weight. He had pulled it away at the last moment. He now sat on his knees, holding his hand close to his chest as he quivered.

"I'm sorry," he said. "I'm so sorry. I chickened out. Let's... let's try again. On three."

He laid his hand back down on the floor.

Amy shook her head. "It's okay. Mom's right. We need to stay together. We'll come up with something else. We have time."

***

The staff lounge was always cramped and dim. Some staffers speculated that it was probably the communal section of an old bomb shelter built beneath The Venue.

Pool tables and couches filled the center of the space. Along one wall were bunk beds with privacy curtains for napping — the various jobs required long shifts and late nights. The other end of the lounge had a bar and several tables where the kitchen would bring in food for mealtimes.

An array of screens were mounted on the far wall, broadcasting the hidden camera feeds from within The Venue.

This was the dead time for most of the staff. They were technically on the clock, but there really wasn't much for them to do while the guests entertained themselves.

Some played pool or ping-pong in the corner. Others snacked on the leftover prime rib from dinner. But most sat on the couches, their feet propped up and their vests and ties loosened, as they watched the big display screens. The Control Room cycled through feeds of interesting developments for them.

Right now, everyone watched the girl in the gymnasium (Guest Number Forty-Five) get down on the floor and hug her father (Guest Number Forty-Eight).

No amputation. No smashed bones. No fiddling with the bracelet enough to trigger a detonation.

A chorus of boos rose from the staff. Some threw popcorn at the screens. Others exchanged money from a wager regarding whether or not the guest would go through with the amputation.

The screens switched over to a new show.

A large man sat huddled by himself in the lobby, hiding behind a plant. Somehow, he had gotten his hands on a small screwdriver. His bracelet was just loose enough for him to angle the screwdriver beneath the bracelet's main casing. A quarter turn at a time, he began removing the screws.

A murmur rose among the staff as they watched the man.

Money changed hands.

***

The Event Planner crossed her arms.

She stood behind her operators in the Control Room, watching the man unscrew his bracelet. With no one at this party being particularly aggressive on the whole "kill someone by the end of the night" rule, he had a good chance of escaping the premises unscathed.

The man never should have been allowed so much slack on his bracelet. The shift manager needed to be more vigilant when he scanned the guests at the beginning of the reception. It would only take a quick clutch of a person's wrist to "accidentally" tighten their bracelet, just as she had *shown* the manager multiple times.

"Should we issue a warning to Guest Eighteen?" one of the operators asked.

"Do we know where Guest Eighteen obtained the tool from?"

The second operator scanned through recorded footage of the man. He rewound various videos of the man at the reception, at the service, and then finally all the way back to the man getting dressed in his hotel room.

"Eye glass repair kit," the operator announced. "He tightened some screws on his glasses, put the screwdriver in his coat pocket and forgot all about it."

The Event Planner nodded. It was a good enough explanation. She didn't believe any of her staff would have *handed* him the tool. Thank god no one had left a tool kit unsupervised either.

"Was it clearly stated in the rules that the control devices must not be removed?" she asked. She probably should have known the answer, but she was tired. All that hassle with the clients in the bridal suite had disrupted her schedule.

The secondary operator pulled up a video of the groom announcing the rules to their guests. A transcript also appeared on the screen. "Just so you know, anyone who doesn't have blood on their hands by midnight will face a penalty," the operator read from the transcript. "Also, anyone who tries to leave The Venue *or tries to remove their tracker bracelet* will face the same penalty."

"Good," the Event Planner said. She was glad the groom actually said it out loud. This couple had been so emotional and distracted that it wouldn't have surprised her if they neglected a simple task like explaining the rules to their guests. "Issue a warning."

The primary operator punched a few commands on his terminal. "Issuing warning to Guest Eighteen."

On the screen, the man's bracelet lit up. It flashed red lights, looking very much like one of those "your table is ready" alert devices.

The man dropped his screwdriver and leapt to his feet. He didn't seem to know what to do, as he appeared to both want to run away from his own arm while also wanting to tuck it toward him to protect it.

"Guest Eighteen, twenty seconds to detonation. Nineteen... eighteen... seventeen..."

Ultimately, all the man could think to do was freeze in place. He stared at the flashing bracelet on his wrist. His eyes stayed wide, and his face pulled tight, as though all his muscles were trying to pull themselves away from the blast.

"No, no, no!" he shouted to no one in particular.

"That should be a sufficient warning," the Event Planner told her operators. "Disarm."

"So... detonate?" the primary operator responded.

The Event Planner looked at him, confusion on her face.

The primary operator spun in his chair and flashed her a wide grin. "Get it? 'Disarm.' Dis-*arm*. Like, 'disarm' him?" He pantomimed pulling off his arm as he spoke.

The secondary operator shook his head and chuckled.

A wide grin broke across the Event Planner's face. She gave both her operators good whacks on the shoulder. "Dis*arm*! Oh my. Why have we never made that joke before?"

The screen lit up with a flash, washing out the entire image. It took a moment for the cameras to readjust. When the image returned, the man lay on his side, half his body singed. His arm gone. Blood pooled out of the stump where his arm had been, traveling along the grout in the tile floor, speeding away as though it were its own lifeforce, still trying to get out the door.

The Event Planner knew that she should have cared that the warning had escalated to a detonation, but it was late, and a little morale boosting humor among the staff never hurt anyone. Except the occasional guest.

"Dis*arm*," the Event Planner said again, shaking her head. "You guys."

She realized she probably found it so amusing because a deep exhaustion had overtaken her. Most of the staff only saw her as stiff and proper, but back home, with a couple drinks on a late night, she was prone to get the giggles.

Tonight appeared to be one of those nights.

She gave another little laugh that turned into a snort.

The operators both smiled.

"I need coffee," she said, rubbing her eyes.

But before she could leave for a quick trip to the kitchen, something on one of the screens caught her eye.

"Well, well, well. Sleeping Beauty is awake," she said pointing to a camera feed from the women's restroom.

Sure enough, Guest Thirty-Two — the Event Planner believed her name was Tiffany — slowly raised her head off the toilet seat. She spat the few remaining chunks of vomit out of her mouth into the bowl. Then she grabbed a few squares of toilet paper, held it to her nose, and blew out a wad of bile-filled snot.

"Oh, this will be good," the primary operator said, sending the video to the main screen.

Tiffany, who had downed three drinks *before* the wedding service, had passed out on the toilet just after dinner. In the meantime, three of the other restroom stalls had filled with terrified, hiding guests.

But Tiffany slept through it all. It helped that the other guests had stayed completely silent.

The Event Planner had kept an eye on Tiffany. She didn't want any of her staff to miss this reveal.

This should be fun, she thought.

CHAPTER 17

Caleb smiled, but it was a forced smile. He felt the muscles in his cheeks having to pull the edges of his mouth up.

But smile he did.

The screen inside the photobooth counted down from ten.

Nine... Eight... Seven... Six...

Lilith stood to his right, a smile on her own face larger than Caleb had ever seen from her. Between them, they held up the body of Freddy, although Lilith had taken to calling him "Bernie." As in *"Weekend At..."*

Bernie stared daggers at the camera.

Literally.

His eyes were nothing but the handles of two daggers that Lilith had made Caleb stab into him while Lilith held him down. Freddy — er, "Bernie" — had been hired the same year as Caleb. They had gone through their orientation together, and even then, Caleb fantasized about one day killing him.

He was the guy who made Caleb realize that he wasn't cut out for the brotastic world of finance. The guy must've said the c-word at least three times during their sexual harassment training. Whenever a woman spoke, whether it be a female boss or a waitress, Freddy would turn to Caleb and say, "She needs a dick in her mouth."

When Lilith first started interning at the company, Freddy made no attempt to control his wandering eyes from analyzing every inch of her body. He had a habit of coming up behind her to give her a spontaneous shoulder massage, sniffing her hair as he did.

Lilith once stood up to him and told him to stop hitting on her.

Freddy, of course, responded that he wasn't hitting on her. He would never hit on her. Not until she lost twenty pounds. When Lilith stormed off, Freddy turned to Caleb and said, naturally, "Boy, she sure needs a dick in her mouth."

Caleb never told Lilith about that particular catch-phrase. If he did, she probably wouldn't have committed to simply stabbing him through the eyes. Caleb tried to imagine what she would do instead...

Most likely, she'd have held Freddy down while Caleb pulled out all of his teeth. And then, she might have forced Caleb to drop his pants, pull out his dick, and place it in Freddy's gummy, bloody mouth. Because Freddy sure needed a dick in his mouth. Fun times.

Three... Two... One...

"Smile!" Lilith said.

The photobooth snapped off a series of three photos. As planned, they hurried to position themselves for three different poses.

The first was smiling with *Bernie* slung over their shoulders. Caleb gave a thumbs up while Lilith pointed a small sign at the body that read "Party Animal."

The second photo was of Caleb and Lilith actually holding the daggers, pretending to be in the process of stabbing Freddy through the eyes.

The final shot, which wasn't well planned out, was some sort of orgy, sex position with the three of them all entangled and humping up against each other.

As the machine printed the photo card, they set Freddy in a chair. A table of goofy props waited nearby and Lilith took a few moments to put a captain's hat and pink feather boa on his corpse.

The machine spat out their photos. When Lilith picked the card up, her expression immediately turned downward.

"The last one came out blurry." she said. She studied the photo for a bit. "Let's do it again."

"Sure thing."

Caleb went over to Freddy and slung the man's arm around his shoulder, preparing to lift one-hundred and eighty pounds of douche-baggery. He didn't see the point in another photo, though. The Venue already told them that all the photos from the booth would be confiscated and destroyed at the end of the night. It was only here because Lilith wanted a photobooth at her wedding, complete with all sorts of zany props.

Caleb personally detested photo booths. He always felt a weird pressure to be creative, or happy, or to act like a fool. Caleb didn't like acting like a fool. That's when people laughed at him.

But nothing else seemed to be bringing Lilith joy at this point.

They had finished off most of the stragglers in the ballroom about thirty minutes ago. Everyone else had run off.

Caleb had suggested that they could hunt down their guests throughout The Venue, picking them off one at a time, but Lilith shot down that idea.

"Why should we be the ones who have to kill all these people?" she had lectured him. "If I just wanted to kill people, we could have had our wedding in a fucking barn in Pennsylvania and burned it to the ground. Oopsie, the candles got too close to the burlap. What would be the fucking point in that? Are we fucking psychos?"

He had thought she was asking the question rhetorically, but she stopped and stared at him, waiting for a response.

"Uh, no," he finally stammered out.

"These people don't just deserve to die. They deserve to be punished. The most painful punishments — the ones that really last, that really leave a wound — don't come from a knife. They come from a mirror."

"You're right. You're absolutely right."

"Just wait until midnight gets close. When it becomes clear they have no options, they're going to look deep inside themselves. And they're going to tear each other apart."

"Like animals."

"Like fucking animals."

With that, she had grabbed him and kissed him. Passionately. Her tongue went deep into his mouth and her hand slid down into his pants.

He took her back to the room. And sure, they had sex. For all of five minutes. Caleb had imagined his wedding night sex would be a deeply sensual, almost spiritual experience. The type of bonding moment that phrases like "making love" fell short of explaining. In his mind, Caleb expected something beyond an orgasm of the body. He wanted an orgasm of the soul.

But that's not what he got.

Instead, Lilith insisted that they stay mostly clothed, so that they could run out to the balcony and ballroom at a moment's notice. With her silky white dress hiked up to her waist, she pushed him down on the bed and straddled him. She didn't even look at him, though. She faced the other way, toward the TV.

She watched all the various feeds from different rooms and different guests in hiding. There wasn't any action, which seemed to disappoint her. Everyone clutched whatever weapons they could get their hands on and crouched down in various nooks and crannies. Some were hiding only feet from one another. Surely they knew there were other people nearby — people they could kill for freedom.

No one did.

Lilith's motions, riding up and down on Caleb, became mechanical. When she moaned, it was as though she had to consciously remind herself that sex involved moaning.

Caleb peeked around her to see the screen. Maybe he could catch a glimpse of his parents. Or Amy. Where were they all hiding?

But Lilith then climaxed — or pretended to, at least — and climbed off of him. She pulled down her dress and went back out to the balcony. Caleb quickly pulled his pants back on and followed.

Since then, they had been hanging out with some of their guests in the photo booth. But as Caleb prepared to lift Freddy so that they could try a second round of photos, one of the doors to the ballroom creaked open. He turned.

Freddy's date, Tiffany, wandered in.

She had been a last minute plus-one for Freddy, who had actually cycled through three different plus-ones since the Save The Dates went out. Caleb never understood why guys like Freddy always seemed to have a never-ending supply of hot girlfriends. Well, he did have a theory — Freddy was rich and he purposefully sought out stupid girls who were impressed by his riches.

Caleb didn't know much about Tiffany except that she was from some small central Oregon town and moved to New York to follow her dreams of being a Broadway actress. She probably got some praise for a supporting role in a high school musical, and that little bit of validation set her off on a life altering course. He presumed she met

Freddy while she was waitressing in New York and found that sleeping with some rich asshole was easier than an ordinary job.

It occurred to Caleb that Tiffany was one of the few guests he actually pitied. She didn't ask for this. She didn't deserve it. If a simple girl like her had only found a nice guy like Caleb, he could have taken care of her. They could have moved back to her hometown, opened an insurance company or some shit, and started popping out babies, all of whom would love and respect their father.

He could have made her happy. And then she wouldn't have to die. But alas, she chose poorly.

Tiffany walked through the ballroom. Her face was pale, seemingly not from fear or exhaustion but from a wee bit of alcohol poisoning. Her sandy blonde hair had become matted near her scalp and frizzy everywhere else.

She wandered over to Caleb and smiled her drunken smile at him. It was sweet and cute. He could see her pupils struggling to zero in on his face. She apparently didn't see the large pools of blood nor the general disarray of the tables and chairs. To her eyes, it must look like the night had ended and the ballroom was in the cleaning stages.

"Great party," she said, her words slurring ever so slightly.

"Thanks." He smiled at her.

"Thanks for having me." She swayed on her feet and patted down her disheveled hair.

It was so adorable, her trying to pretend that she hadn't spent most of the night with her head in the toilet. Caleb wanted nothing more than to scoop her in his arms, carry her up the stairs to her room, and tuck her into bed. Bring her a few glasses of water. Hold her hair back as she puked. And when she awoke, the first thing she would see would be him, sleeping in the chair beside her bed, protecting her dignity.

Her gaze broke away from his face and looked around the room, still not quite seeing things for how they were.

So sweet, so simple. Caleb took a breath. He couldn't pull his eyes off her.

"Well, well, well. And where have you been, sweetie?" Lilith said as she stepped out of the photo booth and came to stand beside Caleb. The blood that had soaked up through the bottom fringes of her dress and up the lace of her sleeves was hard to miss.

The same with the knife in her hand.

At that moment, Caleb noticed Tiffany's body stiffen. The fine, blonde hairs stood out on her arm from the goosebumps that had suddenly formed.

"I, uh, I was in the bathroom. Just looking for Freddy."

"Isn't that Freddy?" Lilith said with a friendly point.

Tiffany slowly turned in that direction. Freddy stayed slumped in his seat, still wearing the captain's hat and pink boa. Still staring daggers out at the world.

Tiffany didn't seem to have the wherewithal to even form a reaction. She stood, mouth slightly agape, and stared. Caleb could almost *see* her innocent mind churning, trying to fit the pieces together to make sense of what her eyes showed her. *Is this a joke?* she seemed to be thinking.

As Caleb watched her, he felt Lilith's grasp. It wasn't a tender or warm touch. She was slipping something to him — a heavy, metal handle wrapped in a leather grip. He looked down. A sickle had been pressed into his hand. Its rusted blade curved back on itself in a crescent moon shape that came to a sharp tip. He didn't know where she had picked it up from, although he kind of remembered seeing it on one of the tables.

"She's all yours, dear," Lilith whispered in his ear.

He gulped. "I thought we were gonna let everyone else be the hunters."

"Oh, I can make an exception. This is my gift to you. It's *your* special day too." There was something about her tone. Something that said this wasn't optional.

"We got other events to get ready for. I don't want to get too dirty," Caleb said.

The false sweetness dropped out of Lilith's voice. "She is so pretty. Too pretty. Shave off her face."

"You can go ahead and have this one," Caleb offered.

"No."

"Why not?"

"Because I haven't been the one eye-fucking her all weekend."

Caleb's face reddened. He didn't believe that he had necessarily been doing that, but he couldn't argue. Not with Lilith. A shame and embarrassment welled up out of his stomach and washed hot, burning waves through his cheeks.

He gripped the sickle tightly and stepped forward.

It had become abundantly clear that Tiffany could hear them, but the girl continued looking away. She stared out the window. Her body had gone still. It struck Caleb that he was witnessing the extent of Tiffany's fight-or-flight response. If she stood still, perhaps they'd never find her.

Lilith let out a disgusted sigh. Was she annoyed that Tiffany wasn't fighting back? Or was she disgusted at *him* and his hesitation?

"Go on," she said. "We've got a schedule to keep."

Tiffany now broke into tears. Her whole body quivered and her expression contorted into one of terror. She didn't look at Caleb, though. Her body stayed rigid, refusing to move, refusing to give up her hiding place, even if that "hiding place" meant standing in the middle of an empty ballroom. It was all she seemed capable of doing. Even possums knew to lay down when they played dead.

"Wow," Lilith said, shaking her head.

Caleb walked up to Tiffany.

He raised the sickle.

Tiffany's face twisted into a terrified cringe as Caleb swung the sickle's curved blade right across her freckled little nose.

CHAPTER 18

Amy glanced at the clock on the gym wall.

Eleven p.m.

One hour until midnight. One hour until they would be forced to find someone to kill or sit around and wait for someone to kill them.

The Venue had been quiet for a while, the only sounds being the occasional sharp pops of explosions, followed either by more silence or howling screams. In all that time, it didn't seem as though anyone had experienced any success at removing their damn bracelets.

Her parents seemed resigned to the idea that their arms would eventually explode off their bodies. Candice, who had been a school nurse for many years, had fitted all of them with tourniquets near their elbows. She took off both her nylons and then cut them in half so that each person could have a strip of the wide, stretchy fabric.

Candice said that the key to a good tourniquet was the "cone of pressure," meaning the tourniquet needed to sufficiently compress all the blood vessels and muscles in the area. It needed to be wide and tight. A wire or string wouldn't do it.

For several minutes, the four of them practiced pulling their tourniquets. It was a matter of holding one end of the nylon with one's teeth as their free hand pulled on the other end of the nylon. Then they were to take one of the pegs Candice had pulled from the weight machines and insert the small rod into the knot, twisting and torqueing it tight.

Easy-peasy.

... as long as one wasn't writhing on the ground in shock, weak from blood loss, and completely disoriented by the fact that their arm had just exploded.

But Candice assured them that if done properly, a good tourniquet could save their life.

"Ladies and gentlemen, please turn your attention to the north end of the ballroom for the presentation of the wedding cake," the DJ announced, his voice blaring out through the gym and hallways beyond.

Amy jumped at the sound. Her ears had been in a constant state of strain, anxiously listening for approaching feet.

There must be speakers in the ceiling, Amy thought.

And probably cameras.

"This is a red velvet cake with a cream cheese and cyanide frosting," the DJ continued.

Did she hear that right? Cyanide frosting?

"So, if any of you want to kick back and relax for the rest of the night, come to the ballroom and enjoy a slice of cake," the DJ said.

"What the hell?" Mariko whispered out.

"Cyanide kills fast," Roger said. "It's what the Nazi generals used before they could get captured."

"It's a suicide cake," Amy said.

"But why? Why give us the option?" Mariko asked.

Amy shrugged her shoulders, but she believed she knew the answer.

The DJ continued, "I'm being told by the kitchen staff that the cake *does* contain nuts. So, if anyone has an allergy, just eat the cyanide frosting."

Amy glanced toward her mom. Candice's face, which had been so tight with stress, appeared to relax ever so slightly. Amy knew her mom could never hurt, let alone kill, another human. She was destined to be the weak antelope in the herd. The one that the true psychopaths would target. Candice would become someone's ticket to freedom.

Which was exactly what Caleb and Lilith probably wanted to avoid — easy kills for other people. Let the soft ones, like Amy's mom, take themselves out of the equation so that whoever remained could have a true fight to the death. If given the chance, Amy bet her mother would eat the cake.

The DJ continued, "And now, turn your attention to the main stage as Caleb and Lilith have their first dance as a married couple."

A familiar song played through the speaker — *Sweet Caroline*.

Amy loved that song. It reminded her of road trips with her parents. Of all the oldies and classic rock that they listened to in the car, *that* was their song. Whenever it came on, all conversation ceased. All naps would end. The three of them would lean up in their seats and belt out the lyrics together. As a family.

She felt her heart pound and her muscles clench. Caleb and Lilith — those fucking psychopaths — were now twirling on the stage, staring goo-goo into each other's eyes, pausing only to shout out the chorus to *Amy's* family's song. She had probably been the one to teach the song to Caleb back in the day.

Fuck Caleb.

Fuck Lilith.

Fuck this wedding.

"They're on the stage," Amy said, her voice now flat and angry. "They're distracted."

Everyone looked at her. *Her point?*

"We rush them."

Candice was the first to react. "What?!"

But Amy had already started marching to the door, the steak knife — their only non-gym related weapon — clutched firmly in her hand. "I'm not gonna sit here and wait for my arm to explode. I'm gonna grab them. I'm gonna hold them. And I'm gonna *force* them to make this place let us go."

She turned to gauge her family's reaction.

Mariko nodded in agreement. With a bench press bar clutched tightly, she followed after Amy.

Candice and Roger did too.

Amy turned toward the door.

With renewed focus, she stepped into the hallway.

The moment she did, a scream filled her ears.

She leapt to the side just as a woman — her gown drenched in blood — leapt out from behind the door frame and wildly swung an axe downward at Amy, its blade gliding inches from Amy's chest, right at the exact position where she had stood only a moment before.

The woman shrieked loudly, a constant wail that seemed to have been built up and stored deep within her over the course of the preceding hours. She must have been standing there, waiting to attack someone, *anyone* this entire time. That was probably why so few people tried to seek refuge in the gym — they came around the corner and must have seen this woman lying in wait.

The axe blade slammed into the floor.

The woman wasted no time in lifting it and swinging again, this time in Roger's direction. The woman didn't seem to know how to swing an axe; she had probably never done it before in her life. Her movements were just wild, chaotic flails with a heavy object.

Mariko pushed Roger out of the way.

The axe blade struck the wooden door frame of the gym and lodged in tight.

The woman released the axe handle and drew a steak knife from somewhere within her dress. With another scream, she threw herself toward Candice, stabbing with the knife as she did.

By now, Amy had regained her footing. She spun around and grabbed the woman by the hair, yanking her backward.

The woman flailed the knife in Amy's direction. With Amy clutching her hair tightly, the woman twisted and shrieked like a trapped animal. Amy dodged her slashes long enough to steady herself and then she slammed the woman's head into the mirrored wall.

Cracks spider-webbed across the mirror from the impact. The woman slid to the ground. A deep moan rolled out of her lips.

But as Amy stood over her, she could see the woman's chest rising and falling.

The woman was still alive.

Amy bent down and grabbed the knife from the woman's limp hand. She held it out for her mother.

"You do it, Mom."

"Do what?"

"Kill her."

"Amy!"

She looked at her mom. "Just do it. She's right here. If you don't, someone else will."

"This isn't us, Amy."

"She would've killed us, Mom!"

Candice stood her ground and shook her head.

Amy turned to her dad. She held the knife out for him, but he put up his hands and waved her off. "I'm not getting in the middle of this."

"For fuck's sake, people!" Amy said. Next she looked at Mariko. But Mariko also stepped away.

"Come on, Ames. Let's get to the ballroom."

"Someone kill this bitch!" Amy said. "Take the pass. Get out. Go home."

"We're all on the same team, Amy," Candice said.

"We're locked up with psychopaths, Mom."

"We don't have to become one."

"Yes, we do."

"Amy Holgate, you listen to me, and you listen to me now," her mom said in *that voice* of hers. "I have no ill will toward any of these people. It's Caleb and that bride of his who put us here and I'd like to find out why. They're the only ones I care to see pay the price."

"Mom, the rules are—"

"Screw their rules. Screw their game. We're not who they think we are."

With that, Candice stepped past Amy and hurried off down the hall. Her dad followed closely behind. Even Mariko cast one final *Come on, let's go* glance at Amy before quietly jogging away.

Amy hesitated. She looked down at the woman by her feet.

Amy clutched her knife tightly.

The woman had collapsed into somewhat of a sitting position, resting her back against the mirrored walls. Her head lolled to the side so that her cheek rested on her shoulder.

This left her neck exposed.

Vulnerable.

Amy looked around the gym. There were surely cameras in the walls, perhaps even in the light fixtures.

Someone had to be watching her.

Someone could see her plunge the knife into the woman's throat.

If the rules were to be trusted, someone would open a door and let her go wait out the night with Lilith's grandma.

It would be fast. A quick flick of the wrist.

Amy looked down at the woman and her exposed neck. She tried to place the woman. Was she from the bride's side or the groom's? Family, friend, or coworker? She vaguely recalled seeing the woman during the reception. Some other table with some other people with whom Amy hadn't interacted at all.

Blood had splattered all over the woman's dress and face. *Lots* of blood. There didn't seem to be any cut marks or injuries on the woman. This blood must have all come from somebody else.

An image flashed in Amy's mind — the woman sitting at a table with a short, bearded man who had a friendly smile. They seemed to be husband and wife. Amy remembered catching a glimpse of that man charging toward Lilith and getting stabbed in the chest.

The woman's hands were a deep maroon, probably stained trying to stop her husband from bleeding out.

Amy cursed under her breath as she tried to push the sympathetic image from her mind, but it was lodged in tight. She couldn't escape it.

With a sigh, Amy stood.

She turned and ran after her family.

CHAPTER 19

Amy caught up to her family as they ran down the grand staircase.

They tried to keep their footsteps soft, which was easy for Amy and Mariko who had long ago ditched their heels and were running barefoot. Roger's shoes and thick soles, meanwhile, clomped on the stone staircase.

They slowed as they reached the lobby.

The front entrance remained open. Amy could see a few bodies in the dark beyond — people who had sacrificed their arm to escape and only made it so far. Perhaps a guest or two made it further, but the thickness of the night obscured any evidence of it.

Amy turned away from the door and kept running.

They entered the ballroom's foyer. Amy glanced around, feeling exposed. There were no places to hide in this room and the bright lights exposed them to the world.

They crept toward the ballroom doors.

The song neared its end.

Amy crouched by the door and peered in.

She couldn't see much. Unlike the rest of The Venue, the lights in the ballroom were off.

Except for the stage.

A fixed spotlight bounced its light off a revolving disco ball, sending sparkling, magical reflections out onto the stage. The light swirled around the massive three-tiered cake in front of the stage. Its white frosting and pink trim glistened.

Caleb twirled Lilith in circles. Then he brought her toward him in a firm embrace and they swayed in each other's arms.

"They don't have any weapons," Amy whispered, although she could see that their bows and arrows, as well as a small assortment of melee weapons, were stacked on a rectangular hors d'oeuvres table beside the stage.

In the darkness, Amy could barely make out the faint outlines of people seated at the tables, watching the dance. But this audience didn't move. They slumped in their seats. One of the silhouettes seemed to lack a head.

The song began its crescendo to the final chorus.

"Wait for them to kiss," Amy whispered. "Dad and I will take Caleb. Mariko and Mom start with Lilith. Whoever ties down theirs first, helps the other."

Her family nodded and gripped their meager weapons — weight bars and steak knives. They could probably grab a real weapon from the hors d'oeuvres table, but that was on the far side of the stage. They'd lose the element of surprise. Groping along the dark ballroom floor for a weapon didn't seem smart either.

There wasn't much time to look, think, or strategize. The song was about to end and the lights might go up at any moment. Amy concluded that this was their best shot — sneak up quickly and quietly, then tackle them by surprise. Four on two. Not bad odds.

Caleb spun Lilith one final time.

"Get ready," Amy said.

Caleb gathered his bride in his arm and dipped her low.

"Let's go."

Staying crouched in the darkness, Amy ran toward the stage. Her family followed close behind.

Keeping her steps quick, light, and silent, she galloped across the ballroom. Her toes felt the cold hardness of the tile floor, until her foot almost slipped out from under her as it slid across a warm, thick liquid.

Blood. It must be blood.

She could barely see the floor in the dim light. The black-and-white checkered tile had a way of masking the pools that had formed. She hoped she wouldn't trip. She hoped she wouldn't set her bare foot down on a broken wine glass or discarded throwing star.

Despite her fears, she felt her adrenaline kick in. Her speed increased.

Within moments, she pushed past the front row of spectators — knocking their limp bodies to the ground — and leapt onto the stage.

As Amy mounted the steps, Caleb, still dipping Lilith, leaned in and touched his lips to his bride's. His eyes closed. His entire world seemed to vanish in that moment, leaving him unaware of anything other than the woman he held in his arms.

And in that pause, Amy bounded across the stage. She wrapped an arm around his shoulder and used her momentum to pull him off his feet, tackling him violently to the ground.

He dropped Lilith as he fell.

Amy had planned to bring Caleb down and press her knife to his throat before he could respond, but in the tangle of the fall, she found her hand pinned beneath Caleb's body. He tried to scramble to his feet. All Amy could do was wrap her arms around him from behind and hold him to the floor.

"Dad, help!"

Lilith was already back up. She ran toward the weapons table.

"Stop her!" Amy shouted. She hadn't realized how far ahead she had run from her family. Only a few yards, but it felt like much more.

Mariko, who was a few strides in front of Amy's parents, bounded onto the stage and swung the heavy bench-press bar at Lilith's head. Lilith spun around in time to dodge the swing, grabbing the bar as she did. She yanked on it, pulling Mariko in close. In a quick move, she elbowed Mariko in the face.

Mariko fell backwards. She tried to maintain her grip on the bar, but with a confident, twisting maneuver, Lilith wrenched it from Mariko's hands. With the bar all to herself, Lilith twirled it once over her head, building momentum as she swung it hard.

"Mom! Look out!"

Candice had run onto the stage, barreling toward Lilith.

Lilith timed her swing perfectly.

The metal bar slammed into Candice.

Its force sent her off her feet.

Amy could only watch as the bar indented into her mother's head, causing the vessels in her eyes to burst and instantly roll over red.

In mid-air, as she fell, Candice became a rag doll. Her limbs went limp. All fight and all life faded from her in that brief moment in which she fell off the stage, disappearing from Amy's sight. With the spotlight and disco ball shining brightly on the dance floor, a dense blackness filled the rest of the ballroom. It was as if that blackness reached up and took Candice, carrying her off.

Amy couldn't see her land, but Amy knew. She knew her mother was dead.

Elsewhere, Mariko had gotten back to her feet. She wrapped her arms around Lilith and held her from behind. Lilith tried to twist free, but Mariko held on tight. Finally, Lilith pushed off with her foot and threw all her weight to the side, sending both her and Mariko tumbling off the stage where they followed Candice's body to the darkened floor, out of sight.

"Sweetie!" Caleb shouted after Lilith as Amy held him down. He got his arm loose from Amy's grasp and began to push her off him. He didn't seem to actually be fighting her; he was scrambling to get to his wife, to hold and protect her.

As Amy began to lose her grip, Roger rushed over and punched Caleb hard on the side of his face. Caleb's head recoiled and smacked into the stage floor. That seemed to stun him. He stopped resisting. His head swayed side-to-side and Amy could see that his pupils were struggling to focus. Amy didn't think her father had ever thrown a punch in his life, yet it was a good, solid hit.

Roger then pulled off his belt and wrapped it around Caleb's wrists.

"Amy, his legs!" Roger said, quickly yanking the tie off his neck and tossing it to Amy.

Amy looped her father's necktie around Caleb's ankles, wrapping it tightly before binding it off with whatever knots Amy could manufacture. It wasn't perfect, but Amy hoped it would be good enough to hold him.

Fffffft! A flutter of air kissed the back of Amy's neck.

It was an arrow flying past her head.

She turned.

The bright lights of the stage made it so she could barely make out Lilith's silhouette standing among the tables, holding up her bow. Her shadowy figure aimed directly at Amy.

T . J . P A Y N E

"Mariko!" Amy shouted.

No reply came.

Ffffft! Amy barely ducked as the second arrow whizzed by her face.

"Let's go! Get him out of here!" she shouted to her dad.

Roger didn't need any encouragement. He threw Caleb over his shoulder and began to run.

Amy followed right behind.

They descended from the stage and entered what felt like the relative safety of the ballroom's darkness. They ran past tables and chairs. At one point, Amy's bare foot came down solidly not on hard floor, but on a fleshy surface that gave way beneath her weight. Her heel had stomped through a rib cage.

She almost lost her balance, but a decade of dance, and a million miniscule muscle corrections, kept her moving forward.

Ffffft!

Ffffft!

Ffffft!

She couldn't see them. She couldn't even feel them. She only heard the sound of the arrows slicing through the ballroom's stale atmosphere. She had no idea how close they were. The arrows flew by in a flurry; Lilith apparently was not at all worried about accidentally hitting Caleb.

Amy pushed against the back of her dad, propelling him toward the door. The rectangle of light. Escape. It grew bigger. Brighter. They were near to freedom.

Ffffft!

They ran through the door and out into the foyer.

Roger's muscles finally tensed up and he fell to his knees, dropping Caleb into a heap on the floor. There was no time to wait, though.

Amy pulled her father back to his feet. "Grab his ankles. I'll get his arms," she said.

Together they heaved Caleb off the ground.

Amy looked around. The bright foyer left them exposed. No place to hide. No place to interrogate Caleb, to threaten him, to hold him hostage. The moment Lilith walked out that door, she'd have a clear shot.

"The chapel," Amy said.

The entrance was at the end of the hall. They staggered forward, Caleb's weight seeming to multiply with each step they took. His midsection sagged toward the ground and Amy soon felt her grip tire. But they carried on.

He didn't fight. He didn't squirm or shout out.

At one point, Amy assumed he must be unconscious, but when she looked down at his face, she saw him staring right back at her. A small smile danced on his lips as he watched her struggle with his weight.

"Sorry about your mom," he said through that grin. "And your friend."

Mariko. Amy didn't even know what happened to her. She didn't see in the chaos.

Without responding, she threw her shoulder into the chapel door. It swung open, and they ran inside, carrying their new prisoner.

Amy was going to end this. No matter what it took.

She was done fucking around.

CHAPTER 20

Mariko took a mean head-butt to the face when she tried to hold Lilith from behind. The blow broke Mariko's grip and sent her reeling backwards. Just as she managed to steady herself, Lilith punched her square on the jaw.

It sent Mariko sprawling to the ground.

The world went black for a moment.

When her sight returned, it was as though she was looking through a gray fog. A cold breeze caressed Mariko's face, pulling her back to consciousness.

By the time her fogginess cleared, she realized Lilith stood a few feet from her, but Lilith's attention was elsewhere as she fired off arrows into the dark ballroom. Mariko couldn't see Lilith's target, but she knew who it must be.

Lilith nocked another arrow and drew her string taunt. She held it, taking her time to aim. The dark outlines of Roger and Amy shone clearly against the lit doorway as they ran toward the foyer.

Lilith held her breath, leading her target slightly.

Mariko pulled herself to her feet. She threw herself forward into Lilith, knocking her off-balance. The arrow sailed off toward the wall, striking against a piece of mounted weaponry with a loud *clank*.

Lilith wasted no time in spinning around and placing Mariko in a headlock.

Mariko's throat compressed beneath Lilith's strong arm. Mariko flailed her hands behind her, trying to get a finger in Lilith's eye. Anything to break Lilith's grip.

She stomped down hard on Lilith's foot, but Lilith just absorbed the pain.

The headlock grew tighter.

As Mariko's vision blurred, she could see the DJ, dancing in his booth.

"We got people on the dance floor!" he announced. "Let's check out their moves."

Somehow, Mariko's ears were able to register that the DJ had turned on some 90's dance mix, the kind of song that called out the dancer's moves. *Step to the left... step to the right... kick... slide...*

She could swear that Lilith was actually following the directions, yanking Mariko's neck side to side with the beat. She dipped Mariko once... twice... three times to the song.

It had been several seconds now since Mariko had gotten a good gulp of air. Her arms felt rubbery. Her head seemed to float above her body, caught in some gray smoggy layer above the ballroom.

She felt herself being carried forward.

The breeze, which a few moments ago she had only faintly registered, suddenly blew cold wind against her skin.

Instinctively, her arm shot out in front of her. Her palm connected with something hard. She was bracing herself against a wooden frame. The cold breeze blew the foggy film away from her eyes and cleared the world just enough for her to see what was in front of her.

A jagged shard of window glass.

It was the window that Lilith's dad had thrown a chair through in his attempt to escape. The gaping, angry, toothy remains of the window smiled at Mariko.

Lilith put pressure on Mariko's head. She forced Mariko's face to angle forward, pushing Mariko's eye toward one of the pieces of glass that jutted out of the window frame.

Mariko tried to push back, but she could feel her arms buckling. The pointed edge of glass filled her vision, blurring as it got closer. The pressure from Lilith stayed firm and even. Slow. Intentionally slow. At this pace, the glass would enter Mariko's eye one millimeter at a time, slowly deflating it as the shard made its way back into her skull.

"No… no-no-no," Mariko said. It was all she could think to say. Or do.

"Shhh. It's okay, sweetie. It's okay," Lilith responded, as though she were rocking a baby to sleep.

"Please… please…"

Mariko was helpless.

The glass tickled her eyelash.

In a moment, it would slice through her cornea.

Mariko suddenly stopped pushing against the window and instead leaned toward it. The sudden change in momentum sent her body careening to the side, just past the shard of glass. Her shoulder hit the window frame.

The shifting position did little to loosen Lilith's grip.

Lilith's arm constricted even tighter around Mariko's neck.

Mariko threw her left arm out the window.

The light on her bracelet flashed red.

It vibrated.

Mariko reached her arm back behind her. She pressed the flashing bracelet against Lilith's face. Then, Mariko closed her eyes, clenched her body, and waited for—

BOOM!

The blast knocked Lilith backwards.

Air filled Mariko's lungs again. It surprised her that her arm didn't hurt. She didn't feel anything. In fact, she couldn't see or hear anything either.

It was as though the blast had knocked all sense from her body. Her eyes and ears swam in a thick black ocean. Her consciousness detached from her physical self. She sank deeper into the blackness as it swirled around her and prepared to carry her away.

One thought managed to penetrate the numbness of her mind.

The tourniquet.

She had to tighten the tourniquet.

She had to do it now.

Mariko reached her right hand toward her left. She couldn't see. She could barely even feel. Everything felt as though she were touching the world through a thick glove.

Her hand touched something hard and cold. She realized she was on the floor. How long had it been since the blast? Perhaps moments. Perhaps longer. Perhaps she was already dead.

Where was Lilith? Had she left? Had Mariko killed her? Was she standing over Mariko, preparing to finish the job?

It didn't matter. The only thing that mattered was tightening the tourniquet.

Mariko's fingers glided through some sort of slippery residue that covered a tough, wire-like material. The first thought that came to her mind was that she had found Lilith's bow-string, greased up with too much oil. But she soon realized that she was actually fingering her own flesh and tendons.

Right then, she wanted to vomit. The darkness crept closer and she was momentarily glad for it.

But a strange burst of rational thought penetrated the black.

If this is my wrist, then the nylon tourniquet must be a few inches up my arm.

She felt around. When her fingers made contact with a piece of cloth, she grabbed it tight. Her fingers brought the fabric to her mouth and she held it within her teeth. Then her hand went back to find the other end of the nylon.

Perhaps it wasn't the nylon.

Perhaps she had put the hem of her own dress into her mouth.

She didn't know if she was pulling on the right thing. She only knew that she had to pull on something.

She felt another end of fabric.

Between her teeth and her good hand, she pulled the fabric tight. She didn't feel the tourniquet constrict on her arm, sealing off the blood that must be pooling around her.

Mariko didn't feel anything.

The blackness, which had stayed at bay for all these important seconds, now rushed in. It filled her vision.

Once her eyes rolled over and the world went dark, for a split second, her ears compensated. She could hear the world very clearly.

There was music.

The DJ was making up his own lyrics to some techno dance song. "I say, ka-boom went yer hand! Ka-boom went yer hand!"

And then, that too went away. The blackness faded the music into silence.

Thank god, Mariko thought.

CHAPTER 21

Caleb wasn't afraid of death.

Or, at least, he didn't think he was.

There was the slight chance that Amy and her father were going to kill him now, but he doubted it. That wasn't Amy's style. Her dad was a wild card. But Amy? Nah. A little confrontation and she'd wilt like a little dandelion.

He glanced around as they carried him into the chapel.

Unlike the rest of The Venue, the lights in the chapel stayed dark. All the candles in the crystal bowls that outlined the floor — the ones that had lit the wedding ceremony — had long since burned out.

The design of the room, with its high windows along the front wall, allowed moonlight to stream in, casting a blue glow over the pulpit.

Caleb liked this room. Maybe tomorrow, as the cleanup commenced, he would take some time to stretch out on one of the pews and stare at the ceiling. It would be nice to be alone with his thoughts.

Amy and her dad carried Caleb down the aisle.

"The altar," she said to her dad, nodding her head toward the ornate wooden table in the front. It was the only spot in the room where the moon provided any useable light.

He put up no resistance as they lugged him along.

As they passed the darkened pews, Caleb was sure he heard the sounds of scurrying. Maybe some nervous whispers. People must be hiding in the shadows beneath the benches. Like rats.

He wondered who among his friends and family was out there, holding their breath, cowering and shaking in fear.

The purpose of the night had been to reveal the hatefulness of the people who shaped their lives. At least, that was Lilith's stated purpose. But the night had revealed the opposite, and Caleb was just now coming to peace with that.

His friends and family weren't particularly cruel. Or mean.

They were weak.

Maybe that was worse.

Perhaps that was why everyone in Caleb's life spent so much time ridiculing him. Stomping on him. Holding him down.

They were crabs, desperately pulling Caleb back into the boiling pot because it would be better to watch him be cooked with the rest of them than watch him escape. Watch him succeed. Watch him come to the cusp of billionaire status by the age of thirty.

These people were failures. They were losers. They were rats, willing to eat their own to survive.

And now they would have to live with their cowardice for the brief candle flicker that remained of their lives.

As Amy and Roger carried him, no one rose up from their hiding place. No one offered to help ferry the devil to the altar. No one ran forward to kill Caleb and gain their own release. No one set him free in an attempt to curry his favor. They hid in the dark beneath the pews, only shifting to slightly reposition themselves, possibly so they could run if they needed to.

Pathetic.

For all intents and purposes, Caleb was alone with Amy and her dad.

They heaved Caleb onto the altar, dropping him down roughly. It knocked the wind out of him a bit, but he tried not to show it. Instead, he smiled.

Amy stood over him, angling her head so as not to block out the little moonlight she had.

She glared at him.

But seeing anger on her cute little face didn't strike fear into Caleb's heart. It made him want to giggle. Laughing felt mean, though. He should give Amy this moment. Let her have this power over him. This should be fun.

But the more he tried to swallow his mirth, the more the giggle bubbled to the surface, escaping from his pursed lips in little whiffs of laughter. It was like the time when Amy's dad installed a new washing machine and Caleb and Amy crept into the discarded box and hid together, waiting for Roger to finish so they could jump out and scare him.

They were probably five at the time. Maybe six. They sat in that box for what felt like hours but had probably only been two minutes. They stared at each other, excited by their plan.

But, bit by bit, Caleb had begun to crack. Little smiles had curled over his lips. His breathing quickened. Amy had to put her hand over his mouth to keep him from laughing, but that only made it worse. Soon, she also got a case of the giggles.

Little did they know that Amy's mom had been filming the whole thing. The big cardboard box shook with each of their attempts to restrain their joy.

Caleb's chest hurt from suppressing so much laughter. By the time Roger returned to the box, Amy and Caleb were laughing too hard to even say "Boo." They jumped out and then immediately flopped onto the floor, crying as they laughed.

In all his years since, Caleb never laughed so hard. He never experienced so much joy. It was an alchemy of happiness that can only blossom between two soulmates.

He wondered if Amy ever felt that joy again either.

Perhaps today would end that streak of joyless days.

For Caleb, at least.

Amy was fucked.

Seemingly in response to that thought, Amy's hands wrapped around Caleb's throat, squeezing down on his windpipe. Her grip was firm, which surprised Caleb. His lungs strained to push air in and out of his body. He felt his face burn hot as a panic settled into his muscles. He didn't even have the air to fight back.

His vision blurred as he realized that it wasn't just his windpipe that Amy was constricting but the actual blood flow to his head. A blackness seeped in along the fringes of his vision.

"Not *yet*, Amy," Roger said, his voice cutting through the darkness.

Amy's grip immediately loosened and Caleb felt a rush of life pump its way up from his chest through his head and extremities. It took concentration for his lungs to *not* frantically gulp in the needed air. He tried to project calm. Indifference.

"We still need him," Roger continued. "For now." His voice sounded stern. The intonation was unmistakable. He had no problem with her eventually killing Caleb. Just not until they got what they needed.

Amy pulled out a knife and pressed its tip into Caleb's temple.

"Order the staff to deactivate the bracelets," she said.

"Oh, Amy. Amy, Amy, Amy," Caleb said, purposefully trying to make his voice sound as patronizing as possible.

"Do it," Amy commanded.

"You know the rules. Kill someone and you're free to go."

Roger leaned toward Caleb. "Why should we trust you?"

It was a good question; one that Caleb assumed all his guests would ask eventually. But Caleb had rehearsed his answer. "Where's the fun in killing people if they're going to die anyway?" he said. "Why go through with so much hassle? If I simply wanted you dead, I could've hired a bunch of hitmen. It would've been cheaper than this. And if I wanted you to suffer some physical or emotional pain, I could have paid a little extra to have them torture you. What would be the point in that? And, more importantly, what would be the lesson? I *want* as many of you to survive as possible. I want you to have blood on your hands. I want you to carry that with you for the rest of your life."

He tried to gauge from their faces whether they believed him or not. He could always read people's intentions from their eyes; it was one of the gifts that made him a success at business. But he couldn't read theirs. The darkness of the chapel kept their eyes shrouded in shadow.

"You said they'd erase the memories," Roger responded.

"Yes. They have the technology. It's more of a blunt force amnesia. Just clearing out the last forty-eight hours or so. It's mostly for The Venue's protection. They don't like to create a fuss."

"So you said."

"Then what's the problem?"

Roger glared down at him. "If no one remembers, then what's the point in teaching us a lesson?"

"Lilith and I will remember," Caleb said with a smile. "We'll always know. We'll see some of you around, I'm sure. A game night here or meeting up for drinks there. Whatever you people do. We'll see you, out and about in your normal lives. And we'll know. We'll remember. The memory will have burned itself into our minds. We'll have seen you turning into animals. Gutting each other to survive.

"And I believe that deep down, there'll be a tiny itch in your soul. You won't be able to place it. Maybe there will be some dream fragment. Maybe your forehead will inexplicably sweat when you hold a kitchen knife. However it manifests itself, somewhere deep inside, you'll know what you are. You'll know what you did. And what a joy that will be for Lilith and me."

Amy and Roger simply looked down at him.

"What the fuck is wrong with you?" Amy said. It wasn't uttered as an insult. She seemed genuinely confused.

"I'm the only honest one here."

"Let us go," she said, her voice turning cold.

"I wish I could help you, Ames. But if you want the bracelets off, you just have to kill someone."

"Won't be hard." She twisted the knife slightly into his temple, almost like a corkscrew.

He kept his grin, but he felt his muscles strain.

"I'm gonna bore this hole straight through your head. Slowly."

With a bit of added pressure, the knife dug in. It rotated around, scooping out little slivers of his scalp. He tightened his body. He and Lilith had practiced meditation from a pain expert precisely for a moment like this. With calm focus, areas of his brain and their responses to stimuli shut down, exactly as he had been trained.

His smile returned. His gaze again fell upon Amy. She was trying to scare him. Trying to torture him. His eyes rolled over in disgust and he looked away.

"Oh, Amy," he said. "I wish I could believe you had it in you. I wanted you to be one of the few who lived."

"What did I ever to do you? I was your friend."

"My *best* friend. We were so good together. We could have been so happy."

"Is this about high school?"

"It's about more than high school. More than middle school. It's about loyalty. You were my only friend in the world, but the moment we got off that bus in ninth grade and stepped through those doors, what did you do? You were embarrassed by me. You started hanging out with Liza Schwartz and Brandi Halderman. Suddenly, you couldn't bear to be seen with Caleb Hunt. I was alone. Some *friend*."

There was silence.

He still couldn't make out her eyes, couldn't see the realization that must be flashing across her face at the way she rejected him. Abandoned him. Hurt him.

"That's it?" she finally said.

Caleb turned toward Roger. "And you."

"I barely knew you, kid," Roger said.

"I had one chance to reconnect with Amy. I invited her on a road trip to help me move into college. I had it meticulously planned. Cross-country. Stopping at national parks and big cities. I saved for a year to pay for food and hotels. An epic two week adventure. But you and your wife said no."

Roger's face was blank. "What are you talking about? I don't remember any of this."

"Before I left, I came by your house one last time. One last time to say goodbye to Amy. To my best friend. But she was gone. Out camping. With *Ryan Parker*!"

"That name sounds familiar," Roger said.

"You wouldn't let your daughter go on a road trip with *me*, a perfect gentleman. You and your wife never liked me. You never trusted me. You never wanted Amy to be with me."

"You and I have said maybe five sentences to each other in your whole life."

"But I never thought you would feel so threatened by my intellect that you would steer your daughter toward the Neanderthals. The boys who wouldn't make you look like the simple, little man you are. Boys like Ryan Parker. Instead of allowing your daughter to expand her world and realize true love and protection, you opted to let her go off into the woods with some jock. Some walking STD. Because he didn't make you feel inadequate, like I did."

A look flashed between Amy and her dad.

Caleb wished the lighting was better. He wanted to see the realization scroll across their faces. The epiphany. The moment of clarity where they saw their own insecurities laid out before them: Roger and his feelings of stupidity in the face of Caleb's intellect. And Amy and her superficial attraction toward looks and brawn over kindness and love.

The two had sabotaged their own happiness in favor of mediocrity.

Would they see it?

Would they understand?

Caleb waited.

But the looks they cast back down upon him made his hopes fade. They were still confused. Their eyes narrowed as their puny, caveman-like brains tried to put the puzzle together.

"You killed my mom because I went *camping*?"

They didn't get it. They might never get it.

"Because you rejected me and in doing so, you rejected decent humanity."

"That trip had nothing to do with you."

"I loved you. I could have provided for you. Protected you. Treated you like a queen. But you judged me. Not on what was inside. Not on my mind or heart. You rejected me because I wasn't attractive. Because I wasn't athletic. Because I wasn't rich. Because I wasn't cool. Because I—"

"— because *I* wanted to be alone in a tent with Eva Parker, Ryan's sister!"

That name sounded familiar to Caleb. He had vague memories that Ryan had an older sister. She was on the basketball team, right? If she was the same girl Caleb was thinking about, then, yes, she was hot. Was that just another popular girl that Amy had tried to become friends with—?

"I'm gay!" Amy said. "I've always been gay!"

The words took a moment to penetrate Caleb's brain. Instead, they rattled around on the outside. It was like a penny dropping into one of those big funnels, slowly spinning its way down to the center. His mind raced, trying to fit the pieces together.

The grand speech he had been preparing for years, the one where he would really rip into Amy for her betrayal of their friendship, suddenly evaporated from his thoughts.

"No," Caleb said. It was all he could think to say.

"Yeah."

"No. No, really?"

"Yes."

"Even back in high school?"

"Yes!"

"Wait, does that mean... Is Mariko your...?" He felt his face flush.

Had he really missed all the signs? It seemed so obvious now. Who brings just a "friend" to a destination wedding?

Was it true? This whole time?

Did Lilith know? Surely, she had figured it out upon first seeing Amy and Mariko together. Lilith was far more perceptive than Caleb with things like that.

But, suddenly, it all made sense.

It wasn't about *him* at all. It was about her. He just never had a chance. Even when she abandoned him to hang out with the "cool" girls, it wasn't because of anything he had control over. She probably just wanted to fuck Liza Schwartz and Brandi Halderman, as they were the most attractive girls in their grade.

Oh, Amy. Such a little slut.

She didn't love him not because he wasn't particularly attractive... or personable... or athletic.

It was because she just didn't like boys.

Did he really waste four seats at his wedding for this?

Had he brought her and her family here because of a misunderstanding?

How many other misunderstandings had there been?

How many other little narratives had Caleb formed off of only one-sided information? How much anger and resentment had he allowed to calcify over minor perceived slights?

He mentally ran through his guest list.

A strange sensation burned through his roiling stomach.

Doubt.

He pushed it down.

These guests had bullied him. They had rejected him. They had laughed at him and mocked him. They hated him just as much as he hated them. None of them deserved to live.

Except maybe Amy.

He looked back up at her. Her face was still hidden by shadow, but he imagined that she was smiling down at him.

"High school must've been a hard time for you," he said.

"It's hard for everyone. Everyone's dealing with their own shit."

"Are you happy?" he asked. "With Mariko?"

"Yes."

He believed her.

"That's great, Ames. That's really great. I'm happy for you. She seems cool. If it's okay with you, maybe we can meet up for drinks sometime. After this is all over. A double date."

She didn't respond.

"Hey, so..." Caleb began, but he didn't quite know how to express what he was thinking. "I want you to know that I am totally okay with you being gay. In fact, I'm a little upset that you didn't feel comfortable coming out to me until now. We're best friends, Ames. You could have told me anything. You *should* have told me. That kind of mistrust is hurtful. Did you think that I wouldn't understand? That I wouldn't be cool with it? What did I ever do to have you doubt me?"

He didn't mean to raise his voice, but he couldn't help it. What kind of trust was that? Keeping such a deep secret from her best friend all this time. It was a betrayal; that's what it was.

"I... I'm sorry I didn't tell you," Amy said. Her voice didn't sound particularly sorry. "I should have trusted you. And I'm so... uh... so thankful for your approval."

"Of course, I approve. We're friends."

"Yes, we are. We always have been."

He felt her grasping his hand. Her skin was warm and soft.

"As your friend, I'm begging you," she said. "Please. End this. Let us go. Let all of us go."

He looked up and for the first time, he saw her face. She was leaning forward slightly so that the moonlight caught her features. It was the face of his friend. The girl he used to go biking with. The girl who built pillow forts in her living room for their epic Nerf Gun wars. The girl who didn't like following directions for her Legos.

The girl he loved.

Loved as a *friend*.

Only as a friend.

Then he turned to look at Roger.

"For what it's worth, I always really liked you," Roger said, smiling down on him. "Always thought you were a great kid. Whip smart. Loyal. Tough. A man. Any father would be proud to have you as a son."

Caleb nodded.

These were good people. Maybe he misunderstood them.

"You know what," Caleb began. "I think that perhaps we can work out a—"

Something splattered on Caleb's face.

When he looked back up, an arrowhead stuck out from Roger's Adam's apple.

"Dad!"

Roger staggered backwards a bit. His arms flailed around, seemingly unable to decide if they wanted to clutch his bleeding neck or catch his falling body before he collapsed.

Caleb watched Roger stumble. The shadows from the moonlight made his eye sockets look like gaping holes. Soulless holes.

Roger tried to speak, but the air bubble only made the blood gurgle around his neck hole. At some point, Amy had come to his side and was holding him up. Or maybe she was trying to pull him down to safety, but his muscles had become too rigid to bend. Caleb couldn't tell.

Another arrow thudded into Roger's shoulder, spinning him around slightly so that Caleb could finally see his eyes. It was a look of surprise on his face. Confusion.

A new arrow struck him in the chest. The force sent him backwards. He crashed down, knocking over an unlit candelabra which struck the stone floor and sent soundwaves echoing around the chamber.

Amy scurried behind the altar, out of Caleb's view.

He angled his head toward the door, toward the source of the arrows.

Lilith stepped into the moonlight that flooded the aisle, a fresh arrow held nocked and ready on her bow. Even in the darkness, he could see that something was wrong with her. Well, not *wrong* but different. At first he thought that maybe the shadows had shrouded half of her face in blackness, but as she stepped forward he realized that half of her face was actually black. Burned. Her flesh had peeled away leaving exposed and charred tendons from her left ear to her nose.

But she didn't move like she had been injured. Her steps and her posture were as focused and forceful as ever.

All of the complex thoughts Caleb had been feeling toward Amy and her father vanished at the sight of Lilith, advancing up the aisle with her bowstring pulled taut.

Lilith was his life partner. Not Amy.

And Lilith was beautiful. And powerful. And good. And right. He loved her.

And everyone else could burn in Hell.

***

Amy crouched behind the altar. There were no exits on this side of the chapel. The only way out was the way they came in — down the aisle and through the main doors. The only obstacle in her way was the crazed bitch in the wedding dress who was surely readying another arrow into her bow.

Just to be sure, Amy leaned to the side to peek around the altar. An arrow whizzed out of the dark and brushed by her face before clanking off the stone wall behind her. Amy ducked back.

"I've so looked forward to meeting you," Lilith called out in a sing-song voice. "Amy Holgate. Every teenage boy's wet dream."

"I didn't mean to hurt Caleb," Amy shouted to the darkness. "It was all a misunderstanding. He was always a good friend, but it would never have worked between us."

"I'm sorry, but are you hitting on my husband?"

"No. It's just—"

"Because it sure sounds like you're saying that you *could* have had him if only you'd wanted him. Am I getting your cast-offs? Your sloppy seconds? Do you have any other reject boyfriends you think I might like?"

"That's not what I meant." Amy looked around for anything that could be used as a weapon. The altar was too big to move. The candelabra might be useful as a club, but it had fallen toward the pews and Amy couldn't reach it without getting shot.

"Oh, I'm sorry I'm too dumb to figure out what you meant," Lilith said. Her voice sounded closer. She must be slowly advancing down the aisle. "Please educate me. Explain it to me as though I were a love-struck teenage boy. Or a Labrador."

"Lilith, please. I'm gay!" The gay card had never done much for Amy in her life, but it seemed to have almost moved the needle with Caleb just moments earlier. She had been on the verge of convincing Caleb that she stopped talking to him in high school *not* because he creeped out the other kids, *not* because he was weird, *not* because he was a judgmental asshole, but because she just didn't like guys. Classic "it's not you, it's me" strategy.

Her father had gone along with the act so smoothly. They had been so close to being set free.

Her father...

Her dad now lay dead on the other side of this altar. Her mom too. Probably Mariko as well.

And for what?

Because some fucking neighborhood boy had spent the past twenty years building up this twisted narrative in his mind? Because she went camping with another guy? Because her friend from childhood quietly seethed that his life didn't play out like some romantic comedy? Or maybe even a porno?

That was it?

Amy's face hardened. Her limbs, which had felt so weak and empty, filled with a new strength. She crouched on the balls of her feet, like a cat whose entire body was wound tight in preparation to fight or flee, whichever opportunity presented itself first.

Amy wasn't going to die for Caleb's bullshit.

"Oh, sweetie. Of course, you're gay," Lilith said from the darkness. "And, of course, you found the perfect match. Of course, you found love. Because girls like you always get everything they want. There were girls like you at my high school. I even considered some to be my friends at the time. Or rather, I *wanted* them to be my friends. I wanted them to like me. They were so pretty. So confident. So perfect. Just like you."

"You don't know me."

"Oh, I think I do. All Amys are the same. I've met different versions of you throughout my life. And each time, I've had the overwhelming urge to stare into your blue eyes as I carved your perfect nose from your perfect face. To watch as you realize that a knife blade isn't captivated by your flirty smile. A knife knows no lust. It feels no crushes. It won't turn its head when you bat your pretty eyes and flip your pretty hair. It will gut anyone and anything that it touches."

Amy crouched behind the altar, searching for a weapon. All she could see were the crystal bowls that held the candles. Maybe she could throw them. If she got lucky, she might hit Lilith in the face... if Lilith didn't shoot her the moment she stood.

Lilith's shoes clicked against the stone floor, one cautious step at a time. She was getting closer.

Closer to Amy.

Amy heard the dull thud of Lilith's foot kicking into something. A body. Amy's dad. Lilith gave him three firm, solid kicks. The bow twanged out and Amy heard a fresh arrow thud into his corpse. But her dad gave no yell or scream.

Seemingly satisfied with the lack of a reaction, Lilith proceeded up to the altar again. She hummed a few bars of the Bridal Chorus. And then, she began singing it out loud:

"Here comes the bride, all fat and wide.

See how she wobbles, from side to side.
She stepped on a turtle, and the turtle cried."

Amy took a deep breath. She had seconds, perhaps, before she'd have to fight Lilith, one way or another. Maybe if Amy rushed her, she could close the distance before Lilith fired. The bow and arrow would be useless. It would be a hand-to-hand fight. Lilith surely carried some sort of bladed weapon on her. If Amy could get her hands on that, along with the element of surprise, maybe she could win.

Maybe.

She had just seen Lilith slaughter grown men, some of whom had military training. Amy wasn't as tough as them. She wasn't as confident. If they didn't stand a chance, how could she?

Her muscles tightened. Her whole body wanted to pull itself into a shell for protection.

Lilith was faster than her.

Lilith was stronger than her.

Lilith was more psychologically ready to *kill* than her.

How could Amy hope to overpower someone who had spent her entire adult life training for this wedding? This perfect, dream wedding.

Lilith stepped closer.

Amy grabbed a crystal candle bowl. It was the only plan that came to mind — she pulled off her earring and tapped it against the glass.

The sharp *clink-clink-clink* rang out through the chapel.

Lilith stopped moving.

"Um, what the fuck are you doing?" Lilith said.

Amy struck the glass with her earring even more furiously. "When people clink their glasses, the bride and groom have to kiss," Amy said.

T . J .   P A Y N E

"Are you shitting me?"

"It's tradition!" she shouted, striking the glass even faster. "You have to!"

"*This* is your plan?" Lilith said. "You think I'm going to let you run away because I'm too busy kissing?"

"It's bad luck if you don't. This is your magic day. Don't fuck it up!"

All Amy could hear was the clinking. The metal-on-crystal drowned out the other noise. She couldn't even hear if Lilith had continued advancing, tip-toeing around the side of the altar.

Her chest tightened. Any moment, an arrow might plunge through her. Would it hurt? Would it happen in slow motion? Would she feel the arrow progress through her body, going in one side and then out the other?

Maybe Lilith was already behind her.

Maybe Amy's hair was a moment away from getting grabbed, her head forced back, and a serrated steak knife blade was about to start sawing through her neck, tearing out small chunks of her skin in each of its hundred teeth.

But still, she rang on.

Her eyes clamped shut as she listened for any sign, any hint, that she was about to die.

"I like her. She gets us," Lilith finally said.

"Kiss me, sweetie," Caleb said.

Amy faintly heard Lilith's feet step up toward the altar.

"You're beautiful," Caleb said.

Were they actually kissing? Was this a trap?

Over the clinking, she thought she heard the gentle wet sound of lips meeting, but she wasn't sure if it was just her ears telling her what she wanted to hear.

But she had no choice.

Amy burst up from her crouching position, her legs propelling her forward like tightly coiled springs finally being allowed to snap open. Through the sides of her eyes, she thought she saw Lilith's singed, white dress crouched over Caleb. She didn't linger to assess the situation.

Instead, she ran.

As fast as she could.

Her eyes focused on the door, identifiable only by the thin slit of light peeking through the frame. She stared at that door and only that door.

The chapel aisle had grown long, much longer than she remembered. Phantom pains spasmed through her back and legs, as though her body was preparing for the sensation of arrows slicing into her.

Perhaps arrows already had cut into her and it was only her adrenaline that kept her muscles constantly churning, hurling one leg in front of the other. She was sure she felt flying arrows whisper past her head.

But she kept running.

The door seemed to stay at a distance from her, as though it was also running away from Lilith and her arrows. Until, all of a sudden, the door raced up toward Amy and grew large in her vision. She threw her weight against it.

An explosion of light seared Amy's eyes. For a moment, she thought that this must be "the light" they spoke of seeing when one died. Perhaps she actually lay in the center of the aisle, riddled with arrows, as her heart pumped her final ounces of blood out onto the floor.

But her eyes began to adjust.

This wasn't Heaven. It was the well-lit area that connected the chapel to the ballroom. The foyer.

Amy threw herself out of view of the door and out of range of the arrows that she was sure were sailing toward her. She landed on the hard, tile floor. Her hands reached toward her back, her legs, her butt. Searching for arrows. Searching for blood. Searching for wounds.

Nothing.

She spun her head around and peered back through the chapel door. In the faint moonlight streaming through the stained glass, she could see Lilith in her white dress, up on the altar and straddling Caleb. She wasn't nocking a new arrow or even paying attention to her escaped prey.

Amy couldn't tell if the two were simply kissing or actually having sex up there. Some curious, morbid corner of her mind wanted to stare longer and figure it out, but that voice was quickly overruled.

Amy pushed herself off the ground, convinced her feet to keep moving beneath her, and then she ran.

CHAPTER 22

Amy thought about running back to the gym. It was the last place she had felt relatively safe. But she couldn't bring herself to go in that direction. It wasn't that she couldn't run back up that grand staircase; it was that she didn't want to.

She momentarily thought about cinching her tourniquet and running straight out the front door. The road was all downhill. Maybe she could stumble her way to safety before the shock of losing her arm caused her to pass out.

But that didn't feel like much of a plan either.

Really, all she wanted to do was to curl into a ball in the corner of the foyer and hope that death would be quick and painless.

Her legs kept moving, kept carrying her in some forward direction. They didn't seem to want to stop just yet, or at least her mind was struggling to properly relay such orders. And so, on she went.

It occurred to her that sitting down might lead to the one thing she definitely did not want — time to absorb the death of her parents.

The image of her mother's head collapsing beneath the weight of an iron bar...

Her father's blood gurgling up through the arrow hole in his neck...

Amy didn't consciously push the thoughts away. Maybe it was a survival mechanism buried deep in her subconscious that did the work for her. In any case, a grey mist shrouded the memories and carried them from her mind. She'd think about them later.

The leaden weight that had settled into her legs and body drifted off with the memories. Amy found a new strength in the numbness. And it felt good.

She pushed on the nearest door and soon found that she had re-entered the ballroom. A morbid curiosity had overtaken her. Mariko was surely dead in here somewhere. Lilith must have finished her off before chasing them into the chapel.

Mariko was certainly a scrapper. Amy always admired her toughness and calm. But she wasn't a fighter of Lilith's caliber.

Apparently, few people were.

There was a bloodlust in Lilith that Amy had never seen before. She couldn't imagine such hate and callousness existing in a normal person. This was a beast. A monster forged in resentment.

The music in the ballroom played loudly, as usual. This time, it was Frank Sinatra (or maybe Dean Martin — Amy always struggled to tell the difference) crooning about love. The DJ, his sunglasses on, swayed in his booth as he mouthed the words along with the song.

Amy had to shout to make her voice heard above the music. "Mariko!?" she called out. "Mariko?!"

The sound of a door opening made Amy freeze. Part of her wanted to look around for something, anything, that she could use as a weapon. Another part of her wanted to look for somewhere, anywhere, to hide. Her muscles somehow got stuck in the middle of that mental tug-a-war and she ended up standing there, dumbly waiting for whoever had entered to rush over and finish her off.

But it was Caleb's mom and dad who strolled in through the far door. They walked toward Amy.

Mr. Hunt's face was empty. He followed behind his wife as though she were pulling him on a string.

Caleb's mom, meanwhile, fixed her eyes on the arched ceiling that dripped with crystal chandeliers. A blissful smile spread on her lips as she twirled around, swaying her body to the song. She soaked up the moment but seemed determined not to let her gaze drift too low. Even as she slipped slightly on a patch of blood, she regained her footing without ever peering down.

"So beautiful. So, so beautiful," she said to herself.

Amy realized that the DJ had actually lowered the volume of the music, allowing the room to be quiet enough for Amy to hear Caleb's mom speak.

"Mrs. Hunt?" Amy said. She didn't really have anything to say. She didn't even know why she called out the woman's name. It just seemed like she should make her presence known, as Mrs. Hunt clearly hadn't noticed her.

Finally, Caleb's mom's head tilted down. Her eyes went wide with joy as she saw Amy.

"Wasn't it a wonderful wedding, Amy?" Caleb's mom said as she crossed the room to grab Amy's shoulders in a friendly embrace. The smile stretched widely across the woman's face. Her eyes were glassy as her gaze focused intently on Amy, and only Amy.

Amy stood and just stared back at the woman.

"Look at how beautiful it all is," Caleb's mom said. "Lovely. Just lovely. Caleb is doing so well for himself." She then repeated, "Caleb is doing so well for himself. Caleb is doing so well for himself." It was as though her brain had gotten caught in a loop.

T . J .   P A Y N E

Amy looked to the side. At some point, Caleb's dad had peeled off from his wife and wandered toward the cake table in front of the stage. His large shoulders, which Amy always thought looked tight and tense, now slouched in defeat. His head stayed angled up, giving his entire posture the appearance of an old turtle.

This was the man whom Amy had been so frightened of when she was a kid. This was the man whom Caleb could never impress.

Caleb's dad picked up a cake knife and served two slices of cake onto gold-rimmed plates.

"They... they said the frosting..." Amy stuttered. She felt her own mind struggle to make sense of the moment. "It's made with... um..." She couldn't get the word "cyanide" out. She felt as though she were in a dream, trying to speak, trying to scream but unable.

"I know we pushed him hard, but he's grateful to us each and every day," Caleb's mom continued. Her smile somehow grew wider as a proud tear rolled its way down her cheek. "I couldn't be happier. Thank you for sharing this day with us, Amy. You're a true friend."

For a moment, Amy felt like joining Mrs. Hunt in her bliss. She felt like hugging the woman and thanking her for the invite. She felt like closing her eyes and dancing to the music. She felt like having a few drinks too many, then throwing rice and hollering at the bride and groom as they drove off to their honeymoon. She felt like stumbling back to someone's room — Lilith's hot sorority friends, perhaps — and hooking up.

Or maybe not those girls. Maybe someone else.

After all, Amy couldn't let Mariko go back to the room alone. Amy's parents were sure to retire for the night early (they could barely stay up past ten). Amy and Mariko could have a few more drinks and go to the hot tub in their underwear. It wouldn't be long before they'd be making out and fingering each other.

They could go back to the room and... oh, boy... Mariko knew how to get Amy off. And Amy would return the favor. No matter how drunk they got together, each of them always returned the favor.

Oh, sure, it would be awkward in the morning. A bit of shame, a bit of embarrassment, and a whole lot of hangover. She had broken up with Mariko, after all, and Amy was still sure that it had been the right decision.

Why had they broken up again?

It didn't matter.

This was a wedding. Weddings were fun.

Amy should be having fun.

"How are your parents, Amy?" Caleb's dad asked. She looked. He stood beside her, two plates of red velvet cake heaped with white, glistening frosting in his hands.

"Dead," Amy said.

Just saying the word snapped her back to the moment. She looked around for Mariko. She suddenly *had* to see Mariko's body.

"Sorry 'bout that," Caleb's dad muttered. He held a plate of cake toward his wife.

"You rogue. You know I can't eat gluten," she said, playfully slapping him on the shoulder. "Oh, what the heck. It's a cheat day. Our son only gets married once."

She took the plate from his hand. The two of them stepped over to a nearby table and sat down with their cake. Caleb's dad held a fork full of frosting toward his mouth, pausing to stare at it for a moment. He sniffed it. Amy could see a bead of sweat roll down his forehead.

"You know they said it's made with..." Amy began. But she saw the man's eyes go empty again. In a quick burst of will power, he scooped the frosting into his mouth and swallowed it. He grabbed an

T . J . P A Y N E

open champagne bottle from the center of the table and took a long swig.

Caleb's mom, meanwhile, took small, delicate bites of cake. "Mmmm-hmmm." She rolled it around her mouth, savoring the moment. "Lovely," she said.

Caleb's dad suddenly jerked in his seat. His body seized and his face turned red. Then purple. Foam poured from the sides of his mouth as veins bulged in his forehead. He doubled over, coughing out frothy, white bile that was soon streaked with blood.

As her husband seized and gagged, Caleb's mom simply stared off. A wistful light danced in her eyes. "It's such a shame that everyone left so early. They must be jealous. That's it. They're jealous. Do you think any of *their* kids could afford a wedding like this? I don't. It must be hard for everyone to see how well Caleb is doing. They're just jealous. Just jealous. So sad."

Her husband's head thudded onto the table.

Caleb's mom reached out and grasped his hand. "We're such good parents. Such good parents. Such good parents."

And then she burped.

Amy looked away. Something caught her eye. A splash of sea-green fabric peeked out from beneath a blood red table cloth. She recognized that silky dress.

She ran over to the table and pulled back the linens.

There she was.

Mariko.

She lay motionless on the floor. Her skin was pale. Her smooth dress was splattered with blood.

But then Mariko coughed.

Mariko's mind seemed to register that there wasn't a table cloth blocking out the light anymore. Her eyes opened and she stared up at Amy. A confused look flashed across Mariko's face, as though she couldn't quite piece together what Amy was doing welcoming her to the afterlife.

They stared at each other for a moment before Amy crouched down and looped her hands under Mariko's arms. With a heave, she pulled Mariko out from underneath the table.

Mariko's left arm was nothing but stringy tatters of flesh where her wrist used to be. But no blood escaped the wound. The tourniquet seemed to have done its job despite the skin between it and the injury having turned a cold, dead gray.

"I need your help. I'm not strong enough to carry you myself," Amy said, cupping Mariko's face in her hands and shaking her. She didn't know if that's what one was supposed to do to an injured person, but it seemed to work. Mariko's eyes focused in on Amy's.

Mariko didn't say anything, but she managed a nod.

Amy pulled Mariko into a sitting position beside her. She wrapped Mariko's good arm around her. "We'll stand on three," Amy said. "One... two... three!"

Together, they heaved themselves off the tiled floor.

"We have to get out of here," Amy said. "They'll be coming back soon."

Mariko seemed to understand. Her legs began moving, supporting as much weight as they could. Amy's did too. Together, they limped toward the door.

"You have fun, dear," Amy heard Caleb's mom call out to her. The woman's voice was much hoarser than before. A burping and gagging sound interrupted her words. Despite the hoarseness, Caleb's mom still had a pleasant cadence to her speech. "We're going to stay a bit longer. So many people to catch up with."

Amy carried Mariko toward the door without ever glancing back at Caleb's parents.

As they left, Amy was sure she heard the thudding sound of Caleb's mom collapsing to the floor.

CHAPTER 23

With Mariko's arm slung over her shoulder, Amy stumbled out into the foyer. At the far end, the chapel door still hung open.

How long had it been since Amy had escaped Lilith? Several minutes, at least.

Had Caleb and Lilith already left the chapel? Were they elsewhere in the building? Or would they emerge from that foreboding blackness any moment, arrows pulled taut on bows, and shoot them down?

There was nowhere to hide in the foyer. No place for cover.

"Hurry," Amy said softly.

She felt Mariko's weight lift slightly off her. Mariko seemed to be coming to. Perhaps a new burst of adrenaline had kicked into her system. Whatever it was, Amy welcomed it because she didn't have the strength to carry Mariko alone.

Together, Amy and Mariko limped across the foyer, passing in plain view of the chapel door. Amy didn't look, though. If she turned, she feared it would only invite arrows to emerge from the darkness.

On they went. Arm-in-arm.

Their legs tried to keep pace with each other. Mariko's steps were weaker, but her legs were longer. Their stride never quite aligned and Amy worried that one false step, one little leg tangle, would send them both plummeting to the ground, exposed and vulnerable.

But they managed to make it through the foyer and into the main lobby.

The door to the front entrance stood open.

It occurred to Amy that Mariko didn't have a control bracelet anymore. There was no consequence for Mariko rushing out that door and descending the mountain to safety. If Amy tightened her own tourniquet, then she could do likewise.

But at that moment, Mariko's legs buckled. She grew heavy on Amy's shoulder. They'd never make it down the mountain alive.

She looked toward the grand staircase. Despite the number of times she had gone up and down it, those stone steps never seemed as high and insurmountable as they did at that moment.

With no other destination in mind, Amy looked toward the front desk, built in an alcove beneath the grand staircase.

"Over there," she said.

With their legs tripping over each other, they stumbled toward it. The wrap-around desk was solidly built from one end of the alcove to the other. Amy heaved Mariko up onto the desk. Mariko spun her legs around and then climbed down onto the other side.

Amy followed after her.

She expected to see a crowd of guests in hiding, but the area behind the desk was empty. Maybe because it was so close to the ballroom. Maybe because there was a staff door right beside it. Whatever the reason, Amy and Mariko had found a little hidden fortress for themselves. A tight space. But seemingly safe.

Mariko propped herself into a sitting position.

Her breathing stayed low and steady. Her face was pale and her head drooped from exhaustion. But then she looked up and her eyes connected with Amy's. An alertness seemed to retake Mariko's gaze and Amy soon felt that her old friend was studying her, attempting to decipher the answer to the most obvious unspoken question. *What happened to your dad?*

Amy looked down. That seemed to be answer enough for Mariko.

From somewhere overhead, the DJ's voice came out over a speaker. "Heeeey, party people!" the DJ shouted out. "We gonna be wrapping things up here soon. You got about thirty minutes to hit up the open bar, hit up the dance floor, or hit up someone over the head with a hammer. They say, 'Go big or go home.' Well, in this case, it's 'Go bad *and* go home.' You wanna see your kids again? You wanna see your friends? You wanna put this all behind you? Then let's see that kill count rise!"

Amy and Mariko sat there quietly.

"You can kill me, you know," Mariko finally said. Her voice was stronger than Amy expected.

"Oh? You won't mind?"

"Just do it. I'm easy."

"Yeah, you are. Little slut." Amy smiled. Mariko didn't laugh.

"You have a chance, Amy. Take that lamp, hit me on the head, and walk through that door."

Amy looked up. A bronze lamp sat on the desk. It looked dense, heavy.

"How do I know we can trust them?"

Mariko smiled and shook her head. "Well, I think you can trust that they won't let us live if you don't. Why not try Door Number Two?"

"Because Door Number Two involves me bashing your head in."

"I'm sure you've wanted to before."

"Don't joke. Not about this."

Mariko nodded in agreement. "Look, I obviously don't know what happens if you walk through those doors. They might give you a trophy. They might shoot you in the back of the head."

"True."

"All I know is that on the other side of those doors is a chance. On *this* side, all you get is Bridezilla and—" she held up her left arm and tourniquet.

They sat there quietly for a moment.

"I'm gonna die here anyway," Mariko said. "You can make it easy on me. Give yourself a fighting chance. It's a pretty good trade-off."

Amy looked at her. Mariko's gaze stayed firm. It was a look Amy knew well. Mariko wasn't saying what she thought Amy wanted to hear. She had diagnosed the situation and meant every word.

But Amy shook her head. "I'm not killing you."

"Damnit, Amy."

"I won't."

"Just fucking do it."

"No."

"It's right here. Everything you need is right here. And if you pass this up, I swear to God—"

"I can't! Okay? I can't do it."

"If you don't, and someone finds us here, they will."

"No, they won't," Amy said. She heard her mom's voice speaking through her. "We're not the people Caleb and Lilith think we are."

"Amy..."

Amy looked away. They both understood from years of confrontation that Amy was done with the conversation.

Mariko leaned her head back. Her eyes drifted closed. "I'm dying anyway."

"You got hours of blood in you. Don't be dramatic."

"Don't be a pussy."

As Amy was about to respond, a burst of static crackled through the room as the speakers turned on again. It surprised Amy that she didn't hear the DJ's voice calling out through the building. It was a woman's voice. Soft and trembling. "Hello... m-m-my name is Chelsea. Lilith and I are cousins."

Amy and Mariko both looked up. What the hell was this?

***

Caleb sat on the balcony. He held Lilith's hand in his.

He had made a point of sitting to her left so that he could see the char marks from where the explosion had burned the skin from her face. He would never turn away from her. Nothing about her could ever be seen as "ugly" by him.

Even with her injuries, she was as beautiful as ever.

She needed to know that. To always know that.

She said she couldn't see out of her left eye anymore. The explosion had also blown out a few of Lilith's teeth and sent them down her throat. Luckily, she said she didn't need the left side of her mouth to chew and she didn't need her left eye to aim.

After she had cut him free from the altar, they had gone back to their room to quickly disinfect her burns and take a few painkillers. She was lucky that her face barely bled; the blast had fused most of her wounds closed. It must have hurt though, Caleb thought. But he knew his wife was tough.

Lilith didn't want the painkillers to make her too drowsy (there was so much wedding left to enjoy), and so she balanced them out with a few lines of cocaine.

Caleb had also been feeling a little down and lethargic, so he snorted some too. He assumed it was high quality cocaine, as everything at The Venue was the finest. He felt much better now, like he could enjoy himself again.

And so, they had stepped out of their room and back onto the balcony.

It amazed Caleb how Lilith refused to let her injuries slow her. She stood on the balcony and shouted out to the empty room, "We're doing toasts now! Does anyone have anything nice to say about us?"

He wondered if she *wanted* to make this offer to an empty room. The DJ looked like he intended to make a Venue-wide announcement, but Lilith shot him a glare that made him put down his mic.

In the silence that followed, Caleb stared out over the ballroom. A few new bodies had been added to the collection. He recognized the forms of his mom and dad, slouched in their seats. Apparently, instead of fighting or offering up their lives as a sacrifice to their friends and family, his parents had eaten the cake.

Typical. Cowards.

They had, of course, lived down to his expectations, as they always did.

"Anyone?" Lilith called out. "Last chance."

As Caleb took his seat, he heard the screeching of a chair moving across the tiled floor below. Lilith's cousin Chelsea, who was about the same age as Lilith, crawled out from beneath one of the tables.

With her arms hugging herself, and her body angled away from the balcony (probably to make herself as small of a target as possible), Chelsea stood. Even from the distance, Caleb could see the woman's lip quiver. She was terrified.

Chelsea slowly raised her hand. She was volunteering herself.

Lilith gazed down at her with a look of confusion. For the first time, Caleb saw that his bride was speechless. Maybe it was just that her face hurt too much to speak. That was probably it.

In any case, Lilith pointed toward the microphone on the stage.

With slow steps, Chelsea made her way through the fallen chairs and dead bodies.

Caleb didn't really know Chelsea. Lilith hadn't bothered to introduce him around to the family. During the wedding, Chelsea just smiled, shook his hand, and offered some bland platitudes.

He had nothing against her, though.

Chelsea seemed sweet, although Caleb tended to believe that humans used sweet faces and smiles to hide their venom sacs. That was where humans differed from other animals. Snakes and spiders at least *looked* like snakes and spiders. Their coloring declared to the world that they carried poison, and so, no one could be surprised when their bites proved toxic.

Humans were different.

Humans were worse.

Humans were the only species that Caleb could think of whose survival instincts required them to give the *appearance* of being nice. Non-threatening. Non-toxic. Humans were kind to your face. They wanted you to trust them, to believe they were harmless and good. And then, when the smile and pleasantries finished disarming their prey, humans would sink their poisonous fangs into the backs of their unsuspecting "friends."

No other species behaved like that. Not rats, not dogs, not even a scorpion. At least, that's what Caleb believed. Lilith believed it too, he was sure.

And so, he sat and waited to hear what Chelsea had to say for herself.

Lilith set her bow and arrow beside her. Caleb did likewise. A small table had been set up near them with two flutes of champagne and an open bottle. He picked up a flute and was surprised to find it to be chilled. He didn't know when The Venue staff had set it out. They were good. Real good.

He lifted his glass as he stared down from the balcony toward the stage.

Chelsea picked up her own flute of champagne from a table near the steps of the stage. She then climbed up and stood at the microphone.

"Hello... m-m-my name is Chelsea. Lilith and I are cousins," she began. "We used to... used to... spend summers together. Lilith and me."

Chelsea shook so badly that the champagne spilled out of her glass. Her body remained tight as if in a perpetual wince. Due to the distance, Caleb wasn't sure but thought he saw tears reflecting off her cheeks.

"As a child, Lilith was... she was very smart. So smart," Chelsea continued. "When we were kids, Lilith would go into the woods and set traps... the most ingenious traps... for the raccoons. And squirrels. And any animal."

Caleb leaned forward. He hadn't heard this story. And stories about the love of his life, especially her as a child, made him happy.

"She spent a week building this... this big thing. It had pulleys and ropes and nails and a pit. It was so complicated. And it wouldn't just trap the animals. It would, um, it would tear..." she trailed off without completing the thought. "You had to see it. She was so smart. She *is* so smart."

Chelsea took a deep breath and chanced a glance up at Lilith.

Caleb wanted to gaze at her as well. He wanted to see Lilith's reaction. But he thought that might ruin the moment and so he reached out and grasped Lilith's hand instead.

"I... I didn't want to build the traps," Chelsea continued. "I wanted to hang out with my friends. But my parents made me play with Lilith. All summer. I... I yelled at Lilith. I told her she wasted my summer. I called her a loser. I made fun of her for having no friends. I called her stupid. I was the stupid one. Lilith was the smart one. Lilith *is* the smart one. She is amazing. And beautiful. And... and I don't deserve her as a cousin. Or as a friend. I am so, so sorry that I didn't appreciate you."

Finally, Caleb glanced over at his bride.

Lilith moved her hand to clutch her heart as she smiled down at Chelsea. He wasn't quite sure if Lilith was genuinely touched or if this was a misdirect. With Lilith, you could never be sure. And that was why he loved her.

Chelsea raised her glass. Champagne sloshed around and splashed onto the floor as it shook. "T-t-to Lilith and Caleb. May... may their marriage be everything they want and more."

Caleb lifted his glass and tapped it with Lilith's.

"Thank you, Chelsea," Lilith said after letting the silence sit for a moment. "That was very sweet. I love you and I forgive you."

She motioned toward the "Staff Only" door to the side of the stage. It swung open.

"Oh, thank you, thank you, thank you!" Chelsea said. She dropped her glass and sprinted toward the door. She ran through and it slammed shut behind her.

"Let's hear it for the bride's cousin, Chelsea!" the DJ announced. "Do any other guests have something they want to say to our lovely couple?"

Another chair toppled over. A person scrambled out from under a table. A moment later, Tristan, one of Caleb's former co-workers at the firm, ran up to the microphone.

"Caleb is totally the smartest guy I've ever known," Tristan started. He then turned around and rushed back to the steps to grab a champagne flute. He returned to the mic and held his drink aloft. "He's super cool. And really funny. And great. And really awesome. Just a, just a cool, cool guy."

Caleb let out a soft groan.

"Ugh. So disingenuous," Lilith said.

Caleb nodded.

"Allow me, sweetie." Lilith picked up her bow.

***

Amy listened as Tristan's toast was broadcast through the speakers.

"I really wish I was as cool as Cale—"

She heard the whistle of the arrow as it flew down and thudded into him. He dropped the microphone, sending a loud *thunk* through the speakers. The next sounds were of him gurgling and choking out his final breath.

Two more arrows thudded into him until there was silence.

"Let's hear it for Tristan!" the DJ announced.

A smattering of applause came through the speakers. Amy could only assume it was the clapping of the only audience members who mattered — Caleb and Lilith.

"We're nearing the end of this magical night," the DJ said over the speaker. "It's now time for the bouquet toss. But here's a little wrinkle. Whichever lucky girl catches the bouquet won't just be the next girl to get married. She'll be the next girl to get to *live*! So, come on down, girls. Let's fill the dance floor with all the single ladies!"

Mariko looked over at Amy. "Go."

"What?"

"If you won't kill me, then at least catch the damn bouquet."

"No. I—"

"Amy, I want you to leave."

"But you'll—"

"Leave. Now." Mariko leaned forward. With her good hand, she reached out and grasped the back of Amy's head, forcing Amy to look her in the face. Mariko's grip was surprisingly strong and Amy couldn't help but look into her eyes.

"I wanted to spend my life with you," Mariko said. "But I never wanted to hold you back. I never wanted to be something you regretted. Some dead weight that tied you down. I wanted to live with you, but I never wanted to fucking *die* with you. So, go. Catch the bouquet. And give yourself a chance, at least."

They looked at each other for a long quiet moment.

"I mean, if you can," Mariko said, letting her smile break the tension. "Your hand-eye coordination sucks balls."

"If I get out, I'll bring the cops," Amy said. Although, she knew better. She didn't know what would happen on the other side of the staff doors, but she was certain that whatever the European equivalent of dialing 9-1-1 was wouldn't be an option.

If Caleb and Lilith were to be believed, Amy wouldn't remember any of this night. She wouldn't remember her final moments with Mariko. Or with her parents.

Mariko seemed to understand, though. Mariko always understood. Her eyes narrowed and she nodded her head in complete seriousness, letting Amy's promise of retribution be the rationale for her leaving. "Fuck yeah, you will. Get out and then burn this place to the mother-fucking ground," Mariko said.

"I'll... I'll try."

The DJ's voice came back over the speaker. "Close your eyes, Lilith. Caleb, spin your lovely bride around. Get her nice and dizzy."

There wasn't much time. If Amy wanted a chance at the bouquet, she had to hurry.

"Go get it," Mariko said with a grin.

"I..." Amy didn't have any words.

"Later, roomie," Mariko said.

There were many things Amy wanted to say, but all that came out was, "Later, Mariko."

"Now, hurry your ass up."

With that, Amy stood and climbed over the desk.

CHAPTER 24

Amy didn't look back as she ran through the front lobby and past the grand staircase. She thought she heard the sound of shoes clanking on the stone steps, but she refused to check.

She sprinted through the foyer.

The doors to the ballroom had been propped open, allowing her to peek inside.

The disco ball splashed light around the otherwise deserted ballroom. From her spot, she could only see the underside of the balcony. She couldn't see Caleb or Lilith, but she could hear their feet on the metal platform as Caleb spun Lilith around.

Amy scurried into the ballroom and crouched behind the cake table. And then she waited.

"Let's all count together now!" the DJ said. "Three... two... one... Toss!"

The bouquet sailed over the railing of the balcony.

It hung in the air a moment, as though it was refusing to participate with the massacre below. In that instant, it looked like, perhaps, the bouquet would remain in the air, out of reach, forever. Gravity itself had deprived Amy of her chance.

But then, the bouquet reached the peak of its trajectory.

With a delicate, graceful spin, it twirled its way earthward. Its momentum seemingly slowed at the last instant so that it could float down gently to the center of the floor.

And there it rested.

Perhaps thirty feet separated Amy from that bundle of petals and stems.

It was as good as hers.

She balanced herself on the balls of her feet and plotted her course through the tables. She didn't want to make noise. She didn't want to draw attention to herself. She just wanted to get there with as much cover as possible in case Lilith started shooting. And then get out.

She decided that she would scurry to Table Two, and then she'd...

The sound of clomping feet made her head pivot up. A woman, still wearing heels and an elegant black dress, raced in from the bathroom entrance.

A table suddenly tipped over. Another woman had evidentially been hiding there the whole time, waiting for her moment. More tables and chairs shifted. More women leapt from the safety of their hiding places. More competition ran in through the doors.

Amy didn't have time to count the women, but they seemed to be materializing from all sides of the ballroom. In a mad dash, they all converged on the bouquet in the center.

It was now or never.

Amy sprang from her hiding place behind the cake and raced forward. She swerved around a table, jumped over a body, and ran.

One of Lilith's sorority friends veered in front of Amy, cutting her off and taking the inside track to the bouquet. Without even thinking, Amy reached over, grabbed the woman by the shoulder and pushed her to the side. The small bit of force was enough to knock her competition off balance and send her smacking into a chair.

Amy reached the bouquet just as Mrs. Crawford did. The elderly third grade teacher must have been hiding beneath one of the nearby tables and had only now scrambled out to claim her prize. Amy didn't look her in the eye — she couldn't bear to — as she bent down and snatched it out of her teacher's grasp.

Something had come over Amy. Something she couldn't explain. All of her impulses and responding muscle movements were singularly focused on the task of getting the bouquet and getting out of there. The world outside of her immediate goal fell away.

Only survival mattered now.

The scrambling scuffle of feet racing toward her filled her ears. A dozen, maybe more, frantic women charged forward. None of them slowed at the recognition that Amy had already claimed the prize.

As she looked at their twisted faces, she saw their eyes focused solely on the bouquet.

They wanted it, no matter the cost.

She recognized that her own face probably contained the same intensity.

At that moment, the bouquet was life.

And life was blood sport.

"Claim your prize at the door by the stage," the DJ announced.

As Amy turned to run to the exit, a spiked club filled her view.

She ducked, letting the club pass over the top of her head. The woman who swung it lost her balance. Amy gave her a firm shove and sent her tumbling to the floor.

One of the sorority sisters slashed at Amy with a large knife.

Amy dodged to the side and, in a fluid motion, she picked a dinner plate off a nearby table and threw it at the girl's face. It smashed into the side of her head, sending her toppling to the ground.

By now, more people were racing in from all sides.

Amy spun around and ran toward the exit.

She heard the screams of the horde chasing her.

The door was only ten feet away. Nothing stood between Amy and—

WHAM!

With a jolting hit, Amy felt herself flying through the air. All her joints seemed to separate before the elasticity of her cartilage snapped them back into place.

She fell for what seemed like several seconds, but she traveled only a foot or two. She realized that someone had body-checked her so hard that she had left her feet. Her eyes took in a view of a crystal chandelier before everything went white.

But the whiteness wasn't from a concussion or loss of vision.

It was from frosting.

An explosion of white cream that gave way to the red velvet chunks underneath.

Amy had been slammed into the three-tiered wedding cake.

She shut her eyes and held her breath, desperate not to let any of the poisonous glaze into her system. She wiped the frosting from her face then looked around.

The bouquet lay just a foot in front of her.

But a man — the man who had just bowled Amy over — bent down and scooped it up.

It was Father Dave, the priest.

He didn't even look at Amy as he took his prize and began to run toward the open door. But as he took a step, an arrow whistled down from the balcony and plunged into his back. He stumbled forward a step or two and then fell to his knees.

Amy looked up. On the balcony, Lilith still wore her blindfold as she shot arrows randomly down into the crowd.

Amy tried to stand. Her feet slid on the frosting like a car on ice. Over and over again, she dug her toes down for traction. Like running in a dream, every motion, every kick, moved her only a fraction of what it normally would.

But she kept fighting.

Finally, her feet carved their way to the tiniest bit of grip beneath the slick frosting and she pushed off and ran forward.

She could feel the weight of the cake clinging to her dress and skin. She was covered in its thick frosting. Its sweet smell wafted up to her nose. She hoped she wasn't inhaling the cyanide. She hoped the poison wasn't airborne.

A bottle exploded by her feet as she ran. The people chasing her were throwing things to slow her down. But she didn't dare look back.

As she passed Father Dave, lying face down with an arrow in his back, she bent and grabbed the bouquet from his hand. His fingers still had grip and she had to tug at the flowers (what was left of them). He let out a moan in opposition. He was still alive, but Amy didn't wait.

She ripped the bouquet free and ran toward the open door.

Eight more feet.

A pain rippled through her shoulder. Someone had thrown something sharp at her. Maybe it was still stuck in her flesh. She ignored it.

Five more feet.

She blocked out the screams behind her.

She ignored the knives ricocheting off the wall in front of her.

A sudden pain seared into the back of her scalp. Like an asteroid collision sending shockwaves around a planet, she felt the pain first block out all sound before it worked its way to her eyes. Blackness overtook her vision.

Someone must have hit her in the back of the head.

A flying bottle finding its mark, perhaps.

With what little control of her muscles she still had remaining, she commanded her legs to jump forward.

And so, she leapt, or rather tumbled, in the direction of the door.

She prayed she made it through.

CHAPTER 25

The force with which she hit the floor seemed to knock the sound back into Amy's ears.

First came the screams. They grew louder. The thundering footsteps gained on her.

Then came a loud click.

And suddenly the screams went quiet. Muffled.

"Please set all weapons in the provided tray," a male voice said.

It took a few more seconds for Amy's eyesight to adjust. The blackness faded and the room she was in began to take shape. It was completely white and seemingly sterile — almost futuristic. Florescent lights shone down brightly on her. The door behind her was sealed shut.

She took a breath as she realized that she had, in fact, managed to throw herself through the door.

"Please set all weapons in the provided tray," the voice repeated.

Amy looked up. One side of the room had a large glass window and glass door. Two men in red vests, both of whom she recognized as bellhops, stood on the other side of the glass, watching her.

"I... I don't have any weapons," Amy managed to stammer out.

"Your shoulder," the man she remembered as being the head bellhop said.

She suddenly felt a sharp pain piercing her shoulder. She reached behind her and immediately winced as she came in contact with warm metal. A throwing star dangled from her skin. It wasn't deep, though, and by simply tapping on it, she ripped it free and it clanged down onto the floor.

"Put it there."

In the middle of the room was a clear plastic tub. Amy picked up the throwing star and set it inside.

"Now stand."

She rose to her feet. Chunks of cake fell off her dress as she did. The room spun as she stood. Her throbbing head took a moment to adjust. She steadied herself by looking down at her feet. Blood dripped from her shoulder onto the cake and frosting that she had smeared across the concrete floor.

"Please put your hands up. Turn around."

Raising her arms as much as she could, Amy did as told. She turned in a full circle until she came back around and faced the window.

"Do you have any keys or other metal?"

She shook her head.

The head bellhop then slid the window open a few inches.

"Please present your control device."

Amy stepped toward the window. She lifted her left arm and put her hand through the slit. The moment her bracelet moved beyond the glass plane, its lights flashed a red warning and it began to vibrate.

"No, no, no!" Amy cried out. She tried to retract her arm, but the bellhop's assistant grabbed her by the wrist and held her tightly in place.

"Remain calm," the head bellhop said.

On his own wrist, he wore a red staff bracelet. He waved it over Amy's bracelet as though it were a magic wand.

Nothing happened.

The lights on Amy's bracelet flashed more furiously. It started beeping. The vibrations shook their way up her arm until she could feel them in her rattling teeth.

"Wait, please. Let me try again," the head bellhop said as he waved his bracelet over Amy's a second time.

The lights kept flashing. She could feel the vibrations grow in intensity. She shut her eyes and braced herself.

"This damned thing," the bellhop said. "Someone needs to fix this."

"Should we, um, just let it go?" his assistant asked. Amy could hear the concern in the man's voice. He was, after all, the one holding her wrist.

"Just give me a moment. Your name, please?"

"Amy! Amy Holgate!"

The man clicked on his walkie-talkie. "This is Guest Relations. Deactivate control device for Amy Holgate."

Amy reached up to the nylon wrapped around her arm. She put one end in her mouth and gripped the other in her hand. She pulled hard. The fabric constricted, but she kept pulling. Tighter still.

She hoped it wouldn't hurt. She hoped she wouldn't feel it.

The image of Mariko flashed in her mind. Mariko, who had already lost her arm and fought through the pain.

The memory of sitting behind that desk with Mariko, smiling at each other, calmed Amy. Her heart rate and breathing slowed, even as the vibrations increased.

And then...

Click.

Amy opened her eyes. No lights. No beeps. No vibrations.

The bracelet had finally shut down.

The bellhop's assistant undid the clasp and slid the bracelet off her hand. She pulled her arm back through the window and massaged her wrist. The bracelet had never been particularly heavy, but she now realized how much it had been weighing on her mentally. Her arm had been tense since the moment she first saw the power of those devices, and for the past few hours, she had been in a constant state of clenching that side of her body, preparing herself for the moment of explosion.

Now that the bracelet was off, she felt lighter. Her mind, which had been so aching and numb from stress, began to clear.

"I am now going to open this door. When I do, please step through. Be advised that there is a metal detector surrounding the frame of the door. If any weapons are still on your person, The Venue reserves the right to terminate your life."

As the head bellhop spoke, his assistant held up a revolver for Amy to see. It was an elegant, almost antique-looking handgun. He didn't present it in a threatening manner; he seemed to be displaying it more as a formality.

"Do you understand what I have just stated?"

Amy nodded.

"Very well. Opening door."

The head bellhop swiped his bracelet on the door that separated her area from his. The door buzzed and swung open. He motioned for her to proceed.

Amy took a breath and then stepped through the door and metal detector.

Not a beep.

The head bellhop smiled pleasantly at her and then sharply pivoted. "This way, please." With stiff, precise posture, he led the way down the hall.

The bellhop's assistant stood behind her, keeping the gun trained on her back while maintaining a professional smile the whole time. "After you, ma'am," he said.

Amy began walking.

The head bellhop led their little procession down a wide, beige corridor. The area was bland but clean. Occasional unmarked metal doors, all closed and locked behind keypads, dotted the otherwise empty area.

They walked on, turning the many sharp corners of the twisted halls.

As they progressed deeper into the bowels of The Venue, the bellhops' shoes squeaked and echoed around the deserted space.

Well, *almost* deserted.

Amy and her escorts marched past a set of large double-doors. Laughter flowed from the room. People called out to each other in a language that Amy didn't know. It sounded like a frat party.

Two red vested staffers — Amy thought she recalled them serving as waiters — chatted outside the doors. Amy couldn't understand their language, but they smiled and waved to Amy as she passed, and then they continued their conversation.

The bellhops turned a corner and the sounds of the staff faded away.

As they walked, the head bellhop dug into his pocket and pulled out a sheet of paper. He began to read it out loud. "Congratulations on your survival. To protect the interests of The Venue, we require all departing guests to submit to a minor pharmaceutical procedure that will eliminate approximately forty-eight hours of your most recent memories. At which point, you and the nonsurviving members of your party will be placed in an automobile accident scene in a location of our choosing. You will have no recollection of these events. Do you agree to these terms?"

The words entered Amy's ears, bounced around a bit, and then sank to somewhere deep inside her numb body.

"I am afraid I will need to hear your consent before we arrive at the green room. At which point, you may clean yourself. We can even issue you a sedative to help you relax, if you so desire."

A sedative. Relaxation. A shower. A nap.

Amy's mind struggled to think of anything else she could want. Her feet carried her forward, but she didn't feel them. She was now drifting through the hall.

"Do you agree to these terms?"

"Yes," Amy said.

She took a deep breath.

She had survived.

It was all going to be okay.

***

Mariko tried to concentrate on her breathing so that she wouldn't have to concentrate on her pain. She was only somewhat successful.

She wanted to pass out and then drift peacefully into death. She had lost track of time, but she figured the night must be coming to an end soon.

What a day.

As she closed her eyes for what she thought might be the final time, a beefy hand grabbed her shoulder. She felt herself yanked off the floor and pulled up onto the front desk.

Her eyes snapped open, bringing an immediate clarity to her situation. She was looking into a man's eyes. He was young, but he was big. Her brain raced to recall who he was.

A football player…

Lilith's cousin…

Ben?… Bob…?

No.

BRAD.

Linebacker Brad. Lilith's brawny, but simple, cousin.

His hand latched onto Mariko's throat, holding her down against the desk. His other hand raised an old, rusted battle axe above his head.

"No… No…" Mariko croaked out.

She tried to twist free, but his grip was tight. Her good hand swung out, trying maybe to claw at his face or get him in the eye, but his arm was too long and she couldn't strike him anywhere higher than his shoulder.

She looked up at his eyes. He didn't have the cold face of a killer. His lips quivered and his eyes twitched as though they were fighting to close themselves so they wouldn't have to look at what he intended to do. His breaths were quick and panicked.

He was terrified.

And sorry.

"I... I just wanna go home," he said in a wavering voice that sounded like he might be about to cry. "I just wanna leave. I ain't never hurt no one. But if I gotta do this to get out of here. Well... I. I'm sorry. You don't look like you're gonna live long anyway. I'm sorry. I'm so, so sorry."

His eyes clenched shut and he raised the axe.

CHAPTER 26

The head bellhop stopped suddenly. Amy almost walked right into him. He took a step off to the side, toward the wall, and motioned for Amy to do the same.

As she did, she saw why.

They were making way for a woman in a suit and wearing a headset. Amy recognized the woman. Despite the lateness of the night, the woman's hair was still tightly pulled back, her black suit was still crisp, and her posture was still ramrod straight. This was the woman who had hovered behind Caleb and Lilith throughout the reception. They had called her their Event Planner.

The Event Planner marched down the hall, a mug of black coffee in one hand and a croissant in the other. She walked a few steps past the bellhops and then paused at one of the unmarked doors.

She looked down at the keypad and then at her hands, both of which were full. With a pleasant smile, she turned to the bellhop.

"Will you, please?" she said.

He hurried over, waved his bracelet in front of the door's keypad to unlock it, and then held the door open for the woman.

As this was happening, the woman took a moment to examine Amy. A faint grin played on the woman's lips at the sight of the cake and blood encrusted girl who was leaving crumbs and frosting streaks through her pristine hallways. But Amy didn't care. She simply stared right back at the woman. It wasn't out of defiance; she just had no reason to look anywhere else.

"We hope you enjoyed your stay at The Venue," the woman said.

"Thank you," Amy muttered from some subconscious need to be polite.

As the bellhop held the door open, Amy caught a glimpse inside the room.

It was a small room filled mostly with video displays. Two men sat at the displays, working the controls and switching between the various camera feeds. Amy recognized all the locations. The ballroom, the chapel, the hallways, the gym.

This whole time, they had been watching.

The two men at the controls then laughed about something. They pointed to the main screen. They seemed to be making some sort of wager.

At first, Amy didn't recognize the room on the screen. But then her eyes focused in on that metal, twisted lamp.

It was the front desk.

In that instant, the image became perfectly clear. A man was holding a woman down on the desk by her throat. As much as she squirmed and kicked, she couldn't overpower him. He had an axe raised above his head, ready to strike.

Amy couldn't see the woman's face.

But she saw that dress.

That sea-green, silky dress.

The Event Planner walked inside and the door swung closed, blocking out Amy's view.

"This way, ma'am," the head bellhop said, motioning for Amy to continue following him.

She stared at the closed door for a moment.

Mariko was dying.

And for what?

There was no higher mystery to the night. No grand reveal. No dark secret cruelty that Amy had inflicted upon Caleb to deserve this. She could have been nicer, sure, but it was high school. *Everyone* was dealing with their own shit in high school.

Her parents had died because some self-centered kid had gotten his feelings hurt. Mariko, who hadn't even been there in high school, would soon die because that kid had held onto that bitterness.

None of this was proportional.

None of this was fair.

Amy felt her muscles twitch.

The bellhop's assistant motioned with his gun for her to continue.

She started walking.

Her shoulders slumped. Her eyes cast downward. Her feet and body moved with the rigidity of a robot. Or zombie. If anyone were to look at her face at this moment, they would see nothing. Complete emptiness.

Amy had the look and posture of defeat. The spark of life had been extinguished from her frail frame, and now she seemed to only be guided by one impulse — to follow the two men who were marching her toward freedom. Freedom from death. Freedom from memory.

That was what someone would assume by looking at *her face*.

Her hands, meanwhile, moved with a subtle urgency. She hugged herself, stroking her arms while clearing off swaths of the frosting and cake. It was nothing that anyone would notice. The

T. J. PAYNE

bellhop's assistant marching behind her might have assumed it was a young woman's subconscious need to clean off the layer of filth that was crusting onto her.

She had been so covered in the cake that it only took a few wipes of her arms before her fingers were heavy with cream. Then her arms dropped to her front, out of view of the man behind her.

Her fingers rolled the clumps of frosting into a ball, about the size of the balls that her mom would roll dough into when making cookies. It appeared to be an idle movement. Nothing more than a nervous fidget.

Amy wanted it to appear that way.

She slowed her pace ever-so-slightly.

The man behind her walked closer. She could hear his footsteps grow just a bit louder. She could feel his presence just a foot or two behind her.

And then, she spun around.

The bellhop's assistant walked right into her, seemingly startled by the sudden stop. Amy grabbed him by the head and shoved the ball of frosting into his mouth.

The man's eyes grew wide with confusion. He tried to respond by aiming his gun at her, but he was too close. She pinned his arm up under her shoulder. Her other hand, the one that had shoved the frosting into his mouth, clamped over his face, sealing off his lips and nose as best she could.

An instant. That was all it took before she felt him swallow the frosting.

His look of confusion turned to panic as soon as he realized what his throat had done. His eyes narrowed and darted around, searching for help.

Somewhere, Amy heard the head bellhop shouting, but it was as though he were calling out from a great distance. She didn't feel threatened.

She didn't feel anything.

Amy held the assistant in that position for a second or two longer.

She didn't know how long cyanide needed to take effect, but she knew how long fear needed. And it had arrived in the man.

Amy released him, giving him a firm shove in the process.

He fell to the ground. The gun remained in his possession, but he didn't try to aim it at Amy. Instead, he swatted furiously at his own face, trying to wipe away any poisonous residue that remained.

Then, sitting on his knees, he crouched forward and jammed his fingers down his throat. Deep down. Vomiting was his only hope.

The head bellhop rushed up behind Amy and wrapped his arm around her neck. He shouted in her ear as he choked her. She didn't hear what he said. Maybe he was screaming down the hall for help. Amy didn't care. She had gone into a trance. Somewhere in her mind, she probably realized that she was running out of oxygen.

She cleared a handful of frosting from her dress, reached up behind her head, and smeared it over the head bellhop's entire face.

He instantly released her.

As her oxygen surged back, she glanced over at him. He bent down at the waist, holding his breath as he wiped at his face.

By this time, the other bellhop was no longer trying to make himself vomit. He didn't have the strength. He crouched on his hands and knees, quivering, as foamy bile began to pour from his open mouth. His eyes no longer had the awareness to even look up at Amy.

Amy reached down and picked up his dropped gun.

The head bellhop seemed to realize the situation.

T. J. PAYNE

"But... but... you're free," he quietly gasped out, making an obvious attempt not to ingest any of the frosting that covered his mouth.

"I just wanna party," Amy said.

She didn't want to make noise. She didn't want a gunshot to echo down the hall. And so, she swung at the man's head with the gun. The man managed to get his hands up to block the blow, but the gun smacked into his fingers, probably breaking one or two in the process. Amy swung again, and again. Each blow shattered more of the man's hands. Each strike made him crumple down further. First to his knees. Then to the floor.

It was as if she were chopping down a tree with a hatchet. Blow after blow after blow. Pummeling the man's defenses. Quick, decisive strikes.

He tried calling for help, but his unwillingness to inhale the frosting made his voice wispy and weak.

Within a few seconds, the gun made contact with his temple and Amy felt a satisfying crack. The man's limbs gave out and his body slouched down onto the floor. She swung one more time for good measure and was rewarded with a stream of blood that shot out from the man's head and splattered onto the polished concrete.

He didn't react to the hit. He lay motionless on the floor, a stream of white foam pouring from his mouth as the cyanide took hold of his organs.

Amy then knelt down. She grabbed the man's left wrist, the one with the bracelet, and stretched it away from his body. With all her strength, she pounded the gun down onto the man's left hand like a hammer, smashing his bones in the process. She battered down on his hand a few times, hearing the satisfying crack of his joints breaking apart.

THE VENUE

She squished the remains of his hand up tight and easily slid his staff bracelet off his wrist.

Then she stood and walked past the assistant, now convulsing on the floor, looking at him only long enough to determine that he was no threat to her. She left him there. He would be dead soon enough.

Amy marched back down the hall.

Back to the Control Room.

She swiped the staff bracelet at the keypad and was greeted by a green light.

Amy yanked the door open and stepped inside the small space.

The Event Planner stood behind her control operators. None of them seemed startled or concerned that their door had opened. The Event Planner lazily turned her head to see who had joined them.

Amy swung out and smashed the gun into her face.

The Event Planner's nose exploded in blood. She let out a little yell before she doubled over. She swayed for a moment, the blood draining from her shattered nose, and then she crumpled down and collapsed to the floor.

The operators turned in their seats to look. Their eyes barely had time to generate expressions of shock or confusion before Amy pressed the barrel of the gun up against one operator's temple and—

Bang!

Shot him through the head. She pivoted and, at point-blank range — *Bang!* — shot the other. Right in the eye.

Both men slumped down in their seats.

Amy pulled the door closed behind her. She dumped one of the operators out of his chair.

Then Amy took a seat at the controls.

CHAPTER 27

Mariko didn't move.

All she wanted was for the status quo to continue.

Linebacker Brad still held her by the throat, but his grip had noticeably loosened. She breathed easily and felt that she could rip his hand away if she wanted to.

He had lowered the axe a while ago but not in a killing blow. After holding it above Mariko's head for so long, he had finally brought it down to rest by his side. His eyes had clamped shut and for the past several minutes, he had stood over Mariko, shaking his head and trying not to cry.

He looked like a little boy whose father had ordered him to put down the family dog. Some part of him seemed to know that he should kill Mariko. That he needed to. That it made the most sense. But he couldn't bring himself to finish the task.

And now, he and Mariko were locked in no-man's land. He dared not release his ticket to freedom. And he dared not cash it in.

The current situation suited Mariko just fine. And so, she lay there, doing nothing that might result in him changing his mind.

But then, a woman's voice spoke from somewhere behind Mariko's captor.

"Brad... can I have her?" the voice said.

The woman stepped up beside Brad. Mariko recognized her. Her slim figure and long, dark hair. She had been at one of the tables at the front of the reception. The table for immediate family. It was Trina, Lilith's sister — the one who had avoided eye contact as her murderous sister sarcastically toasted her perfection and beauty.

As Brad held Mariko down, Trina stood over her. She had a knife in her hand. But unlike Brad, Trina's hand had no tremor.

"Please..." Mariko managed to croak out. It was the only thing she could think to say.

Trina looked down at her. Despite the stillness of the knife in her hand, her eyes and face seemed remorseful. She then looked away. "I have a baby back home," Trina said. "She needs me. I have to get back to her. Please understand."

Mariko tried to speak, tried to plead, but Trina closed her eyes and shook her head, as if to tell Mariko that words were useless now.

"I'm doing this to get back to my baby. I'm doing this for my baby," Trina said, more to herself than to anyone in the room.

The blade's cold metal pressed against Mariko's neck. She felt it dig in, opening a small slit in her skin. She tried to keep her throat relaxed as she feared that tensing would push more of her flesh into the knife's edge. Without taking a breath, as that too felt dangerous, Mariko tried to calm her heart.

She hoped it would end quick.

And painless.

Click.

Mariko heard it — it sounded almost like a small, electronic chirp — but she had no idea what that tiny sound meant. It was followed by silence.

Brad released his grip on her. The knife moved away from her throat. Suddenly, Mariko was free.

She opened her eyes and twisted her head to look at her captors. Both Brad and Trina stared down at their bracelets. The red lights no longer glowed. Trina tentatively reached over and undid the clasp. It opened easily. She moved slowly, carefully pulling the strap through the clasp one painstaking millimeter at a time.

The bracelet didn't vibrate. It didn't flash red lights.

It slid off her wrist.

Trina let it fall to the floor with a *clunk*.

Upon seeing this, Brad dropped his axe and fumbled to undo his own bracelet. The moment he got it to release from his wrist, he flung it across the room, shuddering slightly as he did, seemingly in anticipation of an explosion.

But no explosion came.

The three of them stayed in those positions, unsure how to proceed. They quietly waited for whatever was coming next.

***

It had taken a little guesswork, but Amy was thankful that the switch she had chosen to flip ended up *deactivating* the bracelets instead of detonating them.

Amy now watched the monitors with satisfaction.

Throughout The Venue, guests timidly examined their bracelets. The ones who removed theirs did so slowly, as though they were diffusing a bomb, which, in a sense, they were. After they were free, they stood in their places, too afraid to move.

The monitors showed dozens of these statuesque people, dumbly remaining in their hideouts, seemingly convinced that this was, perhaps, just another part of the game.

Even at the front desk, Mariko had now lifted herself into a sitting position but nothing more. A silent standoff had commenced between her and the two people who, just moments earlier, had been ready to slit her throat.

"Don't just stand there," Amy said out loud. "Do something, dumbasses."

Something rustled on the floor beside her. Glancing down, she saw the Event Planner, her bashed nose still bleeding, reaching for the headset and walkie-talkie that had been knocked from her face. It lay just out of her reach. She had to pull herself toward it and the buttons on her blazer dragged across the concrete, making a faint scraping sound.

Amy picked the gun up off the console and stood.

The Event Planner rolled onto her side and put her hand up. "No... No," she said. "We budget for these situations. Name your price. Anything you want, I can—"

Amy slammed the gun into the side of the woman's face, sending her head bouncing off the concrete floor.

The woman lay still.

For a moment, Amy watched her, trying to decide if she was merely *acting* unconscious, but she remained motionless. It felt wise to leave such a senior member of the staff alive, just in case, and so Amy kicked the headset across the room and sat back down at the console.

The distraction allowed her to look at the console with fresh eyes because, for the first time, Amy noticed a particular set of switches among the sea of controls.

The label simply read, "Door Locks."

Amy smiled.

***

The hotel manager was the highest ranked employee in the staff lounge.

It was his job to ensure that the various departments — Housekeeping, Kitchen, Front Desk, etc. — were at their designated locations and performing their duties on time.

He usually spent the final hour of an event awakening any staff who were napping, calling an end to the billiard games, and generally getting his crews ready to begin cleanup. The staff would slowly gather in front of the main screens in the lounge and begin the assessment of damages that had occurred throughout the night.

Every broken window, gouged wall, or blood-soaked mattress meant work for someone. It was a good time to take stock and to tease one's coworkers on the level of cleanup that their area required. The pool boy's workload, for instance, was always hit-and-miss. Sometimes the pool would be perfectly clean at the end of the night. Sometimes he would have to drain it, scrub it, and refill it. And sometimes, he would have to sift out an entire family's worth of bloated, decapitated corpses.

You never knew what you were going to get when you worked at The Venue.

The staff lounge usually hummed with conversation at this time. But tonight was different.

The staff lounge had grown quiet as everyone stared in confusion at the screens.

Throughout The Venue, the guests, who had been on the verge of breaking into a bloodbath, let their bracelets fall harmlessly to the floor.

It was weird.

The manager flipped through his copy of the night's schedule of events.

"I don't see this on the agenda," he said, mostly to himself. The rustling of his papers soon became the loudest sound in the room.

Until...

Clunk.

Everyone heard it. The sound was familiar, but nobody could place it — a sharp sound of a piece of metal sliding into, or out of, place.

The manager looked toward the sound.

The doors.

He motioned for the head chef, who stood at the rear of the group and closest to the doors, to investigate.

The chef walked over. The keypad flashed a small green light. He held out his hand and gently pushed against the door.

It swung open easily.

The magnetic locks had been shut off.

Everyone gawked at the swinging door. They all seemed to sense what had happened.

"That's not good," the manager said.

***

Mariko climbed off the desk and into the alcove beneath the stairs. Her legs felt weak, but her mind was focused. She had to know if the sound meant what she thought it meant.

Trina and Brad only watched.

Mariko stepped toward the "Staff Only" door. She gripped its handle and gave a firm pull.

The door swung open.

A steel staircase descended to a concrete hallway that curved beyond her view. Mariko stared.

"Does this mean...?" Trina said. She didn't need to complete the question.

The three of them looked at each other. Mariko felt her muscles tighten. Her blood, which she knew she had precious little of by now, rushed to her face. She felt hot. But it wasn't the nervous, terrified heat she felt before.

This was a heat fueled by anger.

A smile spread on her lips, lighting up her eyes as the blood pumped aggressively through her body.

"We have to tell the others," she said.

CHAPTER 28

Mariko didn't know how long the fatigue would be gone from her. She didn't give a shit about that. She didn't give a shit about anything right now. She strode into the ballroom with Trina and Brad flanking her.

The DJ rocked-out in his booth. Justin Timberlake blared through the speakers. The DJ swayed around, feeling the beat with his very soul.

As Mariko climbed up onto the stage and strutted toward his booth, the DJ put his hands in the air and motioned for her to raise the roof. Mariko grasped the handle on the booth's glass door. She grinned as she gave a little tug.

The door swung open.

The DJ's eyes went wide with shock and confusion. He immediately grabbed the handle and tried to pull his door closed, but Brad jammed his axe blade into the door crack, wedging it open. Using his axe as a lever, he pried on it.

Trina got her fingers in the crack and pulled too.

Yanking together, they ripped it free from the DJ's grasp.

Brad stepped into the booth.

The DJ backed as far away from the door as he could (all of two feet). He put his hands up. "Whoa, man! Wait, wait, wait!"

But Brad didn't wait. Mariko saw no tremble in his hand or axe this time.

In the tight space, he didn't have much room to perform a full swing, so Brad opted for short, choppy, half-swings.

Again and again.

Brad hacked his way through the DJ's outstretched hands.

The DJ screamed. He tried to reach for his controls, his walkie-talkie, anything.

Brad grabbed him by the neck and dragged him out of the booth. He threw the man down onto the stage by Trina's feet. She grasped onto a clump of his hair, yanked his neck back, and slit his throat with her knife.

That wasn't enough, however.

Brad stepped out of the booth, raised the axe over his head and swung it down hard, cleaving the DJ's head off in a single blow.

As Trina stomped down on the DJ's carcass, Mariko stepped into the booth. She wiped the DJ's splattered blood from the controls and turned off the music. Then, Mariko picked up his microphone and traced the cable back to his mixing board. She was looking for a switch. The P.A. system.

She turned it on.

With a crackle of static, she soon heard her own breathing flowing out from the speakers mounted throughout the walls.

Mariko grinned.

"Dear friends and family of Caleb and Lilith," she began. "It may have come to your attention that the bracelets no longer work. The door locks also no longer work. We're not each other's enemies. But we know who the real enemy is. We know who the sick fucks are who invited us here. And we know who imprisoned us here. You and I, we're all on the same team. We always have been. From the moment these games began, it hasn't been us versus each other. It's been us versus *them*. So, meet me in the ballroom. Let's finish this wedding right."

She took a deep, angry breath.

"Let's kill these fuckers."

***

Amy clicked through the various camera feeds.

She watched as the ballroom filled with guests. At first they were timid. Most groups and families seemed to send one member to scout out the situation. Amy couldn't blame any of them for suspecting a trap, but she wished they'd hurry it up.

The scouts crept out, cautiously peering around every corner before proceeding. They ducked and hid if someone else slinked past. Eventually, each group's scout arrived at the ballroom and peeked through the door. They saw other guests grabbing weapons from the wall. They felt the energy in the room. And then, they seemed to sense on some intuitive level that no one in this room wanted to harm them.

A switch flipped in each person at that time.

The timid mice vanished.

Amy watched as they sprinted back through The Venue, back to their group in hiding and announced that, yes, it wasn't a trap. It was real. People were arming up to storm the staff areas.

Faster and faster, Amy watched the guests pour into the ballroom and yank the medieval axes, machetes, and maces from the wall.

Amy clicked through to other camera feeds.

She found a series of camera angles showing the staff corridors.

Her view came to a large room that looked like a beer hall. There were couches and pool tables, although none of them were currently in use. Several dozen red vested staff members gathered in a corner.

A man, whom Amy recognized as the shift manager, stood in front of the group. He flung open a locker, reached inside, and began pulling out handguns. But not just any handguns — antique, ivory-handled revolvers. They were the type of weapon that Amy could imagine an old colonel with a bushy mustache and a monocle sporting on his hip.

The manager passed them out to eager hands.

They were going on the offensive.

They were going to quell the uprising. And then, they would probably come to the Control Room. They would come to stop Amy and kill her.

And yet, at this realization, Amy didn't feel the cold sweat form on her brow. Her hands didn't get clammy. Her breath didn't become short and panicked.

As six staff members, all with guns, set out into the hallways, Amy felt nothing. Either Mariko and the others would kill the staff, or the staff would kill Mariko and Amy.

One way or another, there would be blood.

One way or another, the night would end.

Amy was fine with that.

CHAPTER 29

Brad waved his axe above his head. "Follow me!" he bellowed.

Mariko was first behind him. Her one good hand held a slender sword she had pulled off the wall. She believed it was called a "rapier," but she wasn't sure and didn't really care. It was light and it was pointy. Good enough.

Thirty or so people had gathered in the ballroom by then with more arriving by the second. The men had long since ditched their coats, and the women had rid themselves of their heels. Every person carried a weapon. Many opted for smaller swords or machetes — weapons that they could confidently swing.

Brad let out a roar and ran forward.

Everyone pushed up against one another to follow his lead. The horde crushed against Mariko's back, practically carrying her forward.

They ran through the staff door and entered a white room with a glass window and glass door. The floor of the room was smeared with what looked like blood and frosting. Brad yanked open the glass door and ran out into the hallway beyond. He barged forward and—

Bang!

A bullet struck him in the chest.

More shots followed.

Rage seemed to fuel Brad on a few additional steps.

Three more shots rang out.

Mariko could only watch as the bullets ripped into Brad. She stopped, holding back the other guests in the process.

Brad fell to his knees in the center of the corridor.

From her spot at the glass door, Mariko could see down the hall. About twenty feet away, a group of staff members crouched behind a corner as they fired into Brad.

When Brad's body finally collapsed to the floor, Mariko saw the staff members angle their aim higher.

Toward *her*.

She yanked the glass door shut just as three sharp cracks of gunfire split the air. The bullets struck the glass and violently ricocheted off. But the glass door held.

Mariko gazed through her bullet proof door at the staffers down the hall.

"Well, what's the plan, hon?" someone asked.

Mariko looked. The voice came from Mrs. Crawford, the third grade teacher.

"They have guns," Mariko said.

"So? I don't give a hoot. Ten minutes ago, I was counting myself as dead."

Mariko looked through the elderly teacher's large glasses, still connected to the homemade beaded chain, and into the woman's eyes. Mrs. Crawford's gaze was positively alight with fire. Her eyes danced. In this sweet old lady's hand was a saber that she gripped so tightly that her knuckles were pale.

The image made Mariko smile. She could have laughed out loud. This old woman was ready to charge to the death.

Why tell her no?

"Get a table," Mariko said.

***

The manager gazed down the hall.

He felt that the situation in the ballroom was momentarily resolved.

The staff only had six revolvers among them. The rest of the weaponry, including the shotguns and assault rifles, were hidden in a compartment in the Control Room. Whoever had taken over the Control Room was probably armed with the weapon from the poisoned and battered bellhop he had seen in the hallway.

The manager made a tactical decision to quell the uprising in the ballroom first. Next, he would lead a team to retake the Control Room. Once they accessed the remaining firearms from there, they would sweep through The Venue and put an unceremonious end to the night.

As he debated how many people he wanted to bring with him, he saw a group of guests enter the security chamber, carrying the DJ's body with them.

Using their hands as paintbrushes, they smeared his blood over the window and door. They glopped it on so thick that soon the manager couldn't see through the glass to what was happening on the other side.

"Savages," he said aloud to no one in particular. The armed staff members with him nodded in their own astonishment.

A burst of static crackled through the speaker in the hall. The guests were activating the DJ's announcement system.

"They will try to bargain with us," the manager told his crew. "But they want to do it through a microphone. Because they are afraid."

T . J .   P A Y N E

With his revolver raised, he took a step forward, motioning for his men to follow behind him.

Suddenly, the speakers came to life, set to the highest volume. The manager froze in place and put his free hand over his ear to try to block out some of the deafening noise. It wasn't the voice of a guest that came blaring through. It was a song. A loud, American rap song.

His men stopped moving. The noise seemed to disorient them.

As he debated how to respond, the security room doors flew open. A rectangular hors d'oeuvres table, held upright like a shield, barged through and raced toward them. The top of the table was big, barely able to fit through the door. Several people must have been behind it, carrying it and supporting it. Screams echoed out, blending in with the music.

The manager aimed his gun, as did the other staffers, and fired off a wave of bullets. The tabletop — although made from a fine, thick oak — wasn't nearly bullet proof. The bullets bored through the wood, rewarding the staff with yelps of pain from the people carrying it.

He could see people fall. Their blood splattered onto the floor. The table was a shield, but an imperfect one.

And yet, the forward charge never slowed.

As those who carried the table fell to the ground, the people behind them surged forward to take their places, trampling their fallen comrades in the process. Even the guests who were shot and stomped on didn't seem to care. With their final breaths, they howled in an inhuman fury and urged their side on.

Perhaps a dozen had fallen. But it made little difference.

The table, quickly being shredded by bullets, raced forward.

It closed within ten feet.

Then five feet.

The manager had run out of ammunition several seconds ago. The deafening sounds of blaring music and furious screams masked the fact that his last several trigger pulls produced only inconsequential clicks.

His mind didn't quite register the lack of recoil in his weapon. Much like his revolver, his brain and body had locked up.

He yelled at his men to run. To regroup.

But no one heard him.

His men fumbled in their vest pockets for any spare bullets, but they dropped them to the floor in their haste to reload.

The table smashed into their group.

As it did, a wave of men in suits and women in gowns poured over the top of it. What few rounds remained in the staff's weapons were fired off. The bullets ripped into people, but they slowed no one. The rage fueled the attackers on, making them momentarily impervious to bullets.

The manager turned to run away.

But his legs refused to work. A stinging sensation rippled through his lower back. He looked down and saw the tip of a sword protruding from his stomach. Before his body could even collapse, before gravity could take hold of him, a blunt object connected with the back of his neck, shattering his spine.

His body tried to fall, but someone was holding him up from behind.

A knife... two knives... *three* knives furiously stabbed into him.

It all happened with incredible speed, but the final echoes of his consciousness drew out the experience. The world slowed, and he registered each penetrating strike of steel into his body.

His head drooped. He saw the chef laid out on the floor, staring back at him with glassy eyes as a whirlwind of hatchets and machetes hacked the man apart. The head waiter tried to run, but someone grabbed him and pressed him against the wall, holding him up as blades sliced into him.

Everywhere around him, the manager saw his team cut to pieces. Rabid dogs or a hungry bear would have been gentler, more civilized, in their killings. This was a fury he had never seen and could hardly believe existed in nature.

One final thought slipped through the manager's mind.

What is wrong with these people?

Then his world went black.

***

Amy watched the battle on the monitors.

One of the waiters dropped his gun and tried to run away, but a man whom Amy recognized as Caleb's Uncle Mark tackled him and began slamming his face into the floor. Uncle Mark, despite being in his sixties, ground the waiter's face into the concrete. Time and again, he pounded the man's head, well past the point when it was clear he was dead.

Space became a problem. Not all the guests could fit around the six-or-so staff members, and so some were left with no one to attack. Instead of waiting their turn, they ran off down the hall in packs, hunting for more.

No one tended to the wounded, who didn't seem to mind. They waved their friends and family on.

Amy searched for signs of Mariko, but the bloody sea of humanity was too chaotic and the camera angles were too few.

She turned her attention to the staff lounge. The remaining staff armed themselves with pool cues as they pushed the couches and tables against the door to block it. Unfortunately for them, the door swung both directions. Amy saw some of them arguing, debating how best to seal a door that couldn't be locked.

They never settled on a solution.

A crazed woman, brandishing a knife in each hand, leapt through the door, landed on a waiter, and began stabbing him furiously in the face.

A baggage porter and a line cook fought her off, bludgeoning her with pool cues and bottles. But the woman had done her job. She had distracted the staff from completing their barricade just long enough.

The door opened again and more and more men and women streamed in. They leapt over the couch and slashed at any red vested person they could find.

Amy watched with a quiet fascination as the staff tried to escape.

One housekeeper, probably a few years younger than Amy, slipped out of the staff area through the door by the front desk and crouched exactly where Amy and Mariko had hidden. Amy could see the young woman shake with fear. Her head stayed angled toward the open front door. She clearly wanted to make a run for it but was too scared.

Bit by bit, she inched her way over the desk.

Amy clicked a button that she assumed was the P.A. system. "Housekeeping escaping through front door," she said.

The maid's head jerked up as Amy spoke. She leapt off the desk and ran with a new urgency.

Amy watched. The woman just might make it. She just might escape.

But as she neared the door, a hatchet flew through the air and slammed into her head. It wasn't a particularly good throw; the blade didn't embed in her skull or anything. But it knocked her off her feet. She wasn't giving up, though. She crawled feebly out the door.

A few seconds later, one of Lilith's sorority sisters, along with one of Caleb's cousins, stomped over. They grabbed the maid by her feet and dragged her back inside. Her hands searched for anything to grab hold of. Amy could see the woman screaming, although the sound was off and she couldn't hear it.

They dragged the maid back through the front lobby and through the foyer. She kicked. She screamed. She tried to grab hold of something the entire way.

Amy looked at other monitors. Similar scenes played out across The Venue. Housekeepers, waiters, cooks, and receptionists on the verge of escaping were chased down. They weren't being killed, though. Their pursuers seemed to prefer to drag them off.

No one had coordinated it, but they all appeared to be going to the same destination.

The ballroom.

Inside, the party was in full swing. Guests danced. Guests drank. Guests shouted and laughed.

Throughout the floor, squirming and pleading for mercy, lay the injured staff members. Whenever one of them tried to crawl away, someone danced over and bashed their legs with a hammer. When one would try to fight back, someone would hold them down as other guests stabbed them in the spinal cord.

Near the spiral staircase, a group of ten or so people had gotten together. With knives and swords, they began to advance toward the bridal suite.

Amy took a deep breath.

She was tired.

She was empty.

Amy had been watching revenge play out for twenty minutes now, and the realization had begun to creep in that none of it would bring her parents back.

But she forced herself out of her seat anyway.

It was time to keep the party going and she intended to rally. She crouched down beneath the computer and hunted around until she found the power plug. She yanked it from the wall and the screens went blank.

On the desk was a large pair of metal scissors. Amy picked them up and wrapped the computer's power cord around the blades. She pressed down on the scissor handles, using all her hand strength to slice through the cord's insulation and then its wires beneath.

Soon, she had cut the head off the plug. If some staff member were hiding, they wouldn't be able to reactivate the system. At least not without performing some repairs. The doors in The Venue would remain unlocked forever, as they should be.

Amy stood.

She looked down at the body of the Event Planner. The woman lay perfectly still. Was she faking it? Amy didn't care to get close enough to find out.

And so, she poked her head out into the hall. "I got another one in here!" she shouted.

Within a few seconds, a man and woman who appeared to be husband and wife — Amy thought she remembered seeing them sitting at Table Eleven — marched around the corner. They stepped into the Control Room and each grabbed a fistful of the Event Planner's hair. They tugged her from the room.

The Event Planner either woke up then or she had been awake the entire time because she started bellowing. She looked at Amy as she shouted, "No! Please! Please, mercy! I can take you to the bride and groom. It's them you want. There's a staircase to their suite. I can take you there!"

Amy nodded. There was a part of her that was interested, or at least a part that felt like she *should* be interested. But the words stirred nothing in Amy. She simply shrugged.

"I'm sure I can find it on my own," Amy said.

Then she motioned for the man and woman to take the Event Planner away.

They pulled on the Event Planner's hair and dragged her off down the hall as she kicked and screamed.

Amy wandered off to go find this staircase to the bridal suite.

CHAPTER 30

Caleb was worried about Lilith.

After the bouquet toss, they had returned to the room to watch the final kills for the night, but all they saw on the TV was their guests taking off their bracelets. Caleb tried calling the Event Planner to demand answers, but he got no response.

And so, they sat and watched as their guests armed themselves in the ballroom.

Caleb tried to put a happy spin on the situation. Obviously there was a malfunction, but perhaps it was all for the best. The bracelets had made the festivities too uneven. Too stale.

But now, the ballroom finally had some energy!

They should go out on the balcony and start shooting. Make a real game of it for themselves.

But Lilith didn't respond.

Maybe she was simply coming down off the high from all the drugs she was on. She seemed tired, sure. But also vacant. That empty, glassy look in her eyes was what worried Caleb most.

He tried to egg her on by bragging that he could kill more than her. Lilith still didn't move. She just stared at the TV until the relay was cut off and the screen went black.

Thinking that maybe her injuries were bothering her, he went to the bathroom and got her some lotion for her burned face, as well as a few more painkillers. She rejected them all.

And so, he sat beside her, put an arm around her shoulders, and together they laid down on the bed.

He stared at her face that entire time, gently brushing her stray strands of hair out of her burns. He called her beautiful. He said that he loved her.

But her eyes never connected with his.

He looked at her for ten, maybe twenty minutes.

The party down below grew very quiet. Everyone seemed to have abandoned the ballroom, probably to go attack the staff areas.

But then, a few minutes later, it got loud. Insanely loud. The music and the shouting reached decibels that they hadn't all night. Caleb could hear the screams of what he assumed were The Venue staff being stabbed and tortured.

"Do you want to go down there?" he asked. "Join in the party?"

"What's the point?"

"You could kill someone. I think your Aunt Stacy is still alive. Or Becky?"

"Do I have to do everything? They were all supposed to kill each other."

"Is that what's bothering you? That it didn't go as planned?"

"Nothing's bothering me," she said.

They stayed there for a moment, him staring at her while she gazed off.

"What's wrong, sweetie?" he finally asked.

"Nothing. Just tired."

"Didn't you have *any* fun today?"

For the first time, she actually seemed to consider the question. Her eyes narrowed and her nose scrunched up. It was the cute face she made when thinking — truly thinking. Although, this time, the scrunching up of her nose made her blistered cheek crack and rip slightly. She didn't seem to notice, though.

"I *tried* to have fun," she said. "I *tried* to be happy."

"But?"

She sighed. "But I feel nothing. Just like always. Nothing."

He grasped her hand in his, hoping that the tenderness of his touch would force her to finally look him in the eye. "But what we have isn't 'nothing.' And it doesn't matter if we die right now, or if we go out there and kill them all. What we have transcends tonight. What we have is special. It's a bond. It's an understanding. It's love. True, deep, honest love. And as long as you've lived a life that's felt love, then it's been a life worth living."

At long last, her eyes shifted from whatever spot on the ceiling she had been staring at and she looked at him. But yet, she didn't *truly* look at him. Her gaze seemed to pass straight through him.

"No," she said. "I never loved you. I just needed your money because I couldn't afford this wedding myself." Her face was blank as she said it. Emotionless.

"Wait, what?"

She peeled his hand off of hers and rose from the bed. "Never mind. Let's go kill some people."

With mechanical, weary movements, Lilith slung her quiver over her shoulder, picked up her bow, and dutifully ambled to the balcony door.

"Be a good boy and grab some of these chairs and throw them on the balcony staircase. I don't want anyone to easily charge up at me," she said.

She never looked back at him as she walked off.

Caleb just stared.

Lilith flung open the door. The noise of music and shouting from the ballroom flooded into the suite. Lilith nocked an arrow and immediately fired it off into the crowd down below. She quickly fired another and then another.

Each arrow seemed to awaken her.

"Get up and help me."

Caleb didn't move. He wanted to resist. To stand up to her. To delve deeper into the things she had just said to him.

She never loved me?

Has anyone ever loved me?

"What the fuck, Caleb?!" she screamed as she took aim and released another arrow.

Her voice seemed to reach deep inside Caleb and grab hold of a magical cord. It yanked him from the bed. He soon found himself hurrying around the bridal suite, grabbing heavy wooden chairs and flinging them onto the balcony staircase to build an obstacle for the guests advancing up the steps.

CHAPTER 31

It didn't take Amy long to find the service staircase that led to the bridal suite. There were only so many doors in the underground portion of The Venue, and Amy had gotten a decent orientation of the layout from her time in the Control Room.

She climbed the stairs and emerged at a short hallway.

With revolver in hand, she marched to the large wooden door at the end of the hall.

She could hear shouting from the other side. A commotion. She figured it must be Caleb and Lilith's last stand.

The world had slowed for Amy, or maybe her mind was simply making decisions quicker than it ever had in her life, because she opened the door without hesitating. Part of her recognized that it would be wiser to proceed slowly, if at all. She knew she could hide in the stairwell and probably wait this whole thing out. Just a few hours ago, that's exactly what she would have done.

But she just didn't care anymore.

She only wanted to end this night. She wanted to end Caleb and Lilith's wedding.

The door swung open. Amy could see across the room to the balcony.

Lilith stood near the balcony doorway, swinging her long, spiked hammer weapon at someone. Caleb fought by her side, firing off arrows into whatever crowd appeared to be charging up the spiral stairs from the ballroom. Neither of them looked toward Amy.

Amy's finger tickled the trigger of her gun. She didn't have any real weapons training. Just one trip to a shooting range. She had shot the Control Room operators point-blank, but she didn't trust that she could shoot two moving, fighting people from a distance.

Before she had even made a conscious plan, she found herself silently jogging across the bridal suite, extending the gun out in front of her.

She was going to race over to the balcony. She was going to push the barrel against Lilith's head. She was going to send a bullet into Lilith's brain. Then Caleb's brain. And she was going to do it from a distance where she was sure she wouldn't miss.

But as Amy closed within five feet... four feet... three feet... Caleb turned his head. He looked directly at her.

"Amy?" he said. His voice was light and high, seemingly happy to see that she was still alive.

Lilith heard Caleb's voice and spun around suddenly, swinging out her long-handled hammer in Amy's direction. Amy dodged backwards, but the hammer slammed into the gun, knocking it from Amy's hand.

Lilith advanced quickly, sparing no moment. She swung the hammer again at Amy's head. Amy managed to lean away from it, stepping backwards into the room.

With ferocious but confident swings, Lilith pressed forward, forcing Amy to keep stumbling backwards. There was such power in the strikes that Amy knew she couldn't block them. Lilith's motions were too focused and too purposeful for Amy to dodge to the side.

All Amy could do was back away from the swooping weapon.

Each swing threatened to shatter Amy's arms. Or skull.

It all happened too fast. Before Amy's mind could catch up with her retreating feet, she found her back pressed against the wall.

There was nowhere to run.

No way to evade the next strike.

She glimpsed Lilith's blistered face. The charring had pulled Lilith's mouth into a sneer. One of her eyes had clouded over and didn't seem to work, but her other eye stared back at Amy with an emotionless, dead gaze.

Strangely, Amy realized that she, herself, felt nothing in this moment. No fear, no sadness, no regret. In that fraction of a second, the two women looked at each other with a shared emptiness.

"Say hi to your folks," Lilith deadpanned.

Then Lilith raised the hammer for one final blow to Amy's head...

Amy didn't shut her eyes. She didn't quiver or plead. Her body lost all strength. It was time to die.

Lilith's body lurched.

The hammer didn't swing. Instead, it stayed there in the air. All of Lilith's muscles seemed to have frozen in place.

Amy looked up at her.

Lilith's good eye went wide with shock. Her throat gulped a few gasps of air.

Amy tilted her head down. Toward Lilith's stomach. The tip of an arrow protruded through the bride's abdomen. Redness flowed out from that tip. Like a flood spreading across the land, the redness bloomed out and consumed the white lace of Lilith's dress.

Lilith staggered forward a step, her good eye looking down at her stomach and trying to make sense of the arrow that had appeared.

But then her eye narrowed again, seemingly willing itself to focus on one final victim. One final kill. She looked at Amy.

Amy saw the hammer reel back again, preparing to strike.

Without even thinking, Amy reached into the pocket of her dress. Her fingers tightened around the handle of the scissors she had found in the Control Room. In a quick motion, she pulled the scissors from her pocket and thrust them forward.

The blades jabbed into Lilith's good eye.

The hammer dropped from Lilith's hand. She released a hellish shriek as she stumbled backwards.

Amy didn't let her get away. She grabbed Lilith's arm.

"To have and to hold," Amy said.

She pulled Lilith in close.

"Until death do you go fuck yourself."

With that, Amy slammed her palm into the handles of the scissors, sending their blades piercing deep into Lilith's skull.

Lilith stopped flailing.

She stopped fighting.

She tumbled backwards and crumpled down onto the ground.

Amy watched her body twitch for a moment.

Then she looked toward the balcony.

Caleb stood there, his bow string still slack from the final arrow that he had shot into his wife's back.

He looked at Amy and smiled.

For the briefest moment, Amy saw the smiling face of that boy she knew.

But a crowd of people soon blocked Amy's view. They charged up onto the balcony and tackled Caleb to the ground. Amy saw flashes of several knives sliding in and out of Caleb's back and neck. He screamed. Or, at least, Amy thought she heard him scream. There was so much noise from the crowd that it flooded her senses.

More people ran into the bridal suite from the balcony. They grabbed Lilith and began to stab and hack at her. No one cared that she was already dead. That wasn't going to stop this party.

Amy looked away.

She took a breath and stepped past the group. She walked out onto the balcony, moving past Caleb without even looking down at him. She didn't want to know if he was still alive as a woman began to saw through his ribcage to get to his heart.

CHAPTER 32

Amy stepped off the balcony stairs and onto the ballroom floor.

With the announcement from the DJ booth that the bride and groom had retired for the night, a sense of euphoria overtook the crowd. As the music cranked up louder, the party went into full swing.

The Event Planner was, evidently, still alive. A circle of six guests had formed around her. They smiled as they waved their blades in her face, tauntingly.

"Please... it was a job," the Event Planner pleaded, rising to her feet. "Please. Please."

Amy watched.

No one stated the rules of the game, but everyone seemed to be of the same mind. One at a time, the guests stabbed her. Always in non-fatal places and always being respectful of the next person's turn. When the Event Planner tried to fall, whoever was standing behind her at the time held her up so the stabbing could continue.

The game developed a rhythm. Their stabbing and slashing followed along with the song playing out over the speakers. The DJ booth had been taken over by Lilith's sister, Trina. She danced and swayed to the music.

Someone had broken into the bar (Amy thought she spied a young couple posing in the photo booth with the bartender's corpse) and several people were chugging brands of tequila and whiskey that Amy had never heard of before.

As Amy wandered through the ballroom, she only saw four people *not* engaging in the party. Evidently someone had found and released the guests who had earned their freedom. Lilith's grandma, Coach Sanborn, Angela the sorority sister, and Lilith's cousin Chelsea stood against the wall, their eyes wide as they stared at the scene. Amy didn't know if their memories had been erased yet. She didn't even know if that was possible, as Caleb had promised it was.

But by the horrified looks on their faces, the four definitely didn't understand the circumstances of the celebration.

When Amy walked by them, all she could think to do was to nod her head and say, "Sup."

None of them responded.

Amy continued walking.

She glanced up just in time to see Caleb and Lilith's bodies flung from the balcony. They hovered in the air for a moment, much like Lilith's bouquet, before they plunged down and smashed into the tables below.

Some people went over and lifted them up, holding up their corpses in a dance.

Amy stared at Caleb's face as his body flopped around from side to side. She felt no joy in the moment. No sadness. No nothing.

She stood there for several seconds, trying to will her emotions to resurface. They had settled somewhere near her feet, perhaps even lower, but try as she might, she couldn't bring her feelings back.

She thought of her parents. She thought of Lilith killing her mom and then her dad. She thought of how her old friend trapped her family here — not for any good reason, but because of a twisted narrative he had stewed over for decades. She realized how unfair it all was. She realized how angry she should be.

But tears didn't come. Neither did rage nor laughter.

Amy walked on. She wanted to find Mariko's body, although she didn't know why. It was just something to do.

There was no sign of Mariko in the ballroom. Not in the photobooth, not by the bar, not on the stage.

She had seen Mariko on the monitors, leading the initial charge into the staff hallway. But by the second charge, the tables had blocked her view. She saw the wave of gunfire, though. If Mariko wasn't out dancing with the others, then Amy knew where she must be.

With a heavy step, Amy turned and walked back toward the stage. Toward the door that led to the security room where Amy had escaped with the bouquet.

She pushed open the door and stepped in.

Amy walked through the blood-smeared glass door and into the hallway.

She stepped over bodies.

It wasn't that long ago that having her blood drawn made her queasy. Now, she barely blinked as she kicked a pile of some staff member's teeth out of the way. They bounced across the floor with a satisfying rattle sound.

A fear began to settle into her, if one could call it "fear." Much like her other emotions, fear had become an abstract, academic thought. However she wanted to define it, she "feared" that perhaps Lilith had won. Maybe her goal hadn't been to kill all the people in their lives. Perhaps her goal was to kill the part of those people that Lilith herself lacked.

Because Amy now felt nothing. Perhaps she had become Lilith. Perhaps they all had.

The thought made Amy shrug.

It failed to rile her up and it failed to depress her. She simply turned the corner and kept wandering down the hall.

It was then that she heard a footstep. A rustling sound that echoed down the otherwise empty corridor.

Amy felt no panic. She simply bent down and picked up the nearest weapon — a dull machete —then stood ready to fight the person if they happened to not be friendly.

She stood still; her grip on the machete's handle was firm. Her eyes focused on where the hallway wrapped around a blind corner. From the other side of that corner, Amy could hear deep breaths and a staggering, weakened gait.

The person stepped into view.

Separated by ten feet, the two of them stood and looked at each other.

Amy saw that blood-splattered sea-green dress. That messy black hair. That pale, bloodless face and eyes that struggled to focus. That missing left arm.

"I've been looking for you," Mariko said. A little smile played on her lips as though she believed that this was all just a dream.

She rested her weight against the wall. It was as if she had saved up every last ounce of energy so that she could mutter those words.

Mariko slid down to the ground and let her eyes close.

Amy dropped the machete. She ran the final ten feet down the hall and knelt at Mariko's side. Holding Mariko's head in her arms,

Amy began to sob. She had no control over the tears. They flowed through her and from her in waves.

All she could think to do to anchor herself, to not get swept away in these emotions, was to put her hand on Mariko's chest.

She felt Mariko's pulse.

Her heart was still beating.

Mariko was unconscious.

But as long as she was alive, so was Amy.

CHAPTER 33

It was mid-morning, and Johann was already bored for the day. His summer vacation had been dragging on and there wasn't much to do in his little town. He was on his way to the house of his friend, Karin. Maybe they would watch cartoons today. Or maybe they would work on that tree fort they had designed. Something, anything, to occupy the hours.

Karin's family lived outside of town. It was a bit of a bike ride, but it was better than hanging around his own house by himself. Being around Karin always made the summers more fun for Johann.

But as Johann neared Karin's home, he heard the limos.

Even by the age of twelve, he knew that when the limos passed, he was to stop everything and look away. He wasn't to see the drivers, the passengers, or even the color of the limos or the number of doors on their sides.

The same rules applied to the windowless vans that rolled through the town some days, often filled with cleaning workers in blue coveralls. Johann shouldn't have known that cleaners were in the vans, but word got around. An older brother or someone's uncle would get a job on the mountain. They didn't speak of what they did up there, but they were paid more for a day's work than Johann's father made in a month.

Johann hoped that one day he would be lucky enough to land such a job.

Maybe Karin could get a job there too. He knew they hired women as well as men. Then he and Karin could still hang out during the summers, even as adults.

As the limos turned the corner, Johann stopped his bike and stepped to the side of the road, looking down at his feet as he had been taught.

The limos were moving faster than usual. Their engines louder. Usually they breezed through town with a smoothness that seemed to barely disturb the leaves on the trees. Today, they roared.

The limos drove past him and then screeched to a stop.

Were they stopping for him?

What did he do?

The doors on the limos opened.

Men and women screamed at him. Their words blurred together. Not that Johann understood what they were saying. He thought it might be English, which he only recognized from the movies.

He knew he should leave. Whatever was happening with the limos was bad.

Refusing to look up at the shouting adults, he lifted his leg over his bike and began to pedal away. It was then that a hand grabbed the back of his shirt and yanked him off his seat.

The hand spun him around and soon he was face-to-face with a woman. Her eyes were crazed and her dress was covered in blood.

She shouted something in his face. A word that he understood as "doktor."

He now saw that there were three limos, all crammed together on the narrow road. He tried to keep looking at the ground, but he couldn't help but see that all the shouting adults wore suits and dresses that were splattered with blood. They waved axes and machetes at him as they screamed.

The woman who had him by the shirt collar tugged him toward the last limo. Toward the open door.

Johann didn't want to go. He didn't want to look in that door. He didn't want to be shoved inside and hacked to pieces by this insane, angry, probably cannibalistic group of well-dressed adults. He dug his heels in, but the woman was strong and determined.

She dragged him to the limo and wrenched his head to look inside.

It took a moment for his eyes to adjust to the darkness. But when they did, Johann saw blood. Tons of blood. Men and women had crowded into the back seats. Some were unconscious but many writhed about. They moaned in the red pools that had formed on the upholstery.

The woman twisted his head to look at one person in particular. Another woman. In a greenish dress. She was unconscious, but from the paleness of her face, Johann wondered if she might actually be dead.

Johann was yanked back out of the limo and the woman slammed him up against the side of the vehicle.

She reached into his pocket and pulled out his phone. She held it in front of his face as she said again, "Doktor!"

Johann knew there was a special number to call in situations like this. And it wasn't the number for the doctor. There had been times during his childhood when a person or two made their way down the mountain and screamed for help. There was a reward for calling the special number in those situations, although Johann had never had the opportunity to do it himself. He never dreamed that he would encounter three cars full of such people.

As he looked in the eyes of the woman who held him, Johann's nerves vanished. He had never seen such intensity before. If he didn't get these people to a doctor — a *trustworthy* doctor — he believed that this woman wouldn't just kill him, she would burn the entire town to ash.

Johann was friends with a boy from two towns away. The boy's dad was a doctor. The people of that town knew nothing of what went on at the mountain.

Johann called that boy.

CHAPTER 34

Amy stared out the window.

The view looked out over the treetops. She could see spires of the city dotting the distance. The world looked green and healthy on this summer's afternoon. It had been almost two days since they had escaped The Venue.

She heard the rustling of the hospital bed beside her, followed immediately by a heavy breathing and the creaking of Mariko yanking on the restraints that bound her to the bed. Mariko was working her way into a frenzy.

Amy quickly stood and bent over the bed, putting a reassuring hand on Mariko's shoulder.

"It's okay, it's okay," Amy repeated in a calm voice. "You're safe."

Mariko's head, which had been jerking from side-to-side, stabilized. Her eyes took a moment to focus in on Amy's face. What had been a look of panic became one of confusion.

"Hiya, sleepy-head," Amy said with a smile.

Mariko gulped. She opened her mouth.

"Wait, wait, wait," Amy said. "Have some water first."

Amy reached to an extendable table that was attached to the bed. She rotated it over and lifted a sippy cup that she held to Mariko's mouth. Mariko eyed the cup suspiciously. Amy placed it to her own lips and took a sip, making a show of swallowing the water down. Finally convinced it wasn't poisoned, Mariko put the straw in her mouth.

"We're in a hospital in Bern. It's the fifth biggest city in Switzerland. Cool, huh?" Amy said as Mariko drank. "They had to give you a shit ton of blood, but they say you'll be okay."

Mariko took another gulp and then let the straw fall loosely from her lips. Amy set the cup back down.

"How much do you remember?" Amy asked.

Mariko looked down at her left arm which had been bandaged over at the elbow. Her look said it all — she remembered everything.

Amy nodded. "You've been thrashing around a lot. The nurses said to buzz them when you finally woke up, and they'd take the restraints off. But fuck 'em. I don't have to play by their rules." She reached over and undid the strap that held Mariko down herself.

Mariko stretched her now-free arm. When she opened her mouth, her voice was hoarse. "Wh-what happened? After..."

"Well, the party died down pretty quick after I found you," Amy said. "It was like everyone hit the wall at the same time. Their blood-sugar levels just tanked, or something. Lotta sobbing."

As she spoke, she found that her voice didn't contain any trace of emotion. She wasn't feeling the fear or the sadness or the confusion from her story.

"Go on," Mariko said weakly. "What then?"

"Someone found a garage that had three limos in it," she continued, her words flowing out on autopilot. "It took an hour for us all to find the keys, but Jesse... Did you meet him? He was on Caleb's college debate team. Nice guy. Kinda awkward. But whatever. Anyway, Jesse finally cracked open the box they were kept in. So, we all piled into three limos, bleeding all over the place, and we zoomed down the mountain.

"No one knew where we were going. I didn't really help much. I stayed in the back of the third limo, just trying to keep you warm. Eventually, we came to a town. No one spoke the language and none of us trusted local police. I sort of assumed that we'd be surrounded and shot and then buried off in a field, or something. I think everyone assumed that.

"But we had cracked open the boxes that had our cell phones. And so, everyone just started filming everything. Every interaction. Every person who approached the limos. We uploaded it all. All their faces. Streamed the whole thing. The locals stayed clear of us. A doctor arrived from out of town. He stabilized the critically wounded. Like you."

Amy took a breath.

"Pretty soon, some emergency helicopters came," Amy continued. "They flew us to Bern. And here we are."

"Are we going home?"

"The Embassy is working on that. They interviewed me. They'll come back, I'm sure, and interview you. But, yes, we'll go home soon."

"So... that's it?"

Amy shrugged. "The police took statements from me. The media too. You'll probably want to change your phone number and address as there's a shitstorm of cameras out there. Because of your, um..." Amy motioned toward Mariko's missing arm. "They really want a photo of you. I haven't let them. They'll probably pay."

Mariko looked down at her arm. After a moment, she tilted her head and stared off. Amy's words still seemed to be bouncing around her mind.

"I've been talking to the other survivors. We all agree that the more media attention there is, the safer we feel."

"So, we're... safe?"

Amy nodded. She believed they were safe. Or, at least, she hoped they were.

She had refused to leave Mariko's side, even when the police came to interview her. And they came often. They'd have her describe The Venue. The faces of the staff. The invitation that Caleb had emailed her.

They brought maps for her to try to trace back its location (she couldn't). They brought books of headshots so she could identify a waiter or a bellhop (she couldn't). They forced her to log into her email and find the invitation (she couldn't). After each conversation, the detectives would step into the hall, make a phone call, and speak in a hushed tone.

The doctors did the same. As did the staffers from the American Embassy who stopped by. Everyone seemed to be reporting things back to someone else.

Or maybe Amy was just being paranoid.

She decided that she would wait for Mariko to be a little stronger before she burdened her with that paranoia. No one had threatened her or even appeared to be doubting her. The story of the wedding from hell had spread and no matter how much the police dragged their feet on finding the hidden location, the secret was out.

"But that place... there was a lot of money there," Mariko said, seemingly giving voice to Amy's own fears without Amy having to say anything. "Caleb couldn't have been the first to rent them. They must be well connected. And powerful. What if they come for us?"

Amy took a moment to actually think about that question — a question she'd been avoiding.

Would they ever truly be safe? What kind of life would they have?

She honestly didn't know.

But as she looked down at Mariko, she did know at least one thing.

"We'll just have to learn to live with the unknown," Amy said.

As the two looked in each other's eyes, Amy reached into her pocket. She had prepared a speech. A speech of love. Of the future. Of making each other stronger and better.

Working on the speech had been the only thing that kept her mind occupied during the long hours of guarding Mariko's bedside. She had memorized it and even practiced it out loud once. But at this moment, the moment she needed them, the words had been filed away in some cabinet of her mind and she had lost the key.

And so, Amy pulled the ring from her pocket and pressed it into Mariko's hand.

"I can't really explain why I didn't want to marry you before," Amy managed to say. "I know I said things and made up all these excuses, but the real truth is... the truth is, I was just in my own head. I was figuring my own shit out. Telling myself stories. Never actually talking about it. Never talking with you. And... and I'm sorry. I'm so sorry."

"*This* is how you're proposing?" Mariko smiled.

Amy felt her face blush as she, too, smiled. "You don't have to say anything now," Amy said. "We'll talk through what you want. What I want. We'll be honest. I just... I'm stronger with you. I never want to leave you again."

Mariko looked at the ring. A simple gold band with a small stone. The diamond may have even been fake. In fact, it probably was.

"When did you buy this?" she asked.

But as Mariko held the ring up to the sunlight, Amy could see the recognition flash across her face.

Amy pulled out the ring's companion. A simple, wide silver band. She had made sure to gather them before she left The Venue. She had kept them in her pocket ever since, clutching them tightly whenever feelings of sadness or anger rose in her. The rings calmed her. They made her feel loved and safe.

On the inside of the wedding band was an engraving. *"Together Forever" — 1979 — R & C.*

R & C.

Roger & Candice.

Together forever.

Mariko read the inscription and instantly understood. A tear formed in her eye. She sat up in bed, held out her good arm, and wrapped Amy in a hug.

"I love you," Mariko said.

"I love you too," Amy said between heaving breaths.

They held each other. Amy didn't want to let go.

She vowed she would never let go of a good thing again.

E P I L O G U E

The Event Planner was a tall man and reasonably attractive. But not *too* tall and not *too* attractive. The owners felt that staff who were too tall or too attractive made the male clientele feel insecure. An insecure client only caused problems.

And today, the Event Planner had enough problems on his hands.

He stood in the ballroom, overseeing the cleanup. This wasn't an ordinary scrub-and-repair job, like he was scheduled to perform today. This was a cleanup of a different nature.

The first priority had been to remove all the files and computers from the Control Room and offices. They destroyed them on-site so that they couldn't be intercepted on the road down from the mountain.

And now, sensing that he had a little bit of extra time, his crew performed the next level of cleansing. Cleaners rotated through the ballroom, throwing bodies on wheelbarrows and carting them away. The incinerators in the back parking lot had been roaring for hours now. Time permitting, he wanted to have the pools of blood absorbed by sawdust and sent to the incinerators as well. DNA evidence could be so troublesome.

He ordinarily trusted the cleaners to perform their jobs unsupervised, but time was of the essence today and he felt that his presence in the ballroom added an extra push to their step.

Still, it left him with little to do but stand and watch.

He found himself glancing down at the body by his feet. A woman, or what was left of her. His former colleague. She had been in competition with him for promotion, but despite that, they had stayed on friendly, professional terms. She, like all the other event planners, understood the stress of the job.

"Sir?"

The Event Planner turned. His assistant held out a phone.

"I have Mr. Van Rutherford on the line."

The Event Planner nodded. "I'll take it outside. Less noise."

"Very good. And the Swiss police? What should I tell them?"

"Tell them to delay another two hours. Then they can come investigate. Relay those same instructions to all our contacts in Interpol, the F.B.I., and any embassies and state departments who are involved."

"And the survivors? There are so many of them…"

"Let them go home."

"Sir?"

"Let them talk to the media. Let them tell their stories. Let them live their lives in peace, without our interference. There are to be no threats or bribes. No contact with the survivors of any kind. The coverup is always more dangerous than the crime. Once this building is retired, they will have nothing that connects back to us. If they try to pull on some threads, they will soon discover they all lead nowhere. In the meantime, we have a business to operate."

"Very good, sir."

His assistant walked off to make the calls. The Event Planner took a deep breath. Talking to Mr. Van Rutherford wasn't high on the list of things he wanted to do, but a job is a job.

He unmuted the phone as he walked out of the ballroom.

"Mr. Van Rutherford, I am so sorry for the delay. As I am sure my associate told you, things are a bit chaotic here. It is my unfortunate duty to tell you that there has been a scheduling error at The Venue. Sadly, the Alpine lodge location is unavailable for your family reunion. I am dreadfully sorry. We will provide you with an alternative of your choice. We have a private jungle treehouse venue in Singapore. Or perhaps our castle venue in Luxembourg, which is my personal favorite. If you desire a more urban setting, we operate a skyrise venue in Dubai. If you wish to stay local, there is a rustic farm venue in the Americas."

He paused as the man on the other end cut him off. Fortunately, the man didn't scream insults or threats. The rich could behave brutishly to other service-oriented businesses, but they tended to be on their best behavior for The Venue.

The Event Planner calmly listened to the man's concerns and desires for his family reunion (the rich also tended to be rather long-winded). He stepped out of the building and into the fresh air, having to move to the side to allow a team of cleaners carrying gasoline cans to enter.

He walked off across the parking lot to avoid the noise.

"Might I suggest something?" the Event Planner began when it was his turn to speak again. "We operate a yacht venue that sails from the Cayman Islands. It can accommodate all sixty of your guests. For the inconvenience, we will discount the rate by twenty percent. Does that suit you? Excellent. We will see you on the twenty-third. Thank you for your understanding."

He hung up. Not a bad result. The clean-up on the boat events was always the easiest. Unfortunately, he would need to expense some sea-sickness medication, but it was a small price to pay.

He stood in the parking lot and watched as his friend, the female Event Planner, was carted out the front door and hauled to the incinerator. What a mess.

The Event Planner's eye caught the bronze sign by the front door. Someone had vandalized it in blood so that it now read, "We hope you enjoyed your *SLAY*."

He shook his head. *What kind of guests did the bride and groom invite?* he wondered. *How can people be so cruel?*

He didn't have long to ponder the question, though. There was a building to be burned to the ground and a yacht party to arrange.

The hospitality industry stops for no one.

Luxury takes no vacations.

It would be another busy day.

THE END

Thank you for reading!

I hope you enjoyed *The Venue*.

Please consider leaving a review on Amazon. It doesn't need to be a book report or anything long. Just a sentence will do. Reviews are an important way to support authors and I greatly appreciate them.

Plus, I love hearing from readers!

If you enjoyed *The Venue*, I invite you to check out:

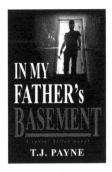

In My Father's Basement
a serial killer novel

Just your average father/son story...
but with abduction, torture and murder.

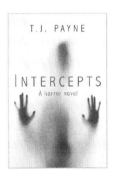

Intercepts
a horror novel

Joe works at a facility that performs human experimentations.
His work just followed him home.

ACKNOWLEDGEMENTS

I've been a bit more introspective lately because, as I write this, the world is gripped in the midst of the Coronavirus Crisis. Some people think that as a horror writer, I should be right at home in the fear and uncertainty of the moment. But the truth is that I write horror not because I like being afraid, but because I so often *am* afraid — afraid that I might lose the people and things that bring me joy in life.

I consider myself a very fortunate person to have been surrounded by so much love and support throughout my life, but there's always the nagging fear that it can vanish in a moment.

Truly, *The Venue* is my version of a love story. A twisted, violent love story, yes. But all the carnage and murder would be empty if it weren't held together by the love between Amy and Mariko, as well as the love between Amy and her parents.

With that in mind, I want to express my gratitude to all the people who have shown me love in my life. Your love has supported me throughout my crazy journey as a writer. My wonderful wife who keeps me grounded and hopeful. My brothers who I know will always have my back. And, of course, my mom and dad who taught me strength and goodness (and hey, for once I didn't write a book about a main character who has severe parental issues!).

If I didn't know love, then I wouldn't know fear.

Thank you for your support.

Made in the USA
Columbia, SC
27 September 2021